# Fault Line

A novel by

KI STEPHENS

Cover Design: Ki Stephens
Editor: Sandra Dee, One Love Editing

This book is intended for an 18+ audience.
For content warnings, please visit www.kistephens.com.

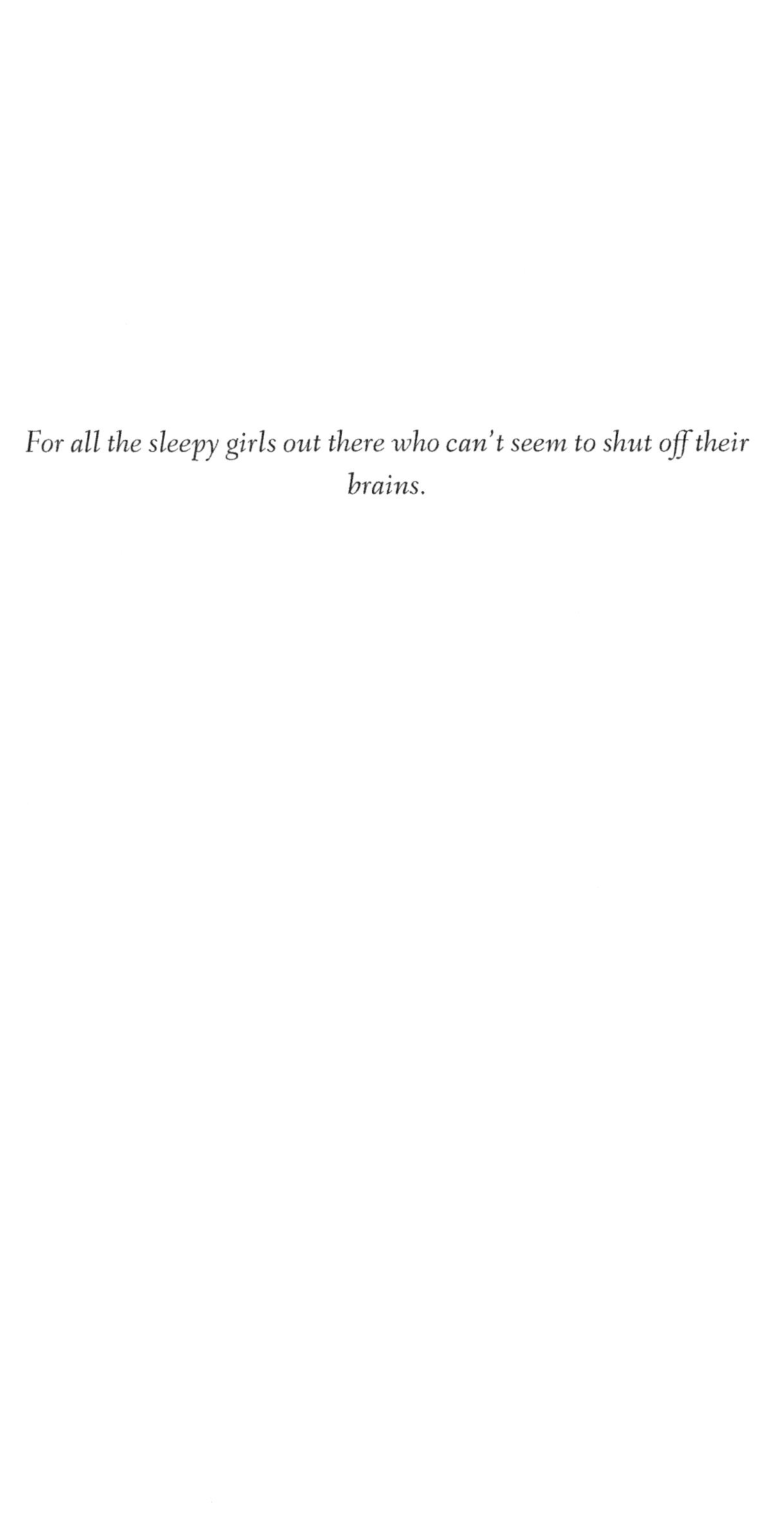

*For all the sleepy girls out there who can't seem to shut off their brains.*

We lived, lulled, on the fault line of chaos. Change could come explosively, and out of nowhere.

WALLY LAMB

# Playlist

| | | |
|---|---|---|
| GLUE MYSELF SHUT \| NOAH KAHAN | ♥ | 3:16 |
| BLOCK ME OUT \| GRACIE ABRAMS | ♥ | 4:09 |
| HEY GIRL \| STEPHEN SANCHEZ | ♥ | 3:05 |
| LAVENDER HAZE \| TAYLOR SWIFT | ♥ | 3:22 |
| MEET YOU IN HELL \| JADE LEMAC | ♥ | 3:07 |
| EXHALE \| SABRINA CARPENTER | ♥ | 2:44 |
| SPEAK TOO SOON \| WILD RIVERS | ♥ | 2:53 |
| SLINGSHOT \| ZACH SEABAUGH, CHANCE PEÑA | ♥ | 2:30 |
| SATURDAY SUN \| VANCE JOY | ♥ | 3:34 |
| DON'T \| WILD RIVERS | ♥ | 3:02 |
| SUNSICK \| BENNETT COAST | ♥ | 2:25 |
| THIS IS ME TRYING \| TAYLOR SWIFT | ♥ | 3:15 |
| WAVES \| DEAN LEWIS | ♥ | 4:00 |
| FAULT LINE \| GRACIE ABRAMS | ♥ | 4:27 |
| MY THOUGHTS ON YOU \| THE BAND CAMINO | ♥ | 3:31 |
| BE \| GARRETT KATO | ♥ | 2:29 |
| DIRTY LOVE \| MT. JOY | ♥ | 2:44 |
| ROSE COLORED LENSES \| MILEY CYRUS | ♥ | 3:43 |
| SAVE ME \| NOAH KAHAN | ♥ | 2:58 |
| LOVE ME BACK \| BEBE STOCKWELL | ♥ | 2:28 |
| TILL FOREVER FALLS APART \| ASHE, FINNEAS | ♥ | 3:42 |

# Chapter One

## KAIA

"I've been thinking about it, and I feel like I deserve to get railed this weekend."

"Jesus Christ, Kaia." My best friend, Elio, scoffs, his usual mellow tone ratcheting up to an unnatural level. "Have some fucking decorum, why don't you?"

I cross my arms with a huff, plopping down onto the edge of my bed across from him. "Coming from the guy who rails people for a living."

Despite his constant attempts to trivialize it, I'm only saying this because it's true. Elio Reynolds—my best friend from childhood and half-willing sober companion—is a well-renowned sex worker. It's not something he enjoys bragging about, but he does make decent money doing it.

According to my estimations, he's made more than enough cash to put himself through college, plus pay off any other debts he's accrued along the way.

"I wouldn't exactly call it a living. Besides, it's one thing for *me* to do it and another to hear about *you* doing it." He tosses his journal down onto my desk, spinning around in his chair to face me. "I think my ears are burning."

"Oh my God, drama queen," I mutter, picking at a particularly nasty split end. "I've actually seen you in the act, you know? That's at least a thousand times worse."

No matter how hard I try, I'm unable to scrub that

disturbing image from my brain. If I remember correctly, it was a balmy June night when I accidentally walked in on him. He was sitting there alone on his couch, manspreading as one does, reviewing a solo scene before popping it up on a subscription site. Thankfully, I clamped both hands over my eyes, screeching out an ungodly sound, before I could witness a full-frontal shot.

And then, you know, the nightmares ensued. For literal months. In fact, I'm still getting over the whole ordeal, and it's fucking September already.

"Alright, so you saw my bare ass through a screen. One. Fucking. Time. And it was an accident." He flippantly gestures toward my chest. "Flash me your tits right now, and we'll call it even."

I lob a throw pillow straight at the center of his forehead. "Go home, E."

"But Kaiaaa," he whines, drawing out my name into three long, annoying syllables. "We only have a few questions left."

We've been working on an assignment for Advanced Calculus for the past three hours. Both of us are deep in the midst of earning our engineering degrees here at Coastal University—electrical for Elio and biomedical for myself. This means that our elective courses occasionally line up.

Luckily for Elio, considering I'm the only one of us holding this fragile team together.

"*You* have a few questions left," I huff. "I've been finished with mine for the last half an hour, waiting for you to catch up and get the hell out of my apartment."

"Okay, Miss Smarty Pants." He waves a dismissive hand, rolling his eyes. "We get it. You're top of the class."

"*Tied* for top of the class." I cough out the spiteful clarification.

"Same shit."

"Hardly."

Leaning back in his chair, he folds his arms together to rest them on his stomach. "Sounds like good ol' Beck's got your panties in a twist again."

Internally, I picture myself drop-kicking Elio out the front door, then hurling his entire backpack full of shit right on behind him. Instead, I say, "*Holden Becker* has nothing to do with my panties, thank you very much."

"You know, I ratted the little hockey superstar out to my sister-in-law the other day." He absentmindedly chews on a cuticle. "She said she'd go hard on him during practice for us."

"Yeah, right." I snort. "I can't imagine Harper going hard on anyone. That girl is like a fairy-tale princess or something. I swear to God."

I'm barely even exaggerating when I say that. Harper Reynolds—his brother's wife and the newest athletic trainer for our school's hockey team—is hands down one of the kindest, most down-to-earth people I've ever met.

Unlike the two of us, I doubt there's even one bad bone in her entire body.

"She's pretty fucking loyal when it comes to family, though," he argues, eyes wide. "You should've seen her the last time I dared to call my brother a pussy. Steam was practically pouring out of her ears."

"Surely not." I suppress my laughter. "Sofia swears she's like the *nicest person ever* . . . which is wild, considering they met while she was still dating Daniel."

"It's funny you should say that because Harper is, like, physically repulsed by your sister. *Still.*"

Oh God, as is her right.

My sister, Sofia, is what I like to call a terminally spoiled serial monogamist. She's also a *seriously* selfish person, with a penchant for dumping her long-term boyfriends at the first sign of trouble. Exhibit A: Elio's brother, Luca, the now-famous NFL linebacker for the Carolina Bobcats.

The two of them were high school sweethearts who started off as middle school friends. I consider their relationship to be her most stable, loving one to date. In fact, they were together for three whole years before she dumped him one night on a visit home, seemingly out of the blue. I'd call it a one-off, except then she moved right on to his best friend, Daniel.

When he was drafted after graduation, she once again decided that she couldn't manage the long distance. She's gone through two other "serious boyfriends" since then.

Now, I wouldn't typically give a shit about my sister's dating history, I swear, but everything she does ruffles my feathers these days.

"Who isn't?" I finally manage to ask, not bothering to mask my contention.

"Ah." The corner of his lip lifts. "So you two are fighting again, then?"

"I'd rather not talk about Sofia right now." I shake my head, clearing my spiraling thoughts. "Also, we've somehow strayed *so far* off the topic of me getting railed this weekend."

It's been a long time coming for me, now that I think about it. I haven't been with anyone since the fall term of last school year, back before I caught my ex cheating on me with his TA. I didn't even like him that much, truthfully, but it still fucking stung.

"Kaia." He clamps both hands over his ears, nose scrunching in visible distaste.

"Fine." I roll my eyes, flipping onto my back to scroll

through my phone. "If you won't talk to me about it, then at least finish your fucking homework so I can check it over."

"Know-it-all," he mutters under his breath.

I turn up my nose. "That's right."

I'M RUNNING on approximately two hours and fifteen minutes of sleep today. After Elio left, I stayed up way too late trying to rework my research proposal. Once I finally crawled under the covers, I tossed and turned in my bed for ages, rifling through thought streams until I could find one pleasant enough to fall asleep to.

My usual coping mechanisms—my weighted blanket (perfectly proportioned at 10 percent of my body weight), my sound machine (playing exactly the right decibel of brown noise), and my 2:00 a.m. snuggles with a body pillow (which I'm fairly certain was designed for a pregnant woman)—were all wildly unsuccessful.

It's okay, though, because I've been expecting this to happen for a long time. On even the best of nights, I have a difficult time shutting off my brain. Last night, one of the worst nights, I let myself ruminate on all the disastrous ways I could screw this up.

*This*—otherwise known as one of the most important days of my life.

There are only fifteen minutes left before my presentation time starts. I'm about to stand in front of a panel of department heads, academic advisors, and esteemed professors. But for now, I'm lingering outside of Weyerhaeuser Hall, tears streaming down one side of my face. Ugly, fat tears that are dripping onto the collar of my Milano silk blouse—the single most expensive piece of clothing I've ever owned.

My palms are sweating, there's an awkward, stabbing ache in my thoracic spine, and I'm about to pop a blood vessel in my left eye. Due to my nearly debilitating lack of sleep last night, it won't stop fucking twitching. This led to me incessantly rubbing and dabbing and blinking, which has caused the situation to spiral so far out of my control.

"*Shit, shit, shit.*" I murmur the words under my breath like some sort of twisted mantra, angrily swiping the tears from my chin. "This is ridiculous, Kaia. Pull yourself together."

I stare at the ragged cobblestone pathway beneath my feet, straining to use my one good eye to focus. There's a faded pattern that I mentally trace, taking three solid, deep breaths while I do.

In through my nose. Out through my mouth.

*Calm down, girl. You've got this.*

I don't even know how long I've been zoning out when I hear a throat clear. It's an abrupt, ragged sound that forces my head to dart up, left eye still pinched shut.

"You good, Karras?"

*Oh, hell no.*

Not now. Not any time, really, but especially not now.

Of course, golden boy Becker would be here to witness my moment of weakness—with his beady brown eyes, his perfect head of sandy hair, and his extremely annoying smile.

Seriously, though, why are his teeth so fucking white? It looks like he bleached them before he rolled out of bed this morning, then sauntered his way through the quad to grace me with his presence.

"Go away," I mutter.

His grin widens. "You're really working yourself up about this proposal, aren't you?"

"Not that it's any of your business, but this"—I angrily

point to my swollen, tear-filled eye—"has nothing to do with the proposal."

"Ah." He gives me a tight-lipped, sympathetic stare. It's one that clearly screams, *I'm not buying it, but sure . . . whatever you say.*

"It doesn't," I insist, resisting the urge to stamp my foot like a petulant child.

"My bad." He holds both hands up in mock defense, giving me a low chuckle. "It was just an educated guess. You know, since you're standing here crying outside of our department building, *oh*"—he glances at what I'm sure is an absurdly expensive watch, raising an amused brow—"about three and half minutes until your presentation time."

"You're kidding." I audibly groan, dabbing under my eye to clear any last lingering tears. "I wanted to get everything set up at five 'til."

He slowly unwraps a peppermint, popping it into his mouth before saying, "Well, looks like you're shit out of luck."

"Yeah, thanks." I scoff, hooking one thumb underneath my backpack strap. "Anyway, I shouldn't waste any more time out here. Good luck following up my proposal, by the way. It's a good one."

"I'm sure it is." There's that smug fucking grin of his again. "I know you always put your *best effort* in."

"Are you really making fun of me for *trying*, Becker?" The snort I let out is not a very pretty one. "What is this, middle school?"

"Not making fun of you at all, Karras." He cracks his widest smile yet. A playful hint of peppermint peeks through the tiny gap in his teeth. "It's one of your best qualities."

I reel back, blinking away the false compliment. "Yeah, okay." In this scenario, no reaction is the best reaction, especially because I know he's trying to get under my skin. "Well, bye, then."

"Hold up a second."

"What is it?" I huff, folding my arms across my chest, impatiently tapping my foot. If he actually makes me late for this proposal, then he won't live to tell the tale. "You have something else to say that'll steer me off course?"

"No." He takes a solid step forward, the rough pad of his thumb swiping across my cheekbone. He draws the corner of his bottom lip beneath his front teeth, a look of pure concentration on his face. "Mascara," he murmurs, rubbing his fingers until the tiny black streak smudges away. "Tends to run when the tears come out."

My eyes narrow as I step away from him, barely managing to suppress a full-body shiver. I blow out a hot breath and quickly recenter myself. Count to three inside my head, mutter a quick thank-you, and then book it inside the building without saying another word.

Fucking strange reaction, I'll admit it. But I suppose when you're running on fumes, even your own body starts to betray you.

# Chapter Two

## HOLDEN

My God, I've never met someone as easily riled up as Kaia Karras. It's likely because I've spent the last three years perfecting the act. Toiling over different ways to get a rise out of her. All I have to do these days is throw her a tiny half-smile, maybe cock my head to the side a little, and her entire body tenses up.

It's one of my favorite pastimes.

Besides, I already know she's going to stroll in front of that panel and knock this shit out of the park. It's just the way she is. She's probably been working on this proposal since the day she was accepted into our major. Meanwhile, I threw my idea together last week.

I know our advisors will like it because it's solid translational research. There are clear, actionable benefits for the population we're serving. Plus, I have community connections.

Professors always eat that shit up.

Don't get me wrong, my idea's a good one, but I'm not going to spend months agonizing over something like this. My final collegiate hockey season is about to start. I need to put on a good enough show to guarantee I'll be signed after graduation.

I was drafted by the Carolina Tornadoes over three years ago, back when I was still a fucking kid. The team's well aware that I want to finish college and secure my degree first, but it feels like there are an infinite number of ways to screw up this opportunity before then.

When all is said and done, the Tornadoes can still refuse to offer me an actual contract. Then, thirty days after graduation, I'll be pushed into the free agent pool, floating around with the rest of the sorry fuckers who couldn't secure a team.

The thought of that happening scares the living hell out of me.

Sure, I'll always have a backup. A fail-safe. I'm graduating next year with a BS in Biomedical Engineering, after all. And, well, there's always the small detail of my trust fund. That's not something I take for granted.

While it hasn't exactly been a walk in the park to get to where I am now, this school shit comes easily to me. Always has. Hockey's where I need to concentrate all my efforts. I'm not saying that I don't have an ounce of natural talent, but I wasn't born into a family of athletes like some of my teammates.

They're the lucky ones.

Instead, I was blessed with a brain that can solve differential equations in my sleep. Not that I'm complaining about that, either. It's an ace problem to have when you're a student athlete, especially one training at my competitive level. I don't have to worry about my grades as much, so it gives me time to put my focus elsewhere.

Since I have a few minutes to kill until it's my turn to present, I settle onto a bench outside Wey Hall. Stretching my legs out, I pull up today's training schedule on my phone. As suspected, I'm slated to stay after practice again today. For some reason, our newest athletic trainer, Harper Reynolds, is riding my ass harder than the rest of the team.

And not in a good way.

She's diagnosed me with something called costochondritis,

which is basically a glorified way to describe my minor chest pains—some inflammatory shit that affects my rib joints. It's a little painful, sure, but it's a pain that I could easily handle on my own. Instead, Reynolds is making me skip out on the good parts of practice, then asking me to stay late for extra rehab.

She's a Coastal U alumni and the wife of a pro linebacker, so she was a shoo-in for this position. Not to mention, Kaia's been dating her brother-in-law for who knows how long. Now that I think about it, that's probably why Harper's treating me like the dirt beneath her shoes. I definitely wouldn't put it past Kaia—nor her parasitic boyfriend, Elio—to tattle on me to Mommy.

It's a sad thing, honestly, considering Kaia's the one pulling all the weight in their relationship. She's the hard worker, the responsible and studious one, and I'm pretty fucking sure she does his homework for him. Whatever. Not my issue.

I just think she could be with someone a little more her caliber, that's all.

Speaking of which, I'm popping another piece of candy into my mouth when she strolls out of our building, head held high. She's in her element now, confidence radiating from head to toe—from her wide smile to her self-assured posture to the notable pep in her step.

She's a fucking vision, isn't she?

"Beck." She clears her throat, tipping her chin up as she steps directly into my sight line. "Good luck wowing them with your half-cocked proposal. Dr. Khatri's eyes were practically sparkling in there."

"I'm so sure they were." I let out a lukewarm chuckle. "You know what's kind of a bummer, though?"

Kaia's been barking up Dr. Khatri's tree since last year, brown-nosing her way into her good graces. But the thing is, we both want her as our dissertation advisor. And I'm not willing to settle to make Kaia happy. This is a competition, after all. The student with the highest-scoring proposal will bid first for their mentor.

Dr. Khatri is my top choice, too. Not because she's my idol, and not because I have some fanatical obsession with her research portfolio, but because she's fucking nice. She gives top marks to students for doing the bare minimum. And that's about all I have to give right now.

"What?" she asks half-heartedly, reaching for the nape of her neck. She gently tugs and twists the shiny, raven strands between her fingers, pulling at the small pieces of her shoulder-length hair.

I lean in, whispering conspiratorially, "I have something you don't."

"Oh, yeah?" She swallows hard, feigning disinterest. "And what's that?"

With an attempt at a casual shrug, I say, "Connections."

"What do you mean?"

"I mean, I have, *what*"—I pretend to do the mental math—"three community collaborators already lined up for this. Plus, a primary contact for sourcing our project equipment."

Her jaw drops. "You're kidding."

"Nope."

"Becker, Jesus Christ!" She swats me on the shoulder, practically huffing and puffing now. "That's the point of having a fucking mentor, isn't it? They're supposed to assist you in bridging connections."

"Yeah, well, when some of the up-front legwork is done, then we can all focus on bigger and better things."

"So what did you do?" She sneers. "Call up Daddy and ask him for a favor this morning?"

I tilt my head, amused at the frustration knitting her brow. Like I said, this girl is easy as hell to rile up. And yeah, I did call up my father last week to ask him for assistance. So what? It was a quick way to find collaborators near Coastal who might be interested in my research question. It's not like I went out of my way to scope this shit out, but I knew that it'd give me a leg up on the competition.

It's all just a bit of friendly fire.

"You act like networking is an issue," I say, pushing back the hair that's flopped onto my forehead.

"*Networking* isn't the issue." Her jaw tightens. "You're using your parents' connections to pull one over on me."

"Not everything's about you, Karras." I can't help but laugh at her contrite expression. She has her hands on her hips now, hackles fully raised. "And besides, I'm simply using all the resources I have at my disposal. It's not my fault if that makes my proposal stand out. Don't tell me you wouldn't do the same."

"I wouldn't." Her eyes narrow in. "You know I've worked my ass off for everything I've accomplished so far."

Her spiteful comment prods at me like a hot poker. As if I haven't worked just as fucking hard in all other aspects of my life. Sure, I have certain advantages because of my family, but it's not like Kaia's lacking privilege, either.

"Oh, please." I barely repress an eye roll. "Spare me the rags-to-riches story. I know your family's well-off, too."

"Whatever." I can see the last embers of her fire wane out. "Go in there with your perfect, golden hair, your shit-eating grin, and all your unmerited *connections*. Just know that when I beat you, it's because I've actually earned it."

"You think my hair is perfect?"

She slaps both hands over her temples, shaking her head. "As always, it's been a colossal waste of time arguing with you."

"Yeah, you're right." I nod, blatantly checking the time on my Audemars Piguet watch. "I better head in. I want to get in there at least five minutes 'til. You know how it is."

"God, you make me so fucking irritated sometimes."

My smile kicks up a few unhealthy notches. "I know."

As PREDICTED, the panel was impressed by my last-minute research proposal. They genuinely appreciated my forethought in reaching out to collaborators. And I could see that fucking sparkle in Khatri's eyes, too. I may not be a shoo-in for top marks, but I'm betting on a near tie between Kaia and myself.

Now that I have that checked off the list, I can refocus my efforts on the more important shit—finding myself a suitable meal before practice.

I shoot off a quick text to one of my wingers, Rai Saito, a guy I've been friends with since we were in diapers. Let's just say the two of us didn't end up playing at Coastal together by chance. And when all is said and done, I wouldn't be surprised if we ended up playing for the same pro team.

Rai Rai also likes to load up on carbs before we hit the ice, so I know he'll meet me here at a moment's notice. Luckily for both of us, there's a dining center directly across from Wey Hall, which I like to refer to as my second home. My first is the rink, and the third and final is my actual house off campus, where I live with Rai and two of our other guys.

By the time he joins me for lunch ten minutes later, I've already scarfed down two full plates of noodles, vegetables, and chicken. I'm on my third round when he slides into the booth across from me, his own plate filled to the brim with food.

"Hey, Becksy," he greets, proceeding to stuff his face before finishing his sentence. "Ow vuv or ruvoval?"

I chuckle at his nonsensical question, raising a perplexed brow. "Come again?"

"Sorry," he mumbles, making a show of chewing his food before clearing his throat. "How was your proposal?"

See, that's one thing I've always loved about Rai. He may not be the brightest, most organized, or cleanliest roommate in the world, but he's a good fucking friend. A solid, dependable sort of guy. He remembers shit that none of the rest of us do, the little things that add up, and he always makes a point to check in.

"Aced it, buddy. Thanks for asking."

"Knew you would, Becksy." He beams. "Did you beat that girl you're always going on about? Kara, right?"

I choke on my own spit, breaking out into a mini coughing fit. "Don't know who you mean."

"Nah, that's right." He snaps his fingers, a lightbulb going off in his brain. "Kaia, no? Kaia Karras?"

Well, *hell*. I guess there's no getting out of this one, is there? I honestly didn't realize I talked that much about her outside of class . . . so much so that my roommate can recite her full fucking name.

"We don't know who came out on top just yet," I say, attempting to downplay my discomfort. "Results to come, Rai."

He gives me an earnest grin, as innocent and clueless as the day he was born. "Well, I'm sure you killed it. You're gonna top your girl Kaia, no doubt."

"I'd definitely fucking like to," I say, grinning at the innuendo that's slipped right over poor Rai Rai's head. "That's one thing I know for sure."

# Chapter Three

## KAIA

HOLDEN BECKER IS such an arrogant little shit. I swear to God he pushes my buttons on purpose because I'm generally an easygoing person.

Okay, maybe that's a bit of a stretch. In certain situations, I can be strung up fairly tight. Meticulous to a fault. But at least I pretend to be easy breezy in front of everyone else. When it comes to him, though, it's like there's this inescapable crack in my façade.

Regardless, I'm not sure how he's fooled the general public into believing that he's some sort of angel. This hapless little puppy who can do no wrong. It's all part of that golden-boy act of his. And unlike the rest of the Coastal U population, I can see below the surface where his claws come out to play.

When it comes to getting what he wants, Holden's just as ruthless and as cutthroat as I am.

If only I could've been a fly on the wall during his proposal today. I bet he charmed the pants right off those panel members. First, by flashing them that perfectly polished smile of his—maybe fumbling around with his notecards just to appear unassuming—and then running his fingers through that thick head of golden hair.

After that, as long as he was able to string a few coherent words together, they probably ate his idea right up.

While he may be an intelligent guy, his entire persona is

the reason he stands out amongst our peers. It's the whole Becker package wrapped up with a neat little bow. As much as it pains me to admit this, even to myself, the man is abhorrently good-looking. He's also a confident, highly capable athlete. And, much to my dismay, the two of us are tied for the highest GPA in our department.

So yeah, all things considered, he's super fucking annoying.

After making it through that eye-twitching proposal this morning, I've spent the last few hours relaxing on my own. Well, my version of relaxing, which includes holing up in my apartment and studying my ass off. Par for the course, I've finished at least half of next week's assignments already.

That's the price I have to pay for partying this weekend. Like I told Elio, I'm both desperate for and deserving of some action. It's basically a deserted wasteland down there. And while I don't usually make an effort to go out with my roommate, Lizzie, it's a sacrifice I'm willing to make tonight.

Lizzie's much more of a party girl than I am, a coed that's devoted to living out all of her college daydreams. We've been sharing an apartment together for over a year now, but the two of us have never been very close. There's nothing wrong with her, per se, other than the fact that she always asks me to pay for her shit. Plus, it can be difficult for me to open up to new people in general.

I still consider myself lucky to have found her, though. We used to be neighbors in the sophomore dorms, and we both happened to be looking for an apartment at the same time. Other than that, our list of commonalities stops right about there.

If I had a legitimate choice in the matter, I would force Elio to take me somewhere instead. He's one of the few people I can always trust myself to let loose around. Unfortunately, he's not interested in attending parties these days. Mostly because he doesn't know if he can handle that type of environment yet.

He's a strong guy—and he hasn't relapsed in nearly three years—but the temptation still lingers in the back of his mind.

So, it'll just be Lizzie and me tonight. I'm sure it'll be a great time as long as I can keep my mind on the mission—finding someone to rail me, that is. Hopefully, well enough that I'm finally able to fall asleep afterward.

"Where is this party, anyway?" I ask Lizzie later that night, nearly tripping as I slip on a pair of comfortable shoes. She said we could trek over to this place on foot, so practicality is my top priority. Thankfully, there's still a warm, coastal breeze here at night, which means we don't have to worry too much about layering up.

"Probably about a mile from here," she says, tossing me an innocent smile from across the hall. "Maybe a little more."

My brow furrows with apprehension. I'm all for cutting back on gas emissions, but I feel a little wary about walking that far in the dark, especially when it's just the two of us girls. "Are you sure we shouldn't grab an Uber?"

"If you want to call one for us, that's cool with me."

As I bring up the app, I resist the urge to heave a sigh. I know I'm the one pushing for it, but with Lizzie's track record, I'm inclined to believe this was her plan from the get-go. "What are the cross streets?"

"Fifty-Sixth and University."

"Fifty-Sixth?" I adjust my skirt in front of our entryway mirror, hiking my stockings up and tucking them underneath the hemline. "Isn't that a few blocks past Greek Row?"

"Exactly."

"Exactly, what?"

She joins me in front of the mirror, swiping a tube of shiny pink gloss across her lips. "That's where all the student athletes congregate."

"Athletes?" I resist the urge to visibly cringe. "Are we talking football, baseball . . . ?"

"Hockey, Kaia." She gives me a playful scoff. "I guess you wouldn't really know, but those guys always throw the best parties."

"How is that even possible?" I run my fingers through my wand-curled strands, securing the tiny wayward pieces, to ensure that my hair's still parted in its rightful place. I like to keep it slightly to the left of center, where I'm able to camouflage the small empty patch. "Aren't they supposed to be focused on winning games or something?"

"Hockey season doesn't start for another week, so this will be their last big hurrah." She smacks her lips together, dabbing the excess gloss from the corner. "I mean, there will definitely be some other parties later on, but nothing like tonight."

"Well, that's just great, then."

"Is there an issue?" She raises one perfectly manicured brow. "I thought you were looking for a hookup tonight, anyway. And believe me when I say that these hockey players are *hot*."

"Yeah, I just—I kind of know someone on the team." My nose wrinkles, discomfort panging in the center of my sternum. "Someone I'm hoping we can avoid tonight."

"What's his name?"

"Uh, Holden? Holden Becker."

"No shit?" Her blue eyes go wide, a soft sparkle in the mirror's reflection. "How do you know him?"

"We share the same major. I might've mentioned him once

or twice before." I wave a flippant hand, feigning nonchalance. "You know that guy who constantly pisses me off?

Her brow scrunches as she racks her brain. "The one who glares at Elio for no reason?

"Yeah."

"*That's* him?" She swats me on the arm. "No freakin' way. Why didn't you mention he was the captain of the hockey team?"

"Didn't feel relevant at the time."

"Girl, that's the most relevant part." She runs her fingers through her strawberry blonde curls, fluffing them to utter perfection. As per usual, her appearance is flawless from head to toe. "Holden Becker is ridiculously hot. You do know that, right?"

"Yes, I'm more than aware."

Her eyes light up at my admission, lips lifting in a not-so-subtle smirk. "Wait, do you have a little crush on him or something?"

"God, no." I let out a humorless snort. "Did you hear what I just said? I can't stand the guy."

She stifles a giggle. "We all know there's a thin line between love and hate, Kaia."

"Sure, in some cases, but not with us. Trust me, there's nothing but a thick, solid, *completely* impenetrable line separating the two of us."

"Yeah, alright." She shakes her head, muttering something about overcompensating under her breath. "So, if we see him tonight, then you don't mind if I shoot my shot?"

"By all means, go right ahead. Just know he has an ego about the size of his daddy's bank account."

My family may be well-off, as Holden so kindly pointed out, but we have nowhere near the level of financial security that he does. He's generationally wealthy. A trust fund baby. And I just happen to have parents who prioritize their careers over their family.

She leans forward, patting me softly on the shoulder. "Aw, it's sweet you think I'd care about his personality."

By the time the Uber drops us off, I've convinced myself that I was worried over nothing. We're not guaranteed to run into Holden tonight. In fact, the house is bound to be too overcrowded to even warrant concern. Or, if we're lucky enough, he'll already be busy showing some poor girl all his little gold medals and first-place trophies.

God knows what kind of bullshit lines he must spew at these parties.

As we hurry across the street, the sound of pounding music blares from the open windows. Lizzie nudges me with her elbow, nodding toward a couple that's practically dry-humping on the front lawn. I give them silent kudos for the spectacle, then quickly divert my eyes to take in the rest of the scene.

Of course, these hockey boys are just as ostentatious as I assumed. Two giant stone pillars line their entryway, topped by a pair of hideous osprey statues. They must be at least three feet tall in height and even bigger in width.

*Holy shit.* I have to crane my neck to see the tips of their wings. It's well known that D1 athletes pride themselves on their school spirit, but surely this is taking things to a whole other level.

Shaking my head at the absurdity, I let Lizzie take the lead. She links our arms together as we approach the front door, ringing the bell with her free hand.

"Do we not just go in?" I ask, confused by the sudden air of formality.

"Not at these parties, Kaia." She gives me a patronizing smile, one that reminds me exactly how clueless I am about this stuff. "They're invite only."

"Invite only? What are these guys—fucking celebrities?"

"I mean, kinda? They have to be careful with who they let inside." Her tone sounds so matter-of-fact, like we should all just agree that hockey players deserve the royal treatment. "One wrong move and it could cost them their spot on the team. And then, eventually, their entire careers."

"Yeah, I guess," I agree with a shrug, unwilling to argue semantics at this time of night.

"Don't worry, you'll—"

She's cut off by the double doors swinging open in front of us. A tall guy with tan skin and dark hair greets us with a smile; it's brilliant and huge, one of the most genuine I've seen coming from a complete stranger.

"Hey, ladies, I don't believe we've met. I'm Rai." He slides a phone out of his back pocket, pulling up what I can only assume is an invite list. He peers down at the device, tapping his foot, casually flicking his thumb across the screen as he asks, "Can I get your names?"

"Lizzie Davis and Kaia Karras," my roommate confidently rattles off, attempting to charm him with a sweet, glossy smile of her own.

Rai's head darts up, one brow shooting skyward. "Sorry, did you just say Karras?"

I rear back, carefully studying his mystified expression. "What, do you know my sister or something?"

His answering grin is nothing short of giddy—there's an almost creepy, unrestrained glint in his eye now—but I have no fucking clue what he could be so happy about. It's strange considering the fact that I've never seen this man before in my life.

"Or something." He rapidly taps out a text before slipping his phone back into his pocket. As he sidesteps next to us, one of his giant arms wraps around our shoulders, guiding us inside the open doorway. "Come in, come in. It's gonna be a great night."

# Chapter Four

## HOLDEN

If I get one more text from Rai telling me to get my ass downstairs, then I'm going to bang my head against my bedroom wall. I already explained that I wanted a chill night to myself for once. I had a rough week, I'm tired, and I don't feel like drinking.

I'd be fine socializing with just the guys, but I don't even know half of the people here right now.

I let Rai and our other roommates, Bodie and Will, host this party because it's a tradition for us. It's the last big drinking night before the season officially starts. And the guys really needed to let off some steam, too. I don't mind the noise or the chaos generally, but Rai needs to learn that no means no.

I'm not going down there, no matter how many times he begs me to.

Stretching my legs out on my king-sized bed, I use my PS4 controller to scroll through Netflix on the big screen. I'm looking for something high-action, with an excessive number of explosions and car chase scenes to drown out the pop music. Something loud and chaotic.

There's never anything good to watch, but at least I'll have some decent background noise while I scroll through my phone.

As I make my final selection, my bedroom door swings open, and a very confused girl stumbles inside. She has dark, shoulder-length hair, a short skirt that accentuates her hips, and legs that go on for days—ones that I'd recognize anywhere.

"Karras?" Cocking an amused brow, I toss my controller to the side, pleasantly surprised—and equally confused—by the intrusion. "To what do I owe the pleasure?"

"Oh, you've gotta be kidding me." She mumbles something unintelligible, but I'm fairly certain it's derogatory. "I'm guessing this isn't the fucking bathroom, is it?"

I chuckle, gesturing toward my splayed-out position on the bed. Inside my room, there's a flat-screen TV and a well-stocked minifridge. My five-level bookshelves are lined with textbooks, trophies, and mementos from the last twenty-one years of my life.

It's enormous, but seeing as I'm the one fronting two-thirds of the rent, the guys let me claim the main bedroom for myself.

"Not sure what kind of bathrooms you've been going in lately."

"Your guy Rai, he told me to come up here." She crosses her arms over her chest with a huff, pushing her tits directly into my line of sight. I strain to keep my gaze focused elsewhere. "Second door on the left, no?"

"That little fuckwit." I can't control my smirk. "He sent you in here on purpose. No wonder he's been messaging me all night."

"Very funny." She stares at me with a blank expression. It takes her a few extra moments to fully register my words before she shakes her head, narrows her eyes, and asks, "Well, then?"

"Well, what?"

"Do you have a bathroom in here or not?"

I push myself off the bed, trying my best not to look like a fucking dweeb as I stretch out in front of her. I've been lounging in bed for the last hour, so my sweatpants hang low on my hips, my T-shirt long gone in the laundry hamper.

"Right this way." I motion for her to step in front of me, guiding her through my walk-in closet. To my slight embarrassment, it's kind of a disaster in here. Thank God I had the foresight to clean up my en suite bathroom earlier this week.

"Would you look at that," she mutters, running her fingertips across a row of my clothing. "A whole damn closet full of shirts you could put on."

I clench my abs, involuntarily flexing at her insinuation. Well, alright, then, it looks like she's not as flagrantly unaffected by me as she pretends to be. "You're the one who barged into my room without invitation."

"Yeah, well, I don't know why you're sitting here alone half-naked while there's a party going on downstairs." She walks fully into my bathroom, turning on her heel to face me. "A party that's being hosted at your house."

"Probably 'cause I can do whatever the hell I want in my own house." I lean against the doorframe, perched up against it with one raised arm. Staring down at her, I add, "In my own bedroom, for that matter."

"Oh, God." She shudders, eyes quickly diverting to the crotch of my sweatpants. Gesturing wildly toward the subtle outline of my dick, she all but whispers, "You weren't about to, like, *you know* . . ."

"No, I don't know." I bite my lower lip, holding back laughter. "You're gonna need to be a little more explicit than that."

"You know exactly what I'm referring to, Becker," she bites out through gritted teeth, cheeks flushed a rosy shade of pink. "Don't pretend you're that clueless."

"You're asking if I was about to fuck myself up here?" I grin at her outraged expression. There she goes again—so easily flustered. "Alone in my bedroom while all of you partied downstairs?"

She nearly chokes, eyes popping wide. "I, uh, I wasn't—"

"What?" I cock my head, feigning confusion. "Rendered you speechless for once?"

"No." There's a fire blazing in her eyes now. "I just wasn't expecting you to be so gross about it."

I lean further onto the frame, propping my head against the crux of my elbow. "So you think masturbating is gross, then?"

"You know what?" She pinches the bridge of her nose, eyes closed as she shakes her head—a frantic little bobble back and forth. Then, placing one hand on the door and the other flat against my chest, she gently shoves me out of the room. "Never mind. Just—just let me use the restroom, and then I'll leave you alone to . . . do whatever it is you were about to do up here."

I clear my throat. "Touch myself, you mean?"

I wasn't, hand to God, but I'm certainly enjoying this anyway. Fighting with her, making her blush, fueling her fire, that is.

She narrows her eyes—tiny green flecks glinting in the fluorescent lights—and scolds me like a child. "Stop it."

Holding my hands up in mock defense, I retreat back to my bed. It doesn't take long to resume my former position, stretching my long legs across the mattress and flicking my movie back into play mode.

Sure, I may have wanted to be alone tonight, but pressing Kaia's buttons is always a welcome interruption.

A few minutes into Tom Cruise's monologuing, I hear the faucet running. It's followed by the faint sound of a door closing, fumbling footsteps, and then the sweet murmurings of Kaia talking to herself. I can't make out most of what she's saying, but I know I hear the words "golden" and "arrogant" mixed in there somewhere.

When she finally pops out of my closet, she says, "Well, thanks for that. I'm gonna go back to the party now."

"Hey," I call, voice soft and low, effectively stopping her in her tracks. "Before you head out, I'm just wondering one thing."

She perches both hands on the swell of her hips. "Do I even wanna know?"

"Probably not, but I'm gonna ask you anyway." I stretch both arms up, folding my fingers together behind my head. Following a casual yawn, I ask, "How would your boyfriend feel about us being alone together up here? You know, with you asking me questions about my dick and all?"

Her head drops back with a groan. "Okay, first off, that's not what just happened. And second, I don't know what *boyfriend* you're talking about."

I perk up at the notion, shifting a little more upright against my headrest. "Little Reynolds?"

"Jesus Christ, Elio is not my boyfriend." There's a deep frown line etched into her forehead. "And he'd kill you if he heard you call him *little*." She gives me a half-smirk of her own, as if she's secretly pleased by my insult. "The two of us have been friends for ages, though, like little kids on the playground type shit. We're *not* together."

"Huh." I press my tongue to the side of my cheek, giving her a noncommittal shrug.

"*Huh*, what?" There's that telltale blush again, but this time, the heat seems to come from a place of anger. "Are you one of those misogynistic weirdos who think that men and women can never *just* be friends?"

"Not at all."

She gives me a look of blatant disbelief. "Then what?"

"I just didn't realize that you two weren't a thing." I scratch the back of my neck. "I thought—well, this whole time, I thought you guys were dating. It's kind of blowing my mind."

"Okay . . . ?" Her tone is skeptical. "Sorry to disappoint."

I grin. "Doesn't disappoint me at all."

"Right." She drags out the word, one hand poised on the doorknob, clearly in a rush to head back to the party. "Well, as entertaining as this has been, I'm gonna go smack your friend Rai upside the head and then resume my mission for the night."

"Mission?"

"I—uh, never mind, actually." Her hand awkwardly moves into her hair. "I shouldn't have even brought it up."

"Ah, but you can't stop there, Karras." Pausing my movie for the second time, I raise a curious brow. "Tell me about this mission of yours."

"And what do I get out of it?"

"I promise not to show you up in class on Monday."

"Hard pass." She shakes her head, giving me an unimpressed frown. "You couldn't even if you tried. We have a guest lecturer this week, and I happen to know them on a personal level."

"I can get Rai Rai back for you," I offer.

"I think I can fight my own battles where *Rai Rai* is concerned."

"Alright." I make one last-ditch effort. "What if I promise to help you, then?"

"Help me?"

"Yeah, on this mission of yours. If you tell me what your goal is for the night, I bet I could help you accomplish it in, like, half the time."

"Yeah, I'm so sure you could." She snorts, her distrustful

gaze flickering across my face. "You know what? Fine. As embarrassing as this is, I'm looking for a hookup tonight. If you have any friends that aren't total jerks, I'd be down for a setup."

At her request, there's an uncomfortable pinching sensation in my chest. For some reason, I'm rattled by the thought of her hooking up with one of my teammates. It's not because I want her for myself—to date her or anything like that—but it's just the principle of the matter.

Kaia Karras is mine to fuck with.

"Hell no," I finally manage to spit out.

She's taken aback by my sudden mood shift, brow creasing in confusion. "What, why?"

I grapple with an excuse, finally settling on, "I'm just not doing that."

"So you don't think I'm good enough for your friends?" She crosses her arms and lifts her chin, indignant. "Is that it?"

"What's that supposed to mean?"

"I get it—you hockey boys are like celebrities on this campus. And what, because I don't usually party with you guys or because I'm not in a sorority, then I'm suddenly not even worth a hookup?"

I bite back a bitter laugh. "Yeah, you're putting a whole lotta words in my mouth that I sure as hell didn't say."

"Whatever." She rolls her eyes, frantically attempting to push my door open. "Forget it. I'll find someone on my own."

"Yeah, have fun with that."

"I will," she flippantly tosses back, not bothering to shut the door on her way out.

"Great," I mutter to an otherwise empty room.

Gritting my teeth, I press play for the third time, cranking up the volume on my TV. It's a dramatic attempt to drown out the party noise and sufficiently distract myself. Unfortunately, it's futile.

The longer I sit here alone, the more and more irritated I become. I'm fully fidgeting now—twiddling my thumbs in my lap, patting the empty space on my mattress, toggling the joystick on my controller.

I'm feeling uneasy, and I'm overwhelmed by the urge to hop back out of bed. I could throw on a shirt, wash my face, and then check out the fucking party for a minute or two. Just to see what's going on down there. Rai, Bodie, and Will would probably appreciate my showing face, at the very least. And I don't even have to drink anything.

No harm, no foul.

# Chapter Five

KAIA

By the time I make it back down to the party, Lizzie's already sitting in Rai's lap, one arm looped around his neck with her head tipped back mid-laughter. I should've known she'd instantly find someone to cling to in my absence.

She's the type of girl who knows exactly what she wants and isn't afraid to go after it. And while I do admit they make a cute—albeit temporary—couple, that doesn't absolve Rai from being on my shit list right now.

With a muffled groan, I squeeze in beside them on the couch, nudging him harshly with my elbow. Lizzie gives me an odd look.

"He's in trouble," I offer by way of explanation.

"Moi?" Rai presses an open palm to his chest, eyes widening in faux surprise. "Whatever for?"

"Don't play coy," I playfully scold, lips rolling together. "You sent me straight into the lion's den."

His sly grin widens. "But he's such a friendly lion."

"Sure he is," I grumble, rolling my eyes. "Actually, now that I think about it, how were you even aware that we knew each other?

He shifts awkwardly in his seat, tension creasing his brow. "Ah, er—he may have mentioned your name in passing once or twice."

My brows shoot up. "Mhm, and you just happen to have a photographic memory?"

"Exactly," he says, nodding as if he's proud of himself for the lie. It's a shitty attempt at diversion, but I'm not going to press him on it. Not here, at least, when he's at least three drinks deep with a squirming girl on his lap.

I'll save my skepticism for his housemate.

Lizzie perks up, her questioning gaze darting between the two of us. "What are you guys talking about?"

"Thanks to this one"—with a sarcastic smile, I pat the offender's bicep—"I just forced my way into Becker's bedroom."

"Oh!" Her eyes spark with mischief, gaze drifting around the party. "Did you convince him to come join us, then?"

I grimace at the thought. "No attempts were made."

She sighs, shoulders falling as she curls further into Rai's open arms. "Bummer."

"You know him, too?" Rai asks, painfully clueless.

"No, but I'd like to," she says in a suggestive tone.

"*Lizzie.*" My jaw drops, her blunt response taking me by surprise. "You're literally sitting on top of another guy right now. You do know that, right?"

"Oh, he doesn't mind." She rests her head on Rai's shoulder, winking as she does. "Right, Rai?"

"Nah, you're good," he says dismissively, his smile unwavering. "I get it. Becksy's a real catch. But you know, he only seems to have eyes for—" He clamps a hand over his mouth, nose scrunched as he attempts to backtrack. "—hockey. Right now, he only has eyes for hockey."

"Hm," Lizzie murmurs, unimpressed. "I'm glad that *hockey* can warm his bed at night. Speaking of, do you have another friend here for Kaia?"

Rai tilts his head. "A friend?"

"Teammate?" Lizzie makes a second attempt. "Kaia's looking for a bed warmer herself."

"Ah." He swallows hard, visibly uncomfortable. "Well, I don't really—"

"Ugh, not you, too," I groan, exasperated by his hesitation. "What's the damn problem with setting me up? I already knew Becker had a stick up his ass, but—"

A throat clears behind me, then, "You talkin' about me again, Karras?"

With a heavy sigh, I slowly tilt my gaze. Holden's standing at the back of the couch now, one hand clasped against Rai's shoulder while the other slicks through his sandy hair. A long-sleeve black shirt and jeans combo replace his half-naked look from earlier.

If I'm being honest, it's not exactly an upgrade.

"Why are you everywhere?" I ask through gritted teeth.

"Again, you're in my house." His lip quirks into a cocky grin. "Go on, then. You know I have a stick up my ass, *but what*?"

"But nothing." I push myself off the couch, discreetly tugging my skirt back into place. At this point, my stockings have inched well below the hemline, and there's little I can do about it. "If neither of you is willing to help me, then I'll just have to help myself."

With a nod of acknowledgment to Lizzie, I turn my back on the boys and wander alone into the crowd. The house is packed but nowhere near the level I'd originally assumed. Apparently, these hockey players take their exclusivity seriously.

It's a wonder my roommate could secure us an invite, seeing as she doesn't personally know any of the players.

Pushing through the living room, I make my way into the

kitchen. There are two kegs near the sidewall, a cooler of chasers, a few handles of hard liquor, and a ten-gallon Gatorade dispenser—undoubtedly filled with jungle juice. I opt for a shot of cheap vodka from one of the unopened bottles on the counter.

To my displeasure, the taste is absolutely disgusting. It's a syrupy strawberry flavor that barely masks the underlying hints of gasoline. A shudder racks through my body as I desperately search for something to wash it down with.

"I can make you a drink," says an unfamiliar male voice.

With a wince, I glance up from where I'm kneeling at the cooler. There's an exceptionally tall man standing at the entryway to the kitchen. He has dark hair, a golden-brown complexion, and a bit of a five-o'clock shadow. He's a tad lanky for my taste, but he's still quite handsome.

"How long have you been standing there?" I awkwardly ask.

"Long enough to see you gag on that Smirnoff."

Soft laughter bubbles out of me. "Not one of my finer moments."

"It's okay." He gives me a polite smile. "I would, too. But I could make you an actual drink if you'd like. Not to brag, but I'm quite the mixologist."

"What's your name?"

"Douglas. Yours?"

"Kaia."

"Pretty." His cheeks draw up into a grin. "So, what do you say? Do you want that drink?"

Oh, I think I kinda like this guy. Although we've barely interacted, I can already tell that he's funny, sweet, and straightforward—a perfect combination of traits for a one-night stand.

"Would you want to dance instead?" I boldly ask. "I should probably cap myself at two drinks an hour."

"Oh." A tinge of red heat creeps up his neck. "I don't really dance."

Uncapping the water bottle I pulled from the cooler, I take a long, slow slip. Then with a shrug, I say, "Okay, your loss."

"But I—I suppose I can make an exception."

Smiling, I set my bottle down and thread our hands together, pulling him out of the kitchen and back into the room of partygoers. There's an upbeat pop song blasting from the speakers. While we dance, his hands come to rest along the curve of my waist while mine wind carefully around his neck.

His touch is featherlight, polite, and reserved. He's a bit too much of a gentleman to pick up on my subtle hints. So if I want to move things in the right direction, I'll need to step up my own game.

Slowly spinning in place, I press my back to his front and lean further against him. Tentatively, his arms snake around my body, caressing me. As the air between us heats up, the song switches to something low and slow.

While we dance, my gaze aimlessly drifts around the crowd. I spot Lizzie and Rai in the same place that I left them. Holden's still there, too, of course, manspreading beside them on the couch, red Solo cup lifted to his lips. It's not long before he notices me staring.

We make eye contact, and his mouth quirks up into a smirk. He lifts his cup toward me, tipping it in a form of silent cheers. Lifting a challenging brow, he takes another slow, deliberate drink, and a prickle of discomfort dots up my spine.

I'm not sure what his aim is here, but at this point, he's successfully disrupted my equilibrium. Shaking my head clear, I attempt to refocus my attention on my dance partner. It's nearly impossible, though, considering I can still feel Holden's gaze smoldering in our direction.

I manage to make it through one more song before my eyes stray back to the scene. But where Lizzie and Rai remain, Holden's nowhere to be found.

*Oh, fucking hell.*

By now, I've lost all semblance of interest in the guy I'm dancing with . . . whose name I can't even seem to recall. So I give up and excuse myself, wandering back over to the cozy couple.

"Alright," I say with a heavy sigh. "I think tonight might be a bust for me, Liz. I kind of want to head out."

"No worries." She nuzzles closer to Rai, sipping slowly from her cup. It looks like she's been nursing the same one for the past hour, so I'm not too concerned about loose inhibitions. "I think I'm gonna stay here, though."

"You sure?"

"Yeah, text me when you make it back to the apartment."

"Let me know if you need anything, okay?" I muster up my most threatening look, pointing an accusing finger at Rai. He lifts an amused brow as I say, "And you, don't do anything that deserves an ass kicking."

"I'll be perfectly safe, *Mom*," Lizzie chides, rolling her eyes. "Don't you worry."

I cut through the crowd, making my way through the front door and back onto their ostentatious porch. As I fumble with my phone, pulling up the Uber app, those ugly bird statues glare down at me, and a sudden shiver racks my body.

"Leaving so soon?"

I freeze in place, spine stiffening at the sound of Holden's irritating voice. My fingers run through the ends of my hair as I turn to face him. He's leaning against the house, partially hidden by the pillar's shadow.

"You really are everywhere."

"Just getting some air," he says, lips pressed into a flat line. "Why?"

He gestures toward the star-painted sky in front of us. It's clear, cloud-free, a midnight blue that glows on the horizon. "It's a nice night."

I shake my head, recalling how he watched me dance from across the room, his eyes burning into us. One minute, he was there. The next, he disappeared. "Yeah, is that the only reason?"

"What other reason would I have, Karras?"

"Never mind." I sigh, nibbling on my bottom lip. I don't know if I'm reading into things I shouldn't, but I'm not going to be the first one of us to crack. I move to step down from the porch and say, "I'll see you in class, Beck."

"Do you need a ride?"

My brow arches as I rear back. "What?"

"A ride?" He assesses me with a smug smirk. "You know, the thing where you get in my car and I drive you home."

"Haven't you been drinking?"

"Water," he says earnestly, forming a quick cross over his chest. "That's it."

I eye him suspiciously. "Why are you being nice to me?"

"Feel like mixing it up."

I contemplate his offer for a long moment. It would be a quick ride back to our apartment, maybe a few minutes spent together in total. It's not like I would owe him anything in return. Plus, I'm a big fan of saving both money and time.

"Yeah, okay," I finally agree. "I'll take a ride."

"My car's just around back."

I follow him around the house to their private parking lot. Of course, this man drives a fucking convertible Ferrari. It's all sorts of extravagant and flashy, especially for a college student. And when you're living in a small coastal town like ours, the smallest of things will draw attention.

Holden must crave it.

But since he's doing me a favor tonight, I bite back all the snarky comments I'd like to make aloud.

"Soo . . ." I trail off instead, an awkward attempt at civil conversation.

"You want to tell me why you're leaving so early?" he cuts in with a blunt question, a direct hit to my already fragile psyche. "I thought you were on a mission tonight."

I swallow thickly. "Yeah, I struck out."

"Really?" He shifts gears as he continues, reversing from the lot. "Looked like you were about to score a home run."

I scratch my forearm. "Wasn't as interested in him as I thought."

"Why not?" He yawns, absentmindedly tapping his thumb against the steering wheel. We pull onto the main street as he adds, "Dougie's a good guy."

"Oh? Should I go back there, then?" I snort a laugh. "Give *Dougie* another shot?"

"Wouldn't go that far."

"How far would you go, then?"

He's taken aback by my sharp tone. "What?"

"You heard me. I said, how far would you go? Because from where I'm sitting, it sure seems like you're determined to cock-block me."

A grunt-snort hybrid escapes him. "The things you dream up in that head of yours, Karras."

"I'm right, aren't I?" I force down a lump in my throat,

steeling my spine with confidence. "For some twisted reason, you want me all for yourself."

"Fine." His grip on the steering wheel tightens, but his gaze stays painfully neutral. "Say you're right. Say I *do* want you. Then what?"

"It's never gonna happen. You know that, right?" My voice drops low, confusion coloring my tone. "You've made it your life's mission to get under my skin. You're annoying as hell, and you're always pushing my boundaries, so—"

"If you want to set real boundaries with me, Karras, I'll respect them. But something tells me you get some sort of sick enjoyment out of our bickering." He licks his lips, his gaze cutting to me for no more than a split second. "I know I sure as hell do."

A thick silence rings through the heavy air between us. I have no fucking clue what to even say to that, so I keep my lips pressed tightly shut.

"If I'm way off base right now, just tell me," he continues, caramel eyes flashing with contrition. "Hand to God, I won't bother you again."

"What do you mean?"

"I won't approach you," he says softly, seriously. "I won't speak to you unless I'm spoken to. In fact, I won't even give you a second look if that's what you want from me."

My shoulders slump. "Oh."

"Is that what you want, Kaia?"

"No." My throat's filled with gravel, the jagged shards burning through me as I swallow. "No, that's not what I want."

# Chapter Six

## HOLDEN

I PULL up to Kaia's apartment building and quietly cut the engine. She may not want me to completely disappear from her life, but I still don't know where that leaves us for now. But what I do know, without a doubt, is that there's a part of her that's inexplicably drawn to me.

The same way I've been drawn to her for the past three years.

Her earlier admission has forged an uneven playing field between us. And right now, for the first time, I'm the one who has the upper hand.

"Well, thanks for the ride." She awkwardly breaks the silence. As she reaches for the door handle, I place a hand over hers, stopping her.

"Can I just say one more thing?"

"What is it?" she asks, impatient.

"I know we don't always get along, but you should know I never want to push you any further than you're willing to go."

"Why do you even care about what I think?" She arches a brow, voice laced with skepticism.

"I just do."

Her expression softens as she sighs. "Beck, you don't even like me."

"That's not true," I say, a small smile playing at the corners of my lips. "There's nothing I enjoy more than riling you up on a moment's notice. Well, that's a lie. First, there's hockey, and then, well, there's actual sex."

Her eyes narrow in response, and I know that she's not amused.

"What do you mean, *actual* sex?"

"Oh, you know, this thing we have going on," I say, gesturing between us. "The way we get under each other's skin. It's a bit like foreplay, no?"

"Wow," she deadpans. "And here I was, thinking we were actually having a nice moment for once. I'll take that as my cue to leave." She lets herself out of the car, patting the top of the door. "Good night, Beck."

"'Night, Karras," I toss back. "Sweet dreams."

Monday morning, I wake up early, my body already tense with anticipation for today's practice. My roommates are fucking dead on their feet, as always, so I do my fatherly duties and bang my fists on their bedroom doors.

One by one, they wake up and join me for a carb-loaded breakfast.

I grab my gear, double-checking that everything is in its rightful place before heading out to the rink. I'm the designated driver, as per usual, since we all like to feel the wind in our hair on the short drive to campus.

It's a fucking beach town, what can I say?

As we drive, the cool morning air pelts into me, but it's a welcome relief from the musky heat of our living room. The guys still haven't completely cleaned up since the party on Friday night. Rai Rai volunteered to do it all by himself, but I told him to make the other guys pull their own weight for once.

And hell, I only joined the party for about ten minutes before dipping out, so it's not my job, either.

Once I find a spot to park outside the rink, the four of us spill out of my convertible and hastily make our way inside.

"Morning, boys," I greet the rest of my teammates, taking my place on the bench beside them.

They give me noncommittal grunts in return, attention clearly focused elsewhere. It *is* seven o'clock in the morning on a Monday, so my expectations weren't set too high in the first place.

Before I can get another word in to cut the silence, Coach Clark blows his whistle, signaling the start of practice. We all take to the ice, our skates carving patterns into the freshly resurfaced rink.

I take my rightful place in the center, skating past my favorite roommate. "So, Rai Rai, you feelin' ready?" I ask, shooting him a grin.

"You know it, man." He laughs, dark eyes shining with excitement. "I've been working on my breakouts all summer."

"I've been working on my slap shot," Bodie chimes in beside us. "You better watch out, Becksy. I might steal your spotlight."

"Says the third liner," I cough under my breath, earning myself a harsh glare.

We turn our attention back to Coach Clark, who's rattling off our practice schedule. We start with a simple passing drill, moving the puck around the rink in a specific pattern.

After a few rounds, Coach switches it up, directing us to work on breakaways. I line up for my shot, taking a deep breath before skating toward the goal. I shoot the puck, watching as it sails past our goalie, Dean, and straight into the net.

Bodie skates up beside me, clapping me on the back. "Nice shot. Maybe I'll let you keep your limelight after all."

I chuckle. "Thanks, man. That's big of you."

We run through a few more drills and plays, sweat beading on our foreheads as we work on perfecting our game. Energy builds in the rink, the excitement of the fresh season warming our blood.

As practice winds down, Clark calls us over for a huddle. "Good work, boys," he says, his breath visible in the frigid air. "We've got a tough season ahead of us." Then he rattles off some more inspirational bullshit before we break, skating off the ice and back to the locker room.

There's a sharp, burning sensation in my chest and a dull, seething ache in my muscles, but it's a satisfying feeling. We've been putting in the work, and it's bound to pay off, the same way it does every fucking year.

As we strip off our gear, a sense of contentment brews inside of me. For the last seventeen years of my life, hitting the ice has always been my favorite way to recharge—my oasis in the desert, my guiding light.

I quickly shower and change before heading off to my morning lecture. As I grab my bag and head for Wey Hall, my mind drifts back to Friday night with Kaia. I'm chalking the whole thing up to a momentary lapse in judgment.

I was shocked to find out that my assumptions about her and Elio were false. And yeah, I am fucking attracted to her. In a big way.

I mean, who wouldn't be?

But the fact that I practically stalked her at the party, offered her a ride home, and then insinuated that our verbal sparring was akin to foreplay—well, it was all a bit much, even for me.

Shaking it off, I make my way inside the lecture hall, scanning the seats for a spot to sit. My stomach dips when I see Kaia sitting near the front, her soft raven hair brushing against her bare shoulders.

I take a deep breath and make my way over to the opposite side of the room. Unable to stop myself, I glance in her direction, trying to catch her eye. But she doesn't even bother to look my way for a split second.

I'll admit, it stings a little.

After our last conversation, I'm confused. She admitted that she doesn't want me to leave her alone, but I'm still struggling to figure out exactly where the line is drawn.

As the lecture begins, I'm easily distracted. I sneak a few more glances toward her, taking in the way her hair dusts across her shoulders and how her eyes light up as she listens to our guest lecturer.

But every time I look over, I see Elio leaning into her—whispering in her ear, jotting notes on her stationery, smirking to himself—and it all makes me feel a little bit queasy.

Elio Reynolds is not a good fucking guy. I wonder if Kaia even knows half the shit he gets up to on the regular, not to mention the stunt he pulled back when his brother was a student here.

It's not as though I'm personally seeking out information about him, but the rumors circulate here at Coastal like wildfire, especially when you happen to have a famous sibling.

As the lecture goes on, I try my best to focus on the material at hand. But my mind keeps wandering back to the non-couple across from me. I know they're whispering back and forth, and I sure as hell would like to know what they're talking about.

Normally, Kaia never lets herself give in to distractions

during class. In fact, it's something she'd usually get on my case about, berating me like some sort of teacher's pet.

So when the lecture finally ends, I pack up my bags and head out, a sense of relief flooding through me as I leave them both behind.

As PART of our in-season training schedule, we're required to hit two walk-in lifts each week—where we work out before or between classes—with a third session being optional. Before I hit my first, I head into the dining hall to grab some food.

I stack my plate, letting the clinking of silverware drown out the ringing in my pocket. It's my father calling, his name glaring at me from the screen, and I debate for a moment whether or not to answer. The man has always been a stickler for formality, and my stomach twists with anxiety just thinking about the ensuing conversation.

Against my better judgment, I answer the call anyway. "Hey, Dad."

His voice is as stiff and formal as it's always been. "Holden, how are you?"

My lips press into a flat line, smile dropping as I say, "I'm good."

I'm almost certain that he doesn't actually care about how I'm doing. There's no need for pleasantries here. I know the robotic attempt is simply a way for him to fulfill his designated role.

He's the loving, supportive Father of the Year type, after all.

"I'd like to take you out to dinner after your game this weekend. I'm coming into town to see you play." The way he phrases it makes my blood boil. It's not a request; it's a demand. But I know better than to argue with him.

"Sure, that sounds great."

"Excellent. I'll see you after the game, then." He hangs up before I manage to get another word in edgewise, leaving me to stew in my own irritation.

I know he means well. He's always been proud of me, my successes with hockey and with school. But I still feel like a pawn in his game. A way for him to show off his successful son to all his rich pals.

I take a deep breath, trying to relieve the sinking feeling in my gut. My father's looming presence always feels like a weight on my shoulders, dragging me down. But I can't let it distract me for too long. I need to focus on the shit I *can* control and try to ignore the pressure of my family's picture-perfect image.

I grab a drink and find a booth to slide into, shaking off the resentment.

I've been playing this role for my parents for as long as I can remember. The perfect son. The shining star. All the things my younger brother, Harris, sure as hell won't bother with.

As I take a bite of my food, my mind dwells on my father's stilted attempts at connection. It's tough to ignore the strain that's cut between us for the last five years. We both pretend like it doesn't exist, but it's an ever-present storm cloud looming in the distance.

Hockey is my escape, my one indulgence, and the driving force behind my pursuit of excellence in all aspects of my life. When I step into the rink and onto the ice, it's the only time I truly feel like myself.

Running a ragged hand through my hair, I make a concerted effort to erase thoughts of my father's visit from my mind. There's a game this weekend to prepare for and a dissertation to work on, and I need to stay sharp and focused if I'm going to stay on top.

My teammates, my coach, my peers—they're all counting on me to succeed. So, I paste on a smile, tucking all the uneasy feelings away for now.

Out of sight, out of mind.

# Chapter Seven

KAIA

As I LIE awake in bed, a heavy weight presses down on me, suffocating me slowly. I've been trying to sleep for hours, but my brain's playing like a broken record, ruminating on all the same endless thoughts.

My mind drifts to schoolwork, the never-ending pile of assignments and deadlines that seem to cast an everlasting shadow. Right now, I can easily manage my workload, but even the thought of falling behind sends a jolt of tension through my spine.

It's not just school—the perpetual fear of failure—that weighs me down. My thoughts inevitably wander to my parents. For the most part, I try to keep them from entering my panicky, late-night thought spirals.

I doubt I even cross their minds on a good day.

I know this because they gallivanted off to Greece only a couple of years after Sofia graduated high school. It was meant to be a temporary thing, but they ended up moving there for good and leaving me behind. It's like they were waiting for their prodigal daughter to finally leave the nest.

And once she was gone, my future was in my own hands.

They acted like they wanted me to come along, but I knew I'd be burdening them with my presence. A nuisance to their careers. So, I stayed in Boyer, the tiny town that sits a few exits off the nearest coastal highway.

This place is all I've ever known. My aunt let me stay with her until I finished high school myself. And now, here I am, on my own again in college.

Well, Elio's here to keep me company, at the very least.

But God, he was acting so fucking strange in class earlier today. He didn't speak to me all weekend, and then he shows up to our lecture completely strung out.

I don't want to automatically assume the worst, but still, the worry grips me like a vice, refusing to let go. I can't help but wonder if he's fallen back into old habits.

But he'd tell me about it if he had, right? He'd confide in me, ask me to pull him up from beneath the murky water. Because we promised we wouldn't go back there again. We said we'd always lean on each other when the temptation became too strong.

*Oh shit.*

If I let myself, I could spend the whole night agonizing about what kind of trouble Elio's getting himself into. Worrying is futile. Instead, I shift course, attempting to think happy thoughts.

What's something carefree and weightless? Something that can help me drift off to sleep at a reasonable hour.

Like a light in the darkness, my thoughts unwillingly stray to Holden.

He spent our entire lecture this morning stealing glances at me and glaring in Elio's direction. He thinks I didn't notice him, but I'm more perceptive than that.

I try to push him out of my head, but he won't relent. His golden hair. That devilish grin. The sound of the rasp in his voice when I first stumbled into his bedroom. He's quickly invading my every thought.

I envision his lips forming those teasing words: "*This thing we have going on . . . It's a bit like foreplay, no?*"

In reality, I'm still alone in my bed. But in my mind, I'm in his car again.

It's Friday night. I can feel the sharp sting of his hand on my skin. The way he leaned over me, reaching across my lap to stop me from leaving. But instead of letting me go this time, his hand slips onto the curve of my thigh, teasing the hemline of my skirt.

Oh, hell no. *No, no, no.*

Lying in bed, I toss and turn, trying to will my thoughts away. But they keep coming back, like waves crashing on the shore, relentless and persistent. Tonight, like most nights, they seem to have a mind of their own.

In my head, Holden leans closer, his lips making contact with my neck, sending shivers down my spine. His warm breath tickles my skin, and the rough pads of his fingertips slowly inch their way beneath my skirt.

My heartbeat quickens, and a flush of scorching heat creeps over my entire body. I can almost feel the warmth of his hands, the strength of his arms encircling me, drawing me closer.

As he whispers my name into the cramped space between us, I clamp my eyes shut—and my thighs—desperately grasping for some semblance of control over my wandering mind. But my efforts are futile.

So eventually, I relent, allowing myself to surrender to the unwelcome sensations. To succumb to the dirty daydream and finally fall into a blissful sleep.

I WAKE up hours later in a cold sweat, my heart pounding so hard I can feel it in my ears. I take a deep breath and attempt to calm myself down, but it's no use. That fever dream fantasy was too intense, too lifelike, and now I'm left with an empty ache in the pit of my stomach.

I shake my head, trying to clear the disturbing thoughts, but they keep creeping back in. I can still feel the illusion, thick and heavy in my head. The warmth of Holden's body against mine, the way his lips felt on my skin.

The physical aversion I'm feeling now, in the light of a new day, is too much for me to handle. I sit up in bed and rub my eyes, hoping to scrub away the feeling.

The first thing I do is check my email on my phone. Maybe if I distract myself with something else, I can drive the nausea away. But as I scroll through my inbox, I come across a message that makes my heart skip.

It's from the panel members—the message that I've been waiting for for the past four days. I sit up straighter in my bed, kicking my duvet off my body as I comb through it at light speed.

***From:*** *bmengineering@coastal.edu*
***To:*** *kaia.karras@coastal.edu*
***Subject:*** *Dissertation Proposals*
*Miss Kaia Karras,*
*We are pleased to inform you that your proposal has been selected as one of the top submissions for this year. We would like to extend our congratulations to you and invite you to select your top three choices for your dissertation advisor. In the event that your first selection is unavailable, we will attempt to match you with your remaining choices.*
*The Biomedical Engineering Department, Coastal University*

A triumphant smile spreads across my face as I read through the message for the second time. This is exactly what I needed to hear this morning.

I quickly respond, providing Dr. Khatri's name—silently praying that she's available to work with me—and thanking them for the opportunity.

Since dawn is barely breaking, I spend longer than normal completing my morning routine. Reset and refreshed, I slowly make my way to campus, my mind buzzing with anticipation for the day ahead.

As I head into Weyerhaeuser, my nerves officially settle. The good news from earlier is still fresh on my mind, so I don't even allow the sight of Holden's smug face to faze me one bit. In fact, it's like he never even appeared in my dreams at all.

Instead, I attempt to walk right on past him without saying a word.

"Karras." He glances up from his phone, his usual cocky grin pasted perfectly in place. "I'm assuming you received the same *special email* that I did this morning."

I freeze, dread chilling my bones. "What email?"

"The one congratulating us on our proposals."

My heart instantly sinks. "Oh, you got that, too?"

"Yeah." He flashes me a self-satisfied smile. "Did you read through it clearly? Because I hate to break it to you, but it sounds like we're not the only ones."

My shoulders slump. Of course, I should've known I wasn't the only student selected. But the idea of sharing my favorite professor with Holden—with any of our peers—is not something I like to envision.

I try to keep my voice steady, nonchalant, as I ask, "So, who'd you put down, then?"

The corner of his lip lifts. "I think you know."

"Please tell me you didn't."

"It's not a big deal, Karras. We can both work with her."

"No, Beck. It is a big deal." I shake my head, my frustration and disappointment mounting. "This was supposed to be my chance to impress Dr. Khatri. To work one-on-one with the woman I admire the most in our department. Why do you even want to work with her? Just because I do?"

"No, I like Khatri, too. She's cool."

"She's *cool*?" I arch an incredulous brow. "Becker, she's one of the most highly esteemed, well-respected researchers in our field. She's a lot more than just *cool*."

"Okay, my bad. She's *really* fucking cool."

"Jesus Christ, never mind." I rub my temples in frustration. "Again, complete waste of energy attempting to reason with you."

His expression darkens. "I get that you're upset, but I've earned this, too. And it's not like Dr. Khatri only has time for one student. If she so chooses, we can both benefit from working with her."

"But it won't be the same," I protest. "She won't be able to give either one of us her full attention."

Holden sighs. "Sharing the same advisor is not the end of the world, Karras. Stop catastrophizing."

"It's easy for you to say, isn't it?" My frustration spills out in harsh words. "You've got hockey, your daddy's money, and your merry band of boys. But this is it for me, Becker. This is all I have. And now, the one thing I wanted for myself, I have to share with you."

His features pull tight. "You know, that also means I have a lot of responsibilities outside of academics. And if working with someone like Khatri can help alleviate the pressure, then you're damn right I'm gonna do it."

"Yeah, responsibilities." I sigh in exasperation. "You know, that word doesn't ring quite the same bell when you have a safety net that spans a mile wide."

"Look, I'm not gonna fight with you about this anymore. We both earned it, and we can both work with her." His jaw tightens. "It's not that fucking serious."

I give him a sharp look. "Nothing's ever *that* serious to you, is it?"

It may be harsh, but it's the truth. I think back to all of our group projects where he'd goof off, distracting others instead of contributing. Or the countless parties he's attended over the years, prioritizing a good time over studying for an important exam.

And let's not forget how he continues to breeze through presentations, relying on his charm and natural charisma rather than putting in the effort to thoroughly prepare.

It's frustrating to witness someone who's supposed to be my equal just sail through their life. And it makes me wonder if he's ever truly faced adversity or been forced to fight for something he desperately wanted, knowing that failure wasn't an option.

Knowing that he truly had nothing, and no one, to fall back on but himself.

"What the hell do you want me to do?" He throws his hands up in frustration. "It's not like I went out of my way to steal her from you. We both earned top marks. We both wanted Khatri as our advisor. It's not my fault that we might have to share her. Do you want me to email the panel back and tell them I changed my mind?"

I give him a blank stare.

"That's ridiculous," he continues. "I'm not going to make myself look bad just because you're feeling insecure."

I know he's at least half-right, but the worry still gnaws at me. If she allows both of us to work with her, that means she'll have to divide her already limited time between the two of us.

"Well, if we're both her advisees, it could take longer for us to finish our projects. And what if there's a conflict of interest with our collaboration partners? What if she has to choose between us when it comes to resources?"

"Then we'll figure that shit out when the time comes."

"But that sounds awful," I practically whine.

"Oh, poor Kaia." He gives me a faux pout. "*Sharing*. That must be really hard for you to fathom. I swear this is youngest-child syndrome at its finest."

"Could you be any more condescending?" I grit my teeth. "I'm not a child, Beck."

"You're not a child, no, but you sure are acting like a spoiled little brat at the moment."

My jaw drops. "Well, I'd rather be a *brat* than an entitled, trust fund baby."

"That's just great." Holden's eyes narrow. "You know, your professionalism is really going to impress Dr. Khatri. Maybe if you tell her how much of a baby you think I am, then she'll decide not to work with me after all."

I let out a frustrated huff. "Oh, just leave me alone, will you?"

"Gladly," he retorts, his smug grin morphing into a scowl.

Thankfully, the sound of his phone buzzing interrupts our dead argument, and he answers it with a distracted hello. Once he starts to talk again, I slip past him, no longer wanting to eavesdrop on his conversation.

As I enter the lecture hall, I notice our professor, Dr. Francis, already preparing for class. He greets me with a warm smile, and some of my lingering anger begins to fade. Regardless of Holden's potential involvement, I still have the chance to work with one of the most brilliant minds in our department.

I settle into a seat in the front row and take out my notebook and pen. As Dr. Francis continues with his lecture, I attempt to concentrate on the material at hand. But the disappointment and irritation continue to nag at me.

Holden was right about one thing: I don't like to share. And the prospect of dividing my time with him makes the situation infinitely less appealing.

All of this, of course, hinges on whether Dr. Khatri is even available to work with us in the first place.

# Chapter Eight

## HOLDEN

THE CROWD ROARS as the puck drops, signaling the start of our first game of the season. Adrenaline pumps through my veins, the sound of our blades slicing through the ice ringing in my ears.

I'm in my element here.

It feels good. But it would feel a whole lot better if I didn't hear my father's voice echoing throughout the arena, booming out a mix of approval and criticism—much heavier on the latter.

We're in the second period when one of the opposing players checks me hard into the boards. The impact reverberates throughout my entire body, but I quickly shake it off.

Don't get me wrong, my frustration is reaching its boiling point. This guy has been gunning for me all night, and I've been trying my best to ignore it, despite how much I'd like to do the opposite. But my fucking dad is here, after all.

In general, it's difficult for me to keep my cool when we're playing against Dayton U, one of our biggest rivals in the division. These guys fucking hate us, mostly because we're better than them in every way. And we always have been.

Over the past few seasons, we've consistently outperformed these guys. Our team has better coordination, more skilled players, and a winning track record that's tough to beat. It's no wonder they can't handle the pressure of competing against us.

In no time, that same shitty, obnoxious player comes at me

again. This time, I'm ready for him. I dodge his attack and retaliate with a shoulder check of my own. He briefly stumbles but comes back for more.

I skate hard, sweat dripping down my forehead as I pull up next to Will. He shoots a grin in my direction. "You okay there, pretty boy?" he asks, skating on beside me.

I roll my eyes. "I'm good."

He laughs, clapping me on the shoulder as he passes by. "You sure are gettin' a lot of love from DU tonight, Becksy."

I offer him a wry smile. "Yeah, I can feel the love every time I get cross-checked into the boards."

We share a quick laugh while I refocus on the puck. The other team carries on taunting me, the handsy guy from earlier shouting a slew of insults that I don't bother to register. I glare past him and skate faster.

The puck sails toward me, and I lunge for it. That's when I feel the full impact of a hit—hard enough to make me stumble. Turning, I catch the offender red-handed. He's a tall, burly guy with an ugly sneer on his face.

"Watch yourself, *pretty boy*," he says, mocking my roommate.

Blood rushes to my head at the flagrant insult. It's one thing for my teammates and friends to sling shit, but this guy's barking up the wrong tree with me. I skate closer, giving him a harsh shove in retaliation.

"What's your problem, man?"

He glares daggers back at me. There's misplaced anger and frustration in his eyes, and I know he won't give up easily. He attempts to body-check me again, but I deflect, ultimately throwing the first punch. The sound of helmets clashing echoes throughout the arena, and the crowd goes wild.

The referees try to break us up, but we keep going at it.

Heat and sweat pour down my face as we trade blows. Finally, our respective teammates manage to separate us, and we're both sent to the penalty box.

The rush of adrenaline slowly wears off as I sit there, watching the game continue on without my involvement. A mix of emotions swirls inside me—anger, satisfaction, and a hint of regret—as I reflect on the pointless fight and wait for my chance to rejoin my team.

After the penalty's served, I return to the ice, more focused this time. I skate harder, easily checking my opponents and chasing down every puck that comes my way.

The game becomes a blur of sound and motion, a frenzy of sticks and skates and bodies colliding. The score stays close, and tensions run high. Still, these fucking DU guys seem determined to get under my skin, continuing to throw jabs and insults every time they approach me.

I manage to ignore the taunts, concentrating on my own performance and the game's rhythm. We score a goal, igniting a surge of energy amongst my teammates, but it's quickly dampened by a tying goal from DU. The crowd's intensity builds as the clock ticks down, and with only a few minutes left, the pressure mounts.

As the game reaches its final moments, I drive the puck near center ice. I skate toward the goal, weaving around defenders, strategizing the perfect play. With mere seconds left on the clock, I spot a brief opening and take the shot, harnessing every last ounce of skill and power in my possession.

To no one's surprise, the puck sails past their goalie and into the net, scoring the game-winning goal. The crowd erupts in cheers, and my teammates mob me on the ice.

I'm sure my father's thoroughly impressed, and I'm happy to have made an impact despite my earlier showboating.

But as I exit the rink and strip off my helmet in the locker room, the rush of our win fading into the background, my thoughts inevitably wander back to my argument with Kaia. I've been dwelling on it all fucking week, no matter how hard I try not to.

I shouldn't have let my frustration get the best of me on Tuesday, and I definitely shouldn't have called her a fucking brat, at least not to her face. Now, she's been giving me the cold shoulder for days, even more so after we received the official email from Dr. Khatri.

As predicted, we'll be sharing her as our advisor.

I tried approaching Kaia afterward to make things right, but she wouldn't even look at me. And honestly, being ignored like this fucking sucks. I'm not used to it, from her or from anyone. I miss teasing her, making her laugh despite herself, riling her up like usual.

I promised I wouldn't push her too far, but I guess I already fucked that up.

It's weird how much I give a shit, actually. And what's even weirder is that I find myself wishing she were here tonight. I doubt she's ever been to a game before, but I can still picture it perfectly—her sitting in the stands, watching me play, waiting for me outside of the arena so I can gloat about my win.

I know we left things on a shitty note, but a part of me wants to show her how fucking hard I work outside of class. That I'm not just the rich, spoiled asshole she thinks I am.

I shake my head, trying to push thoughts of her out of my mind, but it's pointless. I acknowledge that I shouldn't be fixating on this shit, not after the vile words she spewed right back at me.

We both went too far. I'll be the first to admit it.

But no matter how hard I try to block her out, it seems like thoughts of her—the disappointed look on her face, the tremble of her lower lip, that tiny furrow in her brow—always find a way to slip right on through the cracks.

After debriefing with my team and taking a quick shower, I meet my father at some swanky restaurant he's chosen. When I walk in, he stands up, greeting me with a nod and a firm handshake.

Well, that's real fucking nice, Dad. I guess we're playing the role of business associates tonight.

He takes a long sip of his scotch before addressing me. "So, Holden, how's school been treating you this term? Still top of your class?"

"Yeah, I'm doing well. Those contacts you gave me helped beef up my dissertation proposal. So, thank you again."

He gives me a stiff smile. "Good to hear. And the hockey season seems to be off to a great start, thanks to you. I'm sure the Tornadoes are happy."

"Yeah, we're keeping it tight this year. No concerns there." I change course, unwilling to taint my favorite topic with his twisted bullshit. "Uh, and I've been thinking a little bit more about what I want to do after hockey."

He raises a brow. "Is that so?"

"Yeah, this research thing's been sparking my interest. I think it's a good fallback plan."

"Still no interest in law school?" he jokes.

"Definitely not."

He brushes off the notion with a shake of his head. "You're still young, Holden. You have plenty of time to figure it all out. Just focus on hockey for now and worry about the future later."

I clench my jaw, frustrated by his dismissiveness. "Thank you for the needless advice. I know where my focus lies."

He chuckles, a smug, irritating sound that grates on my already frayed nerves. "I'm just saying, don't lose sight of your goals because you want to juggle too many balls at once."

"I wouldn't worry about that. It's just an option." Deflecting, I turn the conversation to my father's subject of preference. "So, how's work been treating you, Dad?"

"It's been busy, as usual. But I can't complain too much. The firm's doing well."

Of course it is. Did I even need to ask?

My father's currently running Becker & Slate, a New York City-based firm that focuses on corporate and securities law. The company was founded over seventy years ago by my great-grandfather and his best friend. My father, as a given, is the current successor, and he'd much rather the firm go to me than to his colleague's son.

But Monty Slate Jr. has been gunning for partner since he was a kid, and I genuinely have zero interest. Law has never appealed to me. In fact, the idea of working at the firm nearly bores me to tears.

"Glad to hear it." I take a casual sip of water before I continue. "And Alyssa Chambers? I assume she's still doing well."

My father's eyes flicker with annoyance, but he manages a strained smile. "She was recently promoted to associate."

"Oh, yeah? And outside of work?"

"Couldn't tell you." His lip twitches. "Ms. Chambers is nothing more than a business colleague, son."

I smirk, eating up his discomfort. "Oh, right. What was her business with you again? Sharing hotel rooms when you go out of town?"

I can't help but take a dig at my father and his so-called perfect marriage. The truth is, it's far from it; he's been unfaithful to our family for years now. Alyssa isn't the first or the only one. And the worst part is that my mom's more than aware of it.

They both maintain this constant charade, acting as if they're living in a glass house where everyone can see inside, each polished window reflecting their supposed perfection. But I know the truth—all those tiny hidden cracks in between, the fragile foundation that lies beneath the surface.

My father's jaw tightens before he quickly regains his composure. "You know better than to make unfounded accusations, Holden."

"Well, it's not really a secret that you spend more time with her than with Mom."

"Enough," he bites out.

"Apologies." I feign regret, giving him a knowing look. "What would you rather we discuss, Father?"

"Since you seem to have such an interest in my nonexistent romantic pursuits, why don't we discuss yours?"

I roll my eyes at his weak attempt at diversion. It's fucking annoying, especially considering the fact that I've already had this conversation with him a million times.

"Dad, we've been over this. I don't need a girlfriend to complete me and all that garbage," I say, exasperated.

He remains unconvinced. "It's not about happiness. It's about finding a good woman to support you in the next stage of life. It's important to project a respectable image, Holden. You're entering a high-profile career, and having a stable woman by your side is key."

Yeah, exactly. He wants me to find someone who fits into his perfect little box of what a good wife and daughter-in-law should be. And then, on the side, I can have my cake and eat it, too. Just like him.

My frustration rises, but I work to keep my tone even. "I'll settle down when I'm ready, Dad. For now, I'm keeping my focus, just like you wanted. Hockey and graduation. That's it."

As he drones on about the benefits of a stable relationship, my mind drifts. He's so far off base that it's laughable. I don't want a Stepford wife who will willingly ignore my infidelity. Someone that's more worried about tainting their picture-perfect image than protecting themselves.

Don't get me wrong, I love my mom, and I hate the way my father treats her—he's the real asshole here. But she's still not the type of person I'd envision for myself. I want to be with someone bold, outspoken, and confident.

The exact opposite of what my father wants for me.

He envisions someone who's prim and proper, a sweet girl who attends church every Sunday and wouldn't dare speak her mind. I'm suffocated by the image. Frankly, the idea of spending the rest of my life with a person like that sounds about as interesting as watching paint dry.

I want someone who wouldn't let my family steamroll her. Someone who's fiercely independent and who can handle my hockey career. She needs to have ambition, drive, a sharp mind, and an even sharper wit.

And she's not just someone's fucking arm candy, that's for damn sure.

If I really wanted to torture myself, I might admit that my description sounds a hell of a lot like a girl I already know . . . one who won't even bother to look at me right now.

# Chapter Nine

KAIA

I SIT ON MY BED, staring blankly at my computer screen, a wave of frustration and helplessness flooding through me. The last few days have been rough, and I'm still reeling from the argument I had with Holden.

There's a thick line of unresolved tension between us now, and it feels like a balloon that's about to pop at any second. Which is why I've been avoiding him all week.

I'm on my third attempt at rereading the same line of text when Lizzie barges into my room, barely managing a smile. I raise a brow in her direction, waiting for her to spill whatever tea's brewing in that head of hers.

"You remember Rai, right?" she finally asks, dropping her bag on the floor and plopping down on the edge of my mattress.

I roll my eyes. "Who could forget him?"

"Well, he invited me over tonight to celebrate after the game," she says with a hint of detachment.

"Okay?" I didn't even realize they had exchanged numbers after the party last week. She hasn't so much as mentioned his name since, even when I half-heartedly attempted to pry. "I'm happy for you?"

"Well, do you wanna come? It's low-key tonight," she says casually. "Just the guys that live there and a few close friends."

I think about it for a moment. On the one hand, it might be nice to get out of my room for a little while. On the other hand, the idea of sitting around with a bunch of strangers, listening to them boast about their win, doesn't exactly sound appealing.

"I'm not really in the mood to sling praise at a bunch of guys I don't know."

"You know Holden," Lizzie argues, waggling her brows.

"Yeah, that's not a major selling point, Liz."

"Aw, are you still mad about your little tiff from the other day?"

When I came home on Tuesday, stewing in my own self-pity, Lizzie spent an inordinate amount of time listening to me rant about our fight. I'm fairly certain she was only halfway paying attention, but it was nice to have someone to talk to about it other than Elio.

"No, I don't give a shit what he thinks of me." Okay, I might care a little bit, especially because he incidentally used the one insult that I despise with all my heart. But I'm not about to admit that out loud. Not to Lizzie, anyway. "But I am still frustrated about the whole situation in general."

"And that means you have to sit in your room alone all weekend?"

"No, but it *does* mean that I need to work twice as hard to prep for our first meeting."

"It's one night, Kaia," she says, her voice softening. "You don't have to stay for long. And who knows, you might even have a little fun."

I sigh, feeling torn. Part of me wants to take her up on her offer, but the other, much larger part of me is too stubborn to budge. "I'm not going."

"Fine. Suit yourself."

"Have fun," I call after her as she leaves my room, a twinge of regret hitting me as the door clicks shut.

And while I sit here alone, I ruminate on my outburst from

the other day. Deep down, I know I was being harsh, but it's difficult to let go of the anxiety I'm feeling about the whole situation.

The idea of having to share my time with Holden unnerves me, and I can't seem to shake the feeling. It doesn't help that he poked at one of my deepest insecurities, either.

I was only halfway lying to Lizzie earlier. Holden can form whatever opinion he wants about me, and it's not gonna be the thing that keeps me up at night. I'm well aware that I'm not really a spoiled brat, even though my older sister has been hurling that same phrase at me my entire life.

But she's always been wrong, and so is Holden.

What's the problem with wanting everything to go according to plan? Isn't that the purpose of setting goals in the first place? If I've worked hard for something, if I've genuinely earned it, then rest assured, I'll be getting what I deserve in the end.

Every last piece of it.

AFTER A WEEKEND of isolating myself in my apartment, I make my way to Dr. Khatri's office, my stomach in knots. She sent us an email requesting a meeting after class, and it's been eating at me all day. I know it's only preliminary, but my nerves are still getting the best of me.

I've been to her office hours countless times, yet I can't help but be intimidated by her. She's a brilliant woman, and I feel fortunate to have her as my advisor, despite having to share her time.

As I enter the lobby outside of her office, I spot Holden kicking his feet back on the bench, calm and collected as per usual. I take a silent seat next to him, refusing to acknowledge his presence. Some people may deem my behavior petty, but at this moment, I'm beyond caring.

"Hey," he greets me with a tilt of his chin. "Heard you almost graced us with your presence on Saturday night."

The audacity of this man astounds me. He's acting as if nothing happened between us, as if our heated argument was a figment of my imagination. And yet here I am, still reeling from the confrontation.

"Hm." I give him a noncommittal grunt.

"Your roommate, Lucy, said she tried to drag you out of your little hidey-hole." He chuckles, low and deep. "But you just wouldn't budge, would ya?"

"Her name's Lizzie," I say, my frustration mounting. "And did you really think I'd show up? Come congratulate you on your big win? Maybe this time, you could call me a brat in front of all your friends."

"Actually, I was just hoping you'd call me baby again."

I shake my head at him in disgust, but a tiny flush of heat creeps up my neck. "Yeah, doesn't pack the same punch without a trust fund in front of it."

Just as he's about to retort, the office door swings open in front of us. We quietly follow Dr. Khatri inside, and she begins with an overview of our respective proposals.

As I listen to Holden droning on, I realize why this pairing might make more sense than I initially assumed. Dr. Khatri didn't only choose us because we both wanted her but also because our projects are similar in nature.

While Holden's focus is on minimally invasive treatment for Parkinson's, mine's centered around brain stim for depression. It's interesting, actually, the way he describes the implantation through blood vessels. Apparently, it's a viable alternative to the current procedure, which is intrusive, painful, and causes permanent damage.

The method he wants to research would eliminate the need for a craniotomy altogether. Even I'll admit it sounds fascinating, important, well worth the research.

As we delve further into the details, Dr. Khatri asks us about our progress with the lit review process.

"I'm still sifting through the existing literature, trying to better shape my initial research question," I say, straightening my spine. "It's a lot to work through, but I'm slowly making progress."

"I'm also in the same boat," Holden chimes in. "I'm trying to narrow down my question and search terms at the moment."

"Good. Those are crucial steps." Dr. Khatri says, jotting down a few notes on the pad in front of her. "And Holden, am I right in saying that you've already connected with some outside collaborators?"

He nods his agreement. Although it's not a typical requirement for students, I already feel embarrassed by my lack of preparation.

"I was planning on doing that soon," I awkwardly add. "Did you have any suggestions or connections that you wanted to pass along?"

"Definitely," she kindly agrees. "I also have some ideas for you, Holden, if you're open to working with some of my colleagues."

We continue discussing our plans for the lit review, and I notice how well Holden's presenting himself. He's thoughtful and articulate, and it certainly appears like he dedicated some actual effort to this meeting.

As our appointment comes to a close, Holden and I thank Dr. Khatri for her time and make our way out of her office. His gaze lingers on me as we leave, so I turn to him, half expecting another jab at my expense. Instead, he surprises me with a compliment.

"Good job in there," he says, shooting me a small, sincere smile.

"Thank you?"

He clears his throat, studying my face. "Look, I'm sorry about overstepping last week. I should've just let you have your moment. I know this shit stresses you out."

I hesitate for a few more seconds, unsure how to react to his words. It's unusual for Holden to acknowledge his role in our disagreements, let alone apologize for them. "It does," I say. "And, yeah, I suppose I went a little far myself."

"And?" he presses, raising a brow.

"And what?"

"And you're also sorry?"

I let out an exasperated sigh. "Did I not just say that?"

"Don't know if I heard those exact words, no."

"Fine, yes." I roll my eyes, but there's a flicker of amusement thumping in my chest. "I'm *sorry*. Does that make you happy?"

A smug grin spreads across his face. "If you wanted to get down on your knees and beg for my forgiveness, I would also accept that."

"You're such a pig."

"Oh, and here I thought I was a *baby*."

"You're a lot of things, Becker," I say, shaking my head. "All of them particularly annoying."

His expression turns serious again, and my heart stutters as he says, "You know, I missed you last week."

"What?"

"I missed talking to you," he admits, his gaze intense. "This ignoring shit you've been doing? Yeah, it doesn't really work for me."

I'm momentarily speechless. Honestly, I assumed that he didn't care either way if we talked. "Holden," I murmur softly, uncertain of what else to say.

"Kaia." He parrots my tone. "Look, if you're pissed at me, then just tell me. Fight with me. Yell at me. But don't shut me out. I don't like seeing you everywhere, knowing that you're just gonna look the other way."

I stand there for a moment, gazing at him with a mixture of confusion and surprise. Other than last Friday night, I've never heard him talk this way before. He's usually so closed off and sarcastic, and his sincerity's throwing me for a loop.

"Are you being serious?"

"Dead serious. I'm just laying it out there," he says with a shrug. "Take it or leave it."

I pause for a moment, contemplating his words. I have to admit, this side of him is nice—the one that's not afraid to express genuine human emotion. But at the same time, I'm still not sure if I'm ready to open up to him myself.

"Okay," I finally say, my voice barely above a whisper.

His face lights up. "Okay?"

"Yes, okay." I give him a shaky nod, a bit dazed. "I'll take it. If I'm pissed at you again, which I will be, then I won't ignore you."

"Good," he says softly, sincerely. But then, in true Holden Becker fashion, he ruins the moment. "And you missed me, too, right?"

"Don't push your luck, Beck."

# Chapter Ten

## HOLDEN

After a grueling practice, followed by another pointless rehab session with Reynolds, I'm completely exhausted. Still, a sense of fulfillment settles inside me. There's just something about pushing myself to the limit, stretching my body to its breaking point, that always makes me feel a little more alive.

I crave it, but I also need time to fully decompress afterward.

Once we're back home, my roommates and I take quick showers, and then the four of us collapse onto the couch together. We crack open a few cold beers, tuning into some trashy reality TV. All of us are too exhausted to chat or care about what's playing in front of us, so silence hangs heavy in the air.

Without warning, Rai glances up from his phone, sitting ramrod straight in his seat. "I have a thought," he declares, his expression suddenly serious.

"Congratulations," I toss back.

"Oh, shut up, Becks." He gives me a playful glare. "Really, guys, I'm thinking we should head out to Amber Isle tonight. Bring a few beers. Start a fire. Blow off some steam before the game this weekend."

It's been a few weeks since our preseason party, and the idea of a night out together is more than tempting. "Yeah, let's do it," I say, raising my bottle, and the other two hooligans chime in with their agreement.

We collect some firewood, pack a cooler of beer, and hastily stuff ourselves into my car. As we make our way to the shoreline, the weight of this long, draining week finally lifts off my shoulders.

Rai was right. This is exactly what we needed.

Will immediately gets the fire started—our resident Boy Scout—as the rest of us kick back and relax. We're laughing, cracking jokes, and drinking up some ice-cold Bud Light. Just one more for me since I'm the DD.

It's a beautiful fucking night. The beach is alive with the soft, subtle sounds of waves crashing against the shore. The sand shimmers in the flickering light of our bonfire, and the sea breeze carries a salty smell mixed with the scent of burning wood.

It's peaceful, calm, a welcome reprieve for my sore, aching muscles and my overworked brain.

Of course, it doesn't take long for the guys to latch onto some nearby girls. Good ol' Rai Rai's making them all laugh, as per usual, but I actually think he's more interested in Kaia's roommate these days.

Before he invited her over on Saturday, he kept bugging me about "Kaia's pretty little friend." I told him to grow some balls and text the fucking girl. As for myself, I'm feeling the buzz, but I'm not really interested in chatting up strangers tonight.

I'm just here to have a good time with my boys.

After a few hours, we head to the Surfbreak Grill for some food. It's a shitty, local hole-in-the-wall, but they have these amazing burgers. Plus, you can't beat their view of the pier.

As we walk in, I'm taken aback by the sight of Kaia and Lizzie, who are already sitting inside at a booth, sipping on a couple of milkshakes. I train my gaze on Rai, who gives me the biggest shit-eating grin in the world.

Of course, this was his fucking plan all along, wasn't it? It's a classic Rai Rai move if I ever saw one. Some real-life *Parent Trap* bullshit.

"Hey, boys!" Lizzie calls out, smiling as she waves us over.

We make our way to their booth, squeezing in next to them. The girls appear to be a little bit tipsy, but they seem happy enough to see us. Well, Lizzie does, at the very least.

Kaia, on the other hand, has that familiar fire in her eyes. Judging by the furrow in her brow and the slight frown on her full lips, she's clearly unamused by the happenstance.

Her dark hair flows in perfect waves, one side carefully tucked behind her ear. She's wearing this little white tank top, too, the tiny straps accentuating her golden skin.

I can't resist the surge of attraction I feel toward her.

Sure, the girl barely tolerates me on a good day, but we've always had this undeniable spark. There's no arguing the way our energy ignites when we're together, and lately, it feels like there's something different happening between us.

Hell, I straight up admitted that I missed her last week. That I want her in my life, despite our constant bickering. And maybe she feels the same spark that I do. Or maybe I'm inventing something more between us inside my head.

So yeah, she makes my dick hard.

But there's something deeper here, too. I'm drawn to her ambition. Her intelligence. Kaia has always been driven and focused and dedicated, and I find all of those qualities incredibly fucking sexy.

"So, Holden," Lizzie slurs, grinning over at me. "How come you keep messing with my girl?"

"Ah." I crack a grin of my own, directing my attention to

Kaia's sheepish gaze. "Are we sure it's not the other way around?"

"That's not what I hear," Lizzie singsongs, nearly belligerent at this point.

"And what is it that you hear, Liz?" I tease.

"Well, Kaia says—" Kaia sinks down in her seat, tugging on Lizzie's arm to get to her stop. "It's fine, Kai Kai. Let me talk," Lizzie chides before bursting into a fit of giggles. "Oh, my God. *Kai Kai* and Rai Rai, how cute."

We laugh at her ridiculous antics, and she immediately forgets where she was going in the first place. Instead, we all move on, placing our food orders and digging in.

It may be a miracle, but by the end of the meal, Rai manages to sweet-talk Lizzie into coming back to our place. There's barely enough room for her in the car as it is, but Rai kindly offers up a seat on his lap.

When Bodie offers the same thing to Kaia, winking at her as he does, I about lose my shit. But I'm the driver, so I can't very well have a girl sitting on my own lap now, can I?

Kaia, however, respectfully declines—as she should—insisting on calling herself an Uber. "Let me call it for you," I cut in, feeling lousy about the lack of space in my convertible.

Kaia rolls her eyes, immediately declining the offer. "I can pay for my own Uber, Beck."

"I'm not saying you can't," I insist, voice soft. "Just let me do this for you."

"Fine, then." She waves a dismissive hand, yielding to my request. "Have it your way."

"Thank you." I pull up the app on my phone, inputting the details of her apartment complex before saying, "All set. They're pulling around in three minutes. Text me when you get home, please."

"As you wish, Daddy." Her eyes widen, and she shudders, feigning a gag at her own suggestive comment. "Oh, God. Please pretend I never said that."

I allow the corners of my mouth to curl up into a self-satisfied grin. "Couldn't erase it from my brain even if I tried."

"Whatever." She gives me a dramatic eye roll. "Thank you for the Uber. Good night, everyone." She moves to hug Lizzie, waving to my roommates before heading out of the building.

As the rest of us make our way back to the house, I recognize how grateful I am for these little moments. The few seconds where I can forget about the stresses of the game and the pressure to perform and just be a college kid having fun with his friends.

Also, I have to admit it was a real fucking treat to see Kaia outside of the classroom again.

THE NEXT DAY, we have a late-morning practice that kicks my fucking ass. We definitely shouldn't have stayed out as late as we did last night. Not to mention, those two beers I drank aren't sitting well in my stomach, either.

With aching muscles and sweat dripping down my brow, I head back to the locker room. But just as I'm packing up my gear, Harper calls me over.

"Hey, Holden, can I ask you to stick around for a few minutes?"

I lift my chin, still feeling a bit winded from practice. "What's up?"

Harper offers me a warm smile. I'm not trying to be a creep, but she's a very beautiful woman. Her soft brown hair is pulled into a loose ponytail, a wild mix of braids and twists interweaved throughout. Her gray-blue eyes are shining under the harsh, fluorescent lights. She's young and she's gorgeous, and the rest of my teammates have definitely taken notice.

Facts are just facts—there's really no denying her physical appeal. But despite her good looks and sugary-sweet personality, she's starting to grate on my fucking nerves.

Sure, the chest pain used to nag at me, but I should be able to manage it fine without her help now. There's no legitimate reason that I should have to stay late after every single practice.

It's all getting a bit fucking redundant, isn't it?

"I just wanted to do a quick check-in and remediate any lingering pain," she says, leading me over to one of the training tables.

With a sigh, I move to lie down on my back, and Harper starts to work on my chest, pressing down on different points to find any areas of discomfort.

"How's your pain level been?" she asks.

"Almost nonexistent, honestly," I say, self-assured. "I've been doing all the exercises you gave me, and it's made a huge difference."

Her fingers press harder against my chest. "That's great to hear. But we still need to be cautious and make sure we're not missing anything."

It's difficult not to feel annoyed by her words. I've been coming to these extra sessions with her for weeks. And it's starting to make me wonder if she's punishing me for something else and if Elio might be the reason behind it.

"I appreciate your concern," I say, trying to keep my tone polite. "But I really don't think I need all these extra sessions. I'm feeling great."

She looks up at me, and I can see a hint of discomfort in her eyes. "Just want to ensure you're in the best possible condition for the season."

I give her a tight-lipped smile, slightly ashamed of myself for being so defensive. I'm sure she's only trying to help me, and I shouldn't take her dedication to her job personally.

As we finish up the session, I thank her and move to head out of the rink. But before I leave, I turn back and give it one last shot. "Hey, can I ask you something?"

She glances up at me, her eyes curious. "Of course. What's on your mind?"

"Uh, look, I don't want to make any baseless accusations, but I feel like I'm doing everything you've asked me to, and I'm still being treated like I'm not making progress. Is there something else going on here?"

"I just want to make sure you're healthy and ready to play." Harper's expression softens, her eyes crinkling in the corners as she gives me a knowing smile. "If you're feeling great, that's fantastic, and we can talk about scaling back your sessions. But let's not rush into anything, okay?"

I give her a tight nod, still reeling from the forced positivity in her tone. It's clear that she's feeling a little bit uneasy, and I can't shake the idea that there's something off about our sessions. But hell, maybe I am just paranoid.

Besides, I don't want Harper to think I'm questioning her expertise.

So I let it go for now. Instead, I offer her one last quick thank-you and move on. No harm done. As long as I'm in perfect shape for the game tomorrow, that's all I really give a shit about.

# Chapter Eleven

KAIA

It's Friday night, and once again, I'm twisting and turning alone in my bed. Sleep eludes me, and my mind's in overdrive. I just want to fucking pass out already. I'm spread entirely too thin, and I feel like my brain is about to explode.

This summer, it seemed like I was finally able to get a break from relentless insomnia. But now, I'm back to square fucking one.

It's awful, feeling like I can't ever shut off my thoughts. I'm worrying and fretting over shit that doesn't even matter. Things that are way far out of my control. And then, of course, there are things that I deserve to be concerned over, but not to such a drastic degree.

There's the weight of my assignments and dissertation, the pressure to maintain my flawless GPA, and the stress of applying to graduate school. They all take their toll.

And the more I try to push my fears aside, the more they crowd my thoughts.

Sofia's still on my mind, too. She texted me last night while I was sitting in my Uber, out of the fucking blue, saying that she wants to visit me here at Coastal. Honestly, I'm not sure I'm ready for that. It's been ages since we've even spoken, and I don't know what to say or how to act around her.

The truth is the two of us have never been very close. And

I'm not sure I have the space or energy to disrupt my routine for her.

In my opinion, it's simply not worth it. If she really cared about me, about our relationship, she would've reached out before now.

And then, unfortunately, there's the resident golden boy. For some reason, he's been consuming my thoughts lately, and it's driving me up a wall. It's absurd, really. We've known each other for three years now, but he's always been more of an afterthought.

A tiny, prickly thorn in my side.

These days, thoughts of him are more like a dagger straight to the gut . . . nearly impossible to ignore.

My fingers absentmindedly pick at my hair, and I know I need to distract myself before I completely zone out. It's something that happens whenever I get overly stressed. I pick, and pick, and pick until my thoughts finally shut off—until there's nothing to worry about besides the incessant aching of my scalp.

It's a compulsion I can't control. A mindless distraction that I crave.

Instead, I try to focus on happy little thoughts, but my mind drifts back to Holden. Again and again. It's like I only have two coping mechanisms to choose from here: pick at my hair or think of him. It frustrates me, and I try to push my hands under my body, hoping the pressure will help me redirect.

I make a concerted effort to focus on something else, anything else, but my mind won't cooperate.

I remember what my first therapist taught me, and I attempt to use those silly little grounding techniques. Just five things to focus on, one for each of my senses: the softness of my sheets against my skin, the faint scent of lavender from my diffuser, the hum of the air conditioner in the background, the lingering taste of the tea I had earlier, and the dim glow of the streetlights filtering in through my curtains.

Yet, despite my efforts, nothing seems to work. My mind's relentless, a nonstop loop of anxiety and baseless fears, refusing to be anchored.

I huff out a breath. Stare at the wall. Tap my fingers against my forearm, tracing a path from the crux of my elbow, down across my radius, and press a thumb into my wrist.

*Oh, fucking hell.*

I don't want to rely on these thoughts, but it's the only thing that seems to work. Sighing, I turn onto my back and let myself fall into the now-familiar daydream.

It's two weeks prior, and we're back in Holden's car again.

I imagine the low cadence of his voice, the feeling of his hands on my skin, and a flame sparks inside of me. It's wrong, I know it is. All we do is argue, and I have no right to think about him this way. But it feels so good to let go, to forget, just for a little while.

Eventually, exhaustion takes over, and I drift off to sleep, picturing Holden's fingers filling me instead of my own.

I JOLT awake in the middle of the night, heart hammering from the dirty thoughts swirling around in my head. Holden's dark eyes, his lips, his hands, his golden hair—it all reverberates in my mind. This time, it simply wasn't enough to carry me through the entire night.

*Well, fuck.*

I try to shake off the unsavory thoughts, grabbing my phone to call Elio. I can only assume he'll be awake at this hour. He's usually a night owl, especially on the weekends, so I'm sure he's up to no good somewhere.

Thankfully, he picks up after only a few rings. "Kai, you okay?" he asks, his voice groggy with sleep.

"Shit, did I wake you?"

"No, you're good," he assures me. "I just got in bed, and I'm like half-asleep, scrolling through my phone."

My eyes widen, surprised that he's tucked away inside his apartment already. "But it's Friday night."

"Yeah, I know, but I had to film back-to-back scenes earlier."

"Oh," I awkwardly murmur.

"Yeah, *oh*. So, is everything okay?"

I let out a shaky sigh. "I can't sleep, and I feel sick."

"Sick, like you're ill? Or sick like you're anxious?"

"Sick like I wanna pull all my hair out." I attempt to keep the explanation brief, knowing he's well aware of my issues. "I can't sleep, and I can't think about anything helpful or productive. Plus, I had this awful fucking dream . . ."

"About what?" he gently presses.

I hesitate, unwilling to share the intimate details. "Er, it's not important. I just—I wanted to hear your voice. I was hoping you could distract me."

"I can swing by real quick if you want? Is Lizzie home?"

"No, she's having a girls' night with some of her friends. Besides, it's the middle of the night. You don't need to do that."

"Kaia, I'm here."

"No, I know." My voice cracks with emotion. "I know you are. And I'll be okay. I'm just overthinking things."

"That's your MO," he teases, an attempt to lighten the mood. "Look, what if I stay up with you on the phone until you fall asleep?"

A wave of gratitude washes over me. "Okay."

"You have any gossip to share?"

"No, my life's incredibly boring right now. You?"

"Well, it's not really gossip per se, but I think my sister's about to propose to her partner."

"Taylor?"

"Yeah, they've been together a while now. The only problem is they're allergic to Tay's dog."

"Oh, no. That's not good."

"I know." He heaves a weighted sigh. "It fucking sucks because Bentley's on his last legs of life right now. And she doesn't want to lock him up to keep him away from the main living areas. Luc was gonna take him, but they have a lot on their plates already with both Juney and work," he explains, referring to his two-year-old niece. "I don't know, I was thinking of offering up my apartment."

"Oh, yeah?"

"I just—I don't know." He hesitates for a moment, and I can sense his self-doubt creeping in. "I feel like some days I can barely keep myself alive. But what do you think?"

"I think you can handle a lot more than you give yourself credit for."

"So, you think I should do it, then? Let Bentley move in?"

"Honestly, I think you'd make a great dog dad."

"Yeah?" He sounds pleased, and I can't help but smile at his reaction.

"Definitely."

"Okay, then yeah," he murmurs. "I'm gonna go for it. I'll text Taylor in the morning."

"What a good brother you are."

He gulps low in his throat. "Well, I've got a lot to make up for."

"You've already served your penance, E," I say, hoping to ease a sliver of his guilt. He's still trying to make up for past mistakes—ones he made years ago. It's time he finally lets himself move on because I know the rest of his family has. "Stop punishing yourself."

"No, I know. It's all good." He changes the topic, deflecting from his own issues. "What else did you want to talk about? I could tell you about the scene I filmed earlier where—"

"Oh God, please don't make me vomit when I'm already feeling like shit," I hastily interrupt, my stomach turning at the mere thought of hearing about his hookups, regardless of whether or not they're work-related. The last thing I need right now is to be reminded of the physical intimacy that I'm severely lacking.

"I was joking, Kaia," he says with a laugh. "Live a little."

I let out a small sigh of relief. I know Elio well enough to know he's not the type to spill all the nitty-gritty details, but lately, my anxiety's been through the roof.

"Yeah, well, my joke radar's kind of going haywire these days," I admit, pushing through the embarrassment. "I feel like I've been taking everything to heart."

"Well, when you're running on five hours of sleep for an entire week, you're bound to be cranky," he points out. "Don't be so fucking hard on yourself."

I appreciate his kind words and his ability to always see the best in me, even when I can't see it myself. When I'm down, he picks me up. And when he's down—which unfortunately happens quite often—I try my best to return the favor. It's one of the reasons we've stayed so close all these years.

"I know," I quietly murmur, a small smile tugging at the corners of my lips. "I'm trying not to be."

"Good."

I pause, breathe deep, then, "Hey, El?"

"Yeah?"

"Thanks for picking up," I say, my voice barely above a whisper now.

"Welcome," he says gruffly.

"I'm gonna try to sleep now, okay?

"Alright. Night, Kai."

"Good night." A sense of comfort surges through me as I hang up the phone. I turn over in bed, pull the covers up to my chin, and say a silent prayer to whatever god might be listening: please let me fall back asleep, I beg, just this once.

The next night, it's more of the same miserable bullshit. I'm running on a never-ending hamster wheel, and my brain won't allow me to take a single break. It's mentally, physically, and emotionally draining.

A burning exhaustion that melts me down to my bones.

All I'm asking for—dear fucking universe—is one little night of reprieve. Just an opportunity to catch up on some much-needed beauty rest. Maybe if I could fall asleep for a solid twenty-four hours straight, then I could make it through the rest of the semester without sleeping another wink.

It's plausible, right?

But the only way I've managed that in the past is by turning to methods I'm not so proud of. And I won't go back there again.

So, if my usual coping mechanisms aren't working and my fictional, fantasy hookups are less effective, that probably means I need to resort to the real thing this time.

Someone, anyone out there, please just rail me until my brain shuts off.

Fully desperate at this point, I grab my phone off the nightstand and shoot a text to Lizzie.

KAIA

hey, where are you?

LIZZIE

sig tau party. did you want to come?

KAIA

yes, please. any hot guys?

LIZZIE

plenty *winking emoji* *eggplant emoji*

With the address secured, I spring out of bed and start prepping myself. I put in my best effort to look as hot as possible in less than ten minutes and then call for another Uber. Tonight, I'm resolved to make this shit happen, once and for all.

Honest to God, I don't think a willing college girl has ever had this much trouble getting herself laid.

# Chapter Twelve

## HOLDEN

After tonight's win, I'm so tired I can barely keep my eyes open. But Rai's got the rest of the guys all riled up, convinced that we need to head over to the Sigma Tau house to celebrate. It's honestly the last thing I want to do, but I figure I'll tag along for a little while just to see how things shake out.

As soon as we arrive, the frat house is a blur of sound and motion. People are milling around everywhere, their voices overlapping in a noisy hum. It's chaotic as fuck. And much different from the parties we host at our place, that's for damn sure.

There's no rhyme or reason to the guest list, and their house is already a fucking disaster—the floors are sticky, there's trash littering the walls, and the state of their communal bathrooms is something out of a nightmare. From the state of things, it doesn't look like these guys have properly cleaned the place since the early 2000s.

But I suppose no one really gives a shit, do they? They just want a place to party, to drink, and they clearly don't care about the consequences.

I make my way over to their makeshift bar and grab myself a beer, hoping to find some small pocket of quiet in the chaos.

By this point, I've officially lost sight of my housemates, so I make do chatting with a few Sig Tau brothers. They're alright guys, and I'm generally fine with small talk, especially since they seem to want to stroke my ego.

"You were on fire tonight, Becker," one of them says, cheersing me with a flimsy Solo cup.

"Thanks, man." I give him a quick nod, deflecting from the praise. It's easy to get swept up in the hype, but I'd rather not come off like an entitled dickhead for once. "We all played a good game."

They agree and then start droning on about some drama they have going with a nearby sorority. From my half-assed attempts at listening, it sounds like the girls have been sneaking in and stealing their composite photos. They've collected at least ten of them from prior years, and no one can quite figure out who's doing it and when.

I really couldn't care less about the whole situation. I've been trying to find an opening to step away from them for the last ten minutes, desperately scanning the crowd for a familiar face.

And that's when I spot Kaia from across the room.

She's leaning against the wall, her eyes sparkling with laughter as she chats with some guy I don't recognize. They're lost in conversation, their faces inches apart, and I feel a pang of something hot and sour in my gut.

I try to push it down, to tell myself that it's nothing, that I'm being ridiculous. But as the guy brushes Kaia's hair behind her ear, whispering something to her, I lose all semblance of control.

I cut off whatever conversation's happening in front of me, making up some bullshit excuse to leave. Then I push through the crowd toward Kaia, heart racing.

"Hey, sorry to interrupt," I say, directing my attention to the random dude next to her. "One of your brothers just mentioned that you're a big hockey fan. Thought I'd come over to say hey."

"Uh." He gives me an odd look, shifting his eyes and glancing at Kaia like she might be in on the joke. "Yeah, not really. Sorry, man."

*Well, fuck.* That was a shot in the dark that didn't pan out like I'd hoped.

Kaia's eyes widen for a moment and then narrow in my direction. She's not buying my bullshit for a second. "Right, so anyway." She drags out the word, her tone filled with annoyance. "Later, Beck."

As she turns her back on me, a flush of heat creeps up my neck. It's embarrassing how obvious I'm being right now, but I can't bring myself to stop. "So, what are you two talking about?" I cut in again, attempting to keep my voice casual.

The guy turns to look at me now, fully sizing me up. He's tall and muscular, with a perfect head of hair and a million-watt smile.

What a piece of shit.

"Just talking." He raises an irritated brow. "Did you need something, man?"

I'm bristling, my fists clenching at my sides. I'm not sure what it is about this guy, but I can tell that he's trouble. He's been looking at Kaia like she's a piece of meat, and I don't fucking like it.

As the tension between us rises, Kaia grows uneasy. She turns to the asshole beside her and asks, "Hey, how about I just come to find you later?"

His face falls, but he quickly recovers. Reaching out, he gives Kaia a quick squeeze on the arm before stepping away. "Sure, we'll talk then."

Once he's out of earshot, Kaia fixes her heated gaze back on me, both hands perched on her hips. "If I didn't already know you were trying to cockblock me, now I'd be one hundred percent sure."

"Well, isn't this a pleasant surprise," I say, blatantly ignoring her comment. "I've seen you outside the classroom twice in one week. Must be some kind of record."

She rolls her eyes, twiddling the bracelet on her wrist. "Just needed to get out of the apartment for a while."

I clear my throat, taking in the full effect of her appearance. She's wearing a tight-fitting top that accentuates every curve and a tiny little skirt that shows off her long legs. The dim lights of the frat house make her glow, and I'm finding it difficult to concentrate on anything else.

"You're still on the hunt for a hookup," I say, attempting nonchalance.

Her frown deepens. "Is that really any of your business?"

"Just trying to make conversation, Karras," I say, raising my hands in surrender. "Besides, I'm pretty sure you made it my business the other night."

She lets out an exasperated sigh. "Yeah, well, that was an error in judgment."

"Was it?"

"Clearly, since you and your buddies are so unwilling to help me."

"What if I told you that I'm willing now?" I propose, taking a step closer.

"Yeah?" she asks, arching a challenging brow. "Who'd you have in mind, then?"

Surprising myself, I blurt out the word "Me" without a split second of hesitation.

She stares, blinking back the shock. "What?"

"You must know I want you, Karras," I admit, my heart

hammering in my ears. "I've wanted you for as long as I can remember. And if you're looking for just one night, then count me in."

Her expression shifts from shock to confusion to a heavy dose of skepticism. "Is this a joke?"

"The furthest thing from it."

There's a beat of pained silence, and then, "Just one night?"

"Just one," I echo, my pulse jumping into my throat.

She looks at me for a long moment, chewing on her lower lip, contemplating my offer. Finally, she swallows, thick and heavy as she says, "So, you want to give me another ride?"

"A ride?" I tease. "You mean that thing where you get in my car and I drive you home?"

"Yeah. And then afterward, you can even come inside."

"Come on." I take her hand, leading her out of the party and into the darkness. We make it out to the back parking lot in seconds flat. Realizing that she's finally mine—for just a momentary lapse in time—means that I can't resist her for another fucking second. I press her up against the side of my car, placing a hand behind her head.

"You sure you want this?" I ask, giving her every last opportunity to back out.

"Just fucking kiss me already."

As I lean in, a surge of electricity shoots through my veins. Our lips meet. Her mouth is hot and soft against mine, and my heartbeat runs wild as our tongues tangle together. I press tightly against her, the heat between us rising with every passing moment.

She pulls me impossibly close, both hands gripping my shirt as our kiss becomes more desperate, more needy. It's like we're trying to devour each other, to hold on to this moment—this one night—as tightly as we can.

When we finally come up for air, she says, "I don't want to have sex with you, Beck."

I struggle to catch my breath, confusion lacing my tone. "Yeah, and I *don't* want to have sex with you, either."

"No, God. I mean, like, we can do anything *but* sex, okay?" She blows out a heated breath. "Just, I don't want to go that far with you when . . ."

"When what?" I carefully press.

With a sigh, she says, "When we don't even like each other."

"You still think I don't like you?" I lean back, running a frustrated hand through my hair. "Kaia, I fucking adore you."

Her brow furrows. "What?"

"I admire the hell out of you. I think you're smart, funny, witty, beautiful." I stop myself before I get truly carried away. "There's never a dull moment when we're around each other."

"Are you sure you're not just saying that to get into my pants?"

A smirk tilts my lips. "Only if honesty's the kinda thing that turns you on."

"Oh God, Becker, just get in the fucking car already."

By the time we make it back to her apartment, I'm practically jumping out of my seat in anticipation. I attempted to make small talk during the ride over, but she shut me down and blasted the radio instead.

I get it—she's probably trying to silence the noise inside her head. But honestly, my own thoughts are just as chaotic. This almost feels like some sort of dream, like an alternate reality that we're stepping into. It's certainly my version of a fantasy.

That is, I've always taken notice of Kaia.

I can remember the first time I ever laid eyes on her. It was freshman year on the first day of our Organic Chem lab. She had longer hair then, but it was pulled into a loose bun, her hazel eyes piercing even through those ugly lab goggles.

And when she first met my gaze, there was an instant spark of attraction between us. I swear she felt it, too.

But then, in walked Elio. The smug bastard. I didn't even know who he was at the time, but there was something about him that rubbed me the wrong way. I had no claim on Kaia, I know that, but I was pissed to find out she was taken.

Later that semester, when I finally got the chance to talk to her, I said something that unintentionally offended her. For me, it was a throwaway comment, but for her, it set a precedent. Since then, we've been playing a dangerous game.

She lobs a few insults my way, I tease her right back, and then the cycle continues.

I never thought I had a real shot at spending a night with her, other than in my wildest dreams. In my mind, she's always been taken. This forbidden fruit—just something pretty to look at, pine over, and then forget about. But ever since I found out the truth, it's like a switch flipped inside my brain.

Now, I feel like I have to have her.

Just one fucking night together.

That's all it'll take. We'll both get this out of our systems, use each other for a few hours, and then we'll go back to how things have always been.

As I follow her up to her apartment, there's a charged silence that fills the air. Pushing inside, she slowly takes off her shoes at the entryway, and I follow suit. It's like I'm a teenager again, awkward and juvenile, with no fucking clue what to do with his hands.

Shaking my head clear, I grasp her wrist, pulling her

against me. Then, without another word between us, my lips come crashing into hers. I walk her backward until we hit the back of the couch.

"Not here," she whispers, lacing our fingers together, guiding me down the hallway to her room.

Once we're tucked inside, she rushes toward me, and our lips lock in a desperate, frenzied kiss. It's electric, the way our bodies fit together, and I feel myself growing harder with every passing moment.

I need her. I need her so badly that it hurts.

With a sense of urgency, I guide her toward the edge of the bed, pushing her down onto the soft sheets. I drop to my knees in front of her, gazing up at her with a hunger that's impossible to control.

She's drop-dead gorgeous, and the sight of her lying there, vulnerable and exposed, sends a shiver down my spine.

I trace the length of her leg with my fingertips, and her body quivers, trembles beneath my touch.

"It's been a long time since anyone's touched me," she whispers, her voice laced with vulnerability.

"Don't worry, baby," I murmur, sliding my hands up her firm thighs. "I'll be so fucking good to you."

I plant a soft kiss against her there, savoring the feel of her skin against my lips. Slowly, I work my way up her leg, inching closer and closer to the tiny scrap of lace that's separating me from her pussy.

"Tell me, Karras. Do you like to be the one in control here?" I ask, watching her carefully.

She meets my gaze, her eyes dark with desire. "You don't, do you?" I continue, a chuckle escaping me. "Everywhere else, you're in charge. But in here, when you're like this—" I graze my teeth against the soft flesh of her inner thigh, earning myself a tiny whimper. "—you like to let yourself go."

"Mhm," she murmurs, the sound sending a rush of heat through my body.

"Then take off your shirt."

She unbuttons her blouse, revealing her perfect breasts spilling out from the top of lacy, lavender cups. I watch, transfixed, as she unhooks the clasp behind her back, letting the fabric slide down her arms and drop to the floor.

She's bare to me now, except for her stockings and panties, and the sight of her takes my breath away. I take her hand in mine and place a soft kiss on each knuckle. "My turn."

With a sense of purpose, I slide my hands to the top of her hips, hooking my thumbs under the thin elastic of her thong. Slowly, I slide it down her legs, revealing the slick, wet folds of her pussy.

Still on my knees in front of her, I lower my mouth to her stomach, savoring the way her skin feels against my lips. I circle her nipples with my fingertips as she squirms beneath me, desperate for more.

"Please, just make me come already," she whines, her voice full of need. It's intoxicating—the way she wants this so fucking badly.

"God, you're so hot when you're desperate."

"Oh, shut up, Beck."

"Even hotter when you pretend not to like me."

She wrinkles her nose. "Is it really pretending, though?"

With a smirk, I say, "You tell me." Then, ever so slowly, my lips trail back down her body toward her bare cunt. I lick her there, pressing the flat of my tongue against her slit, building up the pressure until she's thrashing, writhing into my mouth, moaning uncontrollably.

"That feels so fucking good," she cries.

"So, you do like me, then?"

"Shh," she begs. "Don't stop."

I keep licking her, my fingers working their way deeper inside of her. She tenses up as her orgasm builds, and I keep up the pace, eager to give her the release she craves. Her body writhes and bucks as she gets closer and closer, her moans growing louder and more urgent. I can feel her wetness slicking over my fingers, and it drives me fucking wild with desire.

When she finally comes, it's like a dam bursting, and I drink in the sounds of her pleasure like a man dying of thirst. I keep my fingers moving, riding out the waves of her orgasm until she's fully spent and limp in my arms.

Once she comes down from her high, I pull back and look up at her, savoring the sight of her flushed and sated body. Her eyes are closed, her breath heavy, but she looks more satisfied than I've ever seen her before.

It feels so fucking good to know that I've given her this, something she clearly hasn't had in a long time—a real release.

# Chapter Thirteen

KAIA

I DON'T THINK I've experienced an orgasm like that in years, or maybe even ever.

My entire body feels sated and alive, and I can't help the insatiable need to get my hands on him myself. I've spent the last couple of weeks dreaming of his fingers inside of me, and now that I've had a real taste, I need more.

As I look at him, fully dressed while I'm still naked, I feel exposed. And the need to see what's hiding underneath his clothes is too much to resist. I lean forward, tugging desperately at his shirt.

He smirks, covering my hands. "I thought I was the one in control."

"I want to see you," I practically beg.

He steps back, waiting for me to comply. There's a challenging look in his eyes, a daring spark that's impossible to resist. God, I think I like this side of him—the one that takes charge. The thought of surrendering to his commands, of shutting off my brain like this, sets my entire body—my soul—on fire.

As I stand in front of him, my nipples pebbling in the cool air, he places a hand on my shoulder. Then, he gently shoves me down to my knees. I lick my lips and blink up at him through thick lashes.

In one swift move, he pulls his own shirt over his head,

revealing the hard, tanned muscles of his upper body. He's built, sculpted by the fucking gods, in all my favorite places. I bite my lower lip, captivated by the subtle clenching of his abs and the trail of dark hair running directly down the middle.

I'm ready to yank off the rest of his clothing now, but he seems to have other ideas.

"Put your hands behind your back," he demands.

I roll my eyes but do as he says, waiting impatiently as he slowly works his pants and boxers off. And there it is. He's thick, painfully hard, and my God, he looks to be the absolute perfect size for me. I ache to get my mouth around his cock, to feel him inside of me, but I can't let myself go as far as the latter.

Not tonight. And not with him.

"Open your mouth," he orders, cupping a hand around my jawline. I comply, sticking out my tongue. I want to use my hands to grip his hips, to regain some semblance of control, but he doesn't allow that either.

"No hands," he says, his fingers weaving into my hair, pulling me forward until my tongue touches his tip. Slowly, he guides himself inside.

"Is this okay?" he asks, softly caressing my head and rubbing his thumb along the back of my neck.

I nod my consent, and he makes a low groaning sound deep in his throat. Then he pulls back and pitches forward, slowly fucking himself inside my mouth.

"That's it," he groans, and holy shit, I need to hear the sounds he makes when he comes. "Just like that."

It's not long before he loses control, rutting against me until tears pool in the corner of my eyes. He catches his breath for a moment, gaze never leaving mine. "Sorry, baby. You can use your hands now."

Free from the invisible shackles, I place one hand on his thigh, using the other to circle around the base of his cock. I continue to lick and suck until he's fully shaking, trembling around me.

"Where do you want me to finish?" he pants, voice thick with desire.

I signal with two fingers to the base of my throat, and he exhales a rough moan at the thought. It's not much longer before he's spilling into my mouth, and I greedily drink every drop.

He takes a few seconds to steady himself, groaning deeply before lifting me up onto my feet. His lips crash into mine with a fierce intensity that leaves me dizzy.

"That was fucking incredible," he murmurs against my lips.

"It was good for me, too."

He grins, eyes sparking with mischief. "I could tell."

"Okay." I attempt to compose myself, unsure of where to go next. "So . . . are we done here?"

"Fuck no," he scoffs.

"I already said we weren't having sex."

"Who said anything about sex? I can make you come in a thousand different ways that don't involve sticking my cock in your pussy."

I have absolutely zero clue what to say to that. But before I can respond, jaw nearly dropped to the floor, he orders, "Get on the bed, Karras."

And without further hesitation, I do.

To my pleasant surprise, it turns out he wasn't lying. He proceeds to make me come—precisely three more times—leaving me so fucking exhausted by the time we're finished. When I finally pass out, I'm not entirely sure how much of my soul is still left inside my body.

MY EYES slowly blink open as I bask in the warm glow of the sun. It's filtering in through the crack in my curtains, casting a tiny little rainbow of heat over us.

Memories of the previous night bombard me, and I can't help but grin to myself. It was exactly what I needed—a mindless night of passion with no strings attached. I have to admit, despite my initial hesitation, Holden was the perfect guy for the job.

I can't even recall the last time I slept this soundly. The best part is we didn't waste any time talking after we finished. I passed out immediately, and I guess he stayed with me throughout the rest of the night.

There might be a small part of me that's disgruntled about the whole thing, but I can't bring myself to regret this. I got what I needed, and it feels damn good.

The bed shifts beneath me, and I jolt fully awake. Holden's sitting up, stretching his arms above his head, then scratching at the back of his neck. I watch, silent, as he gathers his things, and I immediately panic.

Is he really trying to sneak out without even saying a word?

My heart pounds as he tiptoes around the room. But then he stops in his tracks, catching my gaze.

"You woke me up," I say in a raspy voice, failing to hide my embarrassment. I can see the confusion in his eyes, and a blush creeps up my neck.

"Hey, I'm sorry," he says softly, his voice low and gentle. "I didn't mean to."

"How long was I out for?"

"I think we passed out around two in the morning," he says, glancing at his watch. "So, I guess, a little over five hours."

"Oh." I slump back onto the bed. "And you were just gonna head out without saying anything?"

"I was trying to be respectful and let you sleep," he says, and I can hear the sincerity in his voice. "It wasn't my intention to be sneaky."

"Oh." My shoulders droop, and I feel foolish for the accusation. If I'm being honest with myself, I have no reason to care either way. "Okay, then."

His eyes soften at my obvious discomfort. "Kaia, I'm serious. I just have a team meeting, and I need to go. It's early. I thought you could use the rest."

"Alright. Well, um, have a good day, then?"

"Yeah, that didn't come out as sincere as you were hoping for," he says with a slight chuckle. "We're in the same boat, Karras. But it was just one night, right? No need to let it make things awkward."

"Yeah, one night," I agree, feeling a little more at ease. "It's all good."

He walks toward my door, and just before he leaves, he tosses back, "So, I'll see you in class tomorrow?"

I give him a small wave, then, "Yeah. Later, Beck."

Monday's Calc class comes to an end, and I quickly stuff my notebook and pen into my bag, flinging it over one shoulder. Elio does the same, and we move toward the exit of the lecture hall. But in my peripheral, I catch Holden's gaze lingering on me, sending a wave of heat through my body.

We're halfway through the quad when he calls out behind us, shouting for us to wait up.

Elio shoots me a puzzled look. "What the hell does he want?"

My pulse quickens, but I don't have time to respond. "Karras," Holden says once he's in earshot. "Can we talk for a minute?"

I raise a surprised brow. "What's up?"

"Just wanted to check in after yesterday morning, make sure everything's good," he says, wiping a bead of sweat off his forehead.

My stomach drops, and I pinch my eyes shut, muttering under my breath, "I'd rather not do this right now."

"Funny." Holden gives me a humorless snort. "That's not what you were saying the other night."

Heat rises in my cheeks, and my chest tightens with embarrassment. Elio's still standing next to me, and the last thing I want is for him to know about what happened this weekend.

"Can we not talk about this here?" I plead.

Elio watches us, his gaze darting from my face to Holden's, eyes narrowing as he connects the dots. "Oh wow, please tell me you didn't," he finally accuses.

I wince. "I may have."

Elio shudders. "Oh, gross, Kai."

There's a flicker of hurt in Holden's expression, but his tone quickly turns defensive. "You know, that's pretty rich coming from you," he snaps.

"What's that supposed to mean?" Elio asks.

"Considering what you do for a living, I don't think you have any room to judge Kaia's decisions."

Elio falls silent, head shaking, the weight of confrontation visibly bearing down on him. It's not that he's afraid of it, but he doesn't have the capacity—nor the desire—to argue with Holden. Eventually, he turns on his heel and walks away, leaving the two of us here alone.

Taking a deep, calming breath, I turn to him and ask, "Why'd you have to go there?"

He grumbles, looking down at his feet. "He started it."

"He was just joking around. Besides, how do you even know about that?" I ask, crossing my arms over my chest.

"It's not like it's a secret." He cracks his knuckles, resumes his bored expression. "Half the campus knows."

"Really?" I balk. I honestly had no clue that Elio's profession was common knowledge. We're so caught up in our own little bubble that the thought never even crossed my mind.

"Yeah, I mean, he's got a famous brother," he points out. "And his videos are pretty public access."

"But he hides his face."

"That doesn't matter when you're covered in tattoos, does it? Everyone knows it's him, Karras. I wasn't trying to be that much of a jerk." He gives me a tight-lipped smile. "I just didn't realize it was a big deal."

A rush of annoyance hits me at his dismissive attitude. "Yeah, well, he doesn't like talking about it."

"I didn't know."

"Now you do." I steady myself, working to maintain my composure. "So, could you just drop it, please?"

"Fine, consider it dropped." His voice softens, and he leans in a little closer. "You know, I figured you would've told your best friend about our hookup."

My cheeks flush with heat. "You obviously don't like him, and he's not exactly fond of you, so why would I bring it up?"

He's taken aback but doesn't hesitate to respond. "It's not that I have anything against him personally. I just don't trust the guy."

I raise a skeptical brow. "What does that even mean? You barely know him."

"I know enough."

"Like what?"

"I know that he got high, beat the shit out of his older brother, and nearly ruined his football career."

I stop walking, my eyes narrowing in anger. "First of all, that's a major exaggeration. And second, that was five years ago. Why are you keeping such close tabs on Elio's business, anyway?"

"I'm not." His expression shifts. "It's just one of those stories that circulate around, like a cautionary tale. If you're an athlete at Coastal, you've heard about it. That's all."

I cross my arms defensively. "Great, and how would you like it if one of your biggest mistakes was just spread all around campus?"

He rolls his eyes, clearly unimpressed. "It's a little bit more than a mistake, Karras."

I take a step forward, my voice rising in frustration. "Everything turned out how it was supposed to in the end. Luca's wildly successful now, so it's not like he caused any long-term damage anyway."

He shakes his head, expression hardened. "Yeah, well, maybe if Elio had learned his lesson then, it would be a different story."

My eyes widen. "What?"

"I mean, come on. It's pretty obvious he's still using."

My jaw drops, heart pounding. "Why in the world would you think that?"

"I have eyes, Karras. I can see how strung out he is from one week to the next."

"You don't know anything about him."

"Five years ago, he made a terrible error in judgment that affected someone else's life." His voice takes on a condescending tone. "And now he's just coasting by, using you to get through his classes, while still getting high in the meantime."

I pause to center myself, trying—but failing miserably—to keep my emotions in check. "You're wrong."

"Am I, though?"

His question hits me like a sucker punch to the gut. My emotions are in overdrive, and I'm struggling to compose myself. I take a deep breath, gather my thoughts, attempt to find a way to defend my best friend.

But as I think about it more, all of my doubts creep back in. I know firsthand how easy it is to slip into addiction. What Holden doesn't know is that I've been there myself, and I also know how hard it can be to quit for good.

For me, Adderall's the problem. I'd use it to push myself to the limit, to stay up all night studying for exams, and to get a leg up on my peers. Looking back now, I know it wasn't the healthiest choice, but in the moment, it felt necessary.

The rush of focus and productivity was addicting, and I couldn't resist the temptation.

And then, there was the inevitable crash. The lowest lows, where my brain could completely shut off for once. In the end, it was a crutch. A mistake. Something I wish I would've never done.

And Elio was the one who helped me quit.

Now, I realize with a sinking feeling that I may have missed the signs. That I should've been paying more attention, looking for any red flags that my best friend might be using again. But instead, I've been so caught up in my own struggles that I've let him down.

My tears fall, hot and heavy, as I recognize the gravity of the situation. If Holden's right, if Elio's truly slipped up, then I've been oblivious to it this whole time.

A true fucking failure.

# Chapter Fourteen

## HOLDEN

I WATCH in horror as Kaia's eyes well up with tears, overflowing and dripping onto the brick pathway beneath our feet.

*Well, shit.*

Shit, shit, shit. I feel like the biggest asshole on the planet.

My heart sinks as I realize that I've broken through her impenetrable armor. The vulnerability in her eyes is striking, and now that I think about it, I've never actually seen Kaia cry genuine tears before. She's usually so full of fire, so ready to fight.

"Hey, hey, hey," I rush out, stepping closer. "Don't cry. I'm sorry," I say, my voice low and sincere. "I didn't mean to upset you."

She sniffs, wiping at her eyes with the back of her hand. "I'm fine. I just . . . I'm worried that what you said might be true. And I feel like an awful friend for not noticing."

"Hey, don't spiral," I say, swiping the mascara off her cheek with my thumb. "You're a great friend. I was just being a dick."

"But what if you're right?" She twists a strand of thick hair between her fingers, tugging at it in a way that looks almost painful. "What if I've missed the signs? I've been so wrapped up in my own stuff lately that I haven't been paying as much attention as I should've."

I can sense her pain, her worry, her guilt, and it all weighs heavy on my chest. "Kaia, look at me," I say, tilting her chin up with my finger. "You're an incredible fucking friend to Elio. And even if he's going through something right now, it's not your fault. Okay?"

"Yeah," she mumbles, eyes downcast.

"Tell me you know it's not your fault." I don't want her to blame herself for something that might not even be true. And I sure as hell don't want to see her cry anymore, especially not when I'm the cause of it. "It's not your fault," I repeat firmly. "You can't control what Elio does or doesn't do. If he's using again, it's not your responsibility to fix him."

She nods slowly, and some of the tension visibly leaves her body. I wrap my fingers around her upper arm, giving it a gentle squeeze.

"Look, I never should've said anything," I continue, practically begging her to smile again. "You're right. It's none of my business. I'm just an asshole who can't leave things well enough alone."

She grins despite herself. "You *are* an asshole, aren't you?"

"See, we agree on something for once."

"We agreed on a lot of things Saturday night," she says, surprising the hell out of me.

My brows shoot up. "Karras, was that an innuendo?"

She shrugs, and some of that familiar fire returns to her hazel eyes. "Figured it was my turn."

"Yeah, well, it was a good fucking night." My lip quirks. "Wasn't it?"

"Mhm," she murmurs her agreement, and then her expression shifts. "But we probably shouldn't keep bringing it up, especially because it was just a onetime thing."

"Right, one time. Unless . . ." I trail off, wondering if I should push my luck.

Since I left her apartment yesterday morning, I've been replaying the sounds she made inside my head. Those tiny whimpers, those long, drawn-out moans, it's all been swirling around in there like a never-ending record. I had to fuck my fist twice in the shower this morning just to calm myself down.

"Becker, come on." She tilts her head, giving me a small frown. "We both agreed."

"I know, but hear me out. I thought that's what all this tension had been building up to, right? We just needed the one night to get this shit out of our system. Hell, I've been wanting to get a taste of you since the second I laid eyes on you. And I thought, after I did, that maybe I could clear the idea from my head. But it was so fucking good between us, right?"

"It was nice, yeah, but—"

"Judging by the way you were trembling and shaking until you passed out, I'd say it was more than just *nice*."

"Okay, calm down, Casanova." She rolls her eyes. "Yes, I'll admit that it was great. It's clear we have sexual chemistry. And I did sleep like a baby afterward, which is honestly what I was looking for, so—"

I falter back. "Wait, what?"

"I uh—" Her voice trails off as she awkwardly scratches at the back of her neck, pulling at some of the stray baby hairs. "I've been struggling to fall asleep for a while now. It's like my mind just won't stop buzzing, and I can't seem to find any relief no matter what I try. I was hoping that maybe a hookup would help me shut off my brain. Let me get a few solid hours in."

I tilt my head, watching her carefully. I can't deny the way my pulse quickens at the thought of being with her again. "And what, you think one night of sleep is gonna tide you over for the rest of time?" I ask, arching a brow.

"It should do." Her lips quirk up in a small smile, but it doesn't quite reach her eyes. "I feel like a new person already."

I take another step closer, closing the gap between us. "Karras," I murmur, my voice low and soft. "Let me try again for you. Let me be that guy."

She blinks, her gaze flicking up to meet mine. "That guy?" she echoes.

"If you're struggling, I wanna be the guy you call for help. The one who can make you forget about everything else and just . . . be in the moment."

There's a long, stilted silence, the air between us heavy with unspoken tension. Finally, she speaks again, her tone teasing. "So, what you're saying is that you want to be my last resort?"

A smirk tilts my lips. "As long as I'm your something."

She shakes her head. "Not happening."

"Okay, well, you had your shot."

"Oh, yeah?" She snorts, her tone lightening. "What is this—a limited-time offer?"

I can't help the chuckle that escapes me, even though it's laced with disappointment. "I'm a hot commodity, Karras. I won't be on sale for too much longer."

"I think I'll take my chances."

"Your loss." I shrug, letting it go for now. There's no use pushing the issue, not when I'm certain this thing between us is far from over. We both feel it, and I know it's only a matter of time before Kaia willingly admits the truth.

If she's looking for the key to unlock her problems, then I'm exactly what she fucking needs. It's undeniable.

. . .

As I STEP inside the gym, I find my housemates standing in a tight huddle, heads together, chuckling like they're sharing some sort of inside joke. But as soon as they catch sight of me, they all break apart, grinning from ear to ear.

"What's up, Becksy?" Rai asks, clapping me on the back. "We didn't get a chance to chat after the meeting yesterday."

I know what's coming next, and I'm not exactly in the mood for their teasing, but I play along anyway. "Yeah? And what'd you all want to *chat* about?"

They share a smirk, and Bodie elbows Rai in the ribs. "We were just wondering where you went on Saturday night."

"Yeah," Will chimes in, raising a brow. "One minute, you were there chatting with some of the brothers. And then the next, you were gone. Vanished like a fucking magician."

I work to steady my voice. "Just had some stuff to take care of."

"Stuff?" Rai echoes, giving me a pointed look. "What kind of stuff?"

I grab a towel from the rack and start to stretch. "You know, just running some errands. Nothing exciting."

They're not buying it, that much is obvious. Will snickers and says, "Yeah, because everyone runs errands at midnight on a Saturday."

Bodie nudges me with his elbow, a sly grin on his face. "Come on, man. We won't judge. Did you hook up with someone?"

My cheeks burn with discomfort, and I avert my gaze. I don't want to lie to them, but I'm not ready to share the details of my night with Kaia. "Nah, man," I say, brushing him off. "Just had some business to take care of."

They keep pushing, trying to get me to fill them in, but I

manage to deflect their questions. I don't want to share this story with them yet. It feels too personal. And honestly, I'm afraid that if I tell them about Kaia, it'll somehow jinx my chances of a repeat.

Thankfully, they drop the subject as we start our workout. I stack some weights on the bar, trying to focus on my lifts and decompress. But in between each rep, my mind drifts back to the girl with the tear-filled eyes, and I'm haunted by it.

I still feel like a dick for making her cry earlier, for pushing too hard, for poking at an insecurity I didn't even know existed. And I'll be damned if I ever let it happen again.

THE NEXT DAY, I mentally prep for our second dissertation meeting. I managed to organize myself after procrastinating until the very last minute, letting the distractions get the better of me. But despite the delay, I'm not too concerned about it.

If the work gets done eventually, does the timeline really matter?

When I arrive at Dr. Khatri's office, I find Kaia already waiting outside. She seems nervous and uneasy, like she's been fretting over this meeting all night. But as always, she also looks stunning, and an undeniable wave of attraction washes over me.

"Hey," I say, taking a seat beside her on the bench.

She acknowledges me with a quick flick of her wrist, unwilling to offer anything more. Then we sit in silence for a few painstaking moments until Dr. Khatri opens her door and invites us in. We take our seats opposite her desk, and she asks us how we're doing.

"All's good over here," I say, charming her with a wide smile.

Kaia nods her agreement, but I can tell that she's not in a good mood. She seems annoyed, more unsettled than usual, and I can't shake the feeling that it's directed toward me.

On the other hand, Dr. Khatri is her typical calm and collected self. She peers over the top of her glasses, briefly assessing us before she dives in.

"Holden, you've done a great job narrowing down your search terms and defining your concepts," she says, flipping through my paperwork. "You came up with less than a hundred results to sift through, which is fantastic."

A sense of pride floods through me, but I don't want to come across as arrogant in front of Kaia.

"Kaia, on the other hand, you cast a much wider net," Dr. Khatri continues. "We need to work on narrowing down your language and better defining your concepts."

"Of course," Kaia says, radiating her usual confidence. "I'll work on it."

"Great." Dr. Khatri gives her a small nod of approval before turning back to me. "Holden, well done on your initial search. You seem to have a good handle on your project already."

"Thank you," I say, sneaking a glance at Kaia. If she's at all upset about the situation, then she's doing her absolute best to hide it. "You know, I'd be happy to help Kaia workshop her question."

"I think that's a great idea," Dr. Khatri says, her eyes lighting up. "Kaia, do you have time to set something up with Holden?"

"Of course, thank you, Holden." Kaia gives me a tight smile. "That's very kind of you."

Although her tone is irritated, I can tell she's trying to put on a brave face. We spend the rest of the meeting discussing the next stage in the process, but Kaia doesn't spare me another glance.

As we stand up to leave, thanking Dr. Khatri for her time, a sense of unease settles in the pit of my gut, nagging at me that I fucked everything up yet again.

Like a dog on a leash, I follow Kaia out of the building. She's walking at a breakneck pace, and I have to jog a little to catch up with her. Once I do, I casually bump her shoulder.

"Well, that went well, don't you think?" I ask, trying to diffuse the tension.

"Sure," she says through gritted teeth. "If you were trying to make me look even more incompetent."

"Ah." I wince. "That was definitely not my intention."

She stops walking, giving me an exasperated look. "*Oh, Dr. Khatri, I'd be happy to help Kaia workshop her question,*" she mocks in a grating voice.

"Come on, I was being sincere."

"Whatever." She turns on her heel, attempting to walk away from me. But before she can manage, I gently clutch onto her wrist, trying to ground her and make sense of what's going on in her head.

"Kaia, seriously?"

Her response is quick and cutting. "Look, I get that you were trying to help in there. And by the same coin, I'm really *trying* not to be mean to you right now. But I'm feeling overstimulated and really fucking anxious, so can you just leave it?"

I drop her hand like a hot coal, taking a step back to give her space. Despite her biting words, I'm grateful for her honesty and willingness to be vulnerable with me again. "I'll leave it. But we'll talk later, yeah?"

She steadies herself, closing her eyes as if to steel herself for the conversation to come. With the tiniest nod of her head, she says. "Yeah, later."

I sigh as she turns and walks away, feeling like a lost puppy while she disappears from view. Everything in me wants to chase after her, to make things right, and to take away some of her frustration.

But for now, all I can do is stand there and watch.

# Chapter Fifteen

## KAIA

I SLAM the door behind me, the crushing weight of my disappointment bearing down on my shoulders. Dr. Khatri was kind and supportive during our meeting. Of course she was, but that doesn't change the fact that she called me out on my poor performance.

And Holden overshadowed me again. It's not that I'm jealous of him—not in that sense, at least—but it's frustrating to put all that time and effort in just to come up short.

I spent hours poring over the research this past week. And for what? I sincerely thought my question was good, but apparently, it wasn't good enough. Meanwhile, I'm sure the golden boy didn't start his search until the last fucking minute.

I know he says he was being sincere, but his offer to help me felt like the final nail in my proverbial coffin. Yes, I know it's not technically a competition, but everything always is between us. And unfortunately, Holden came out looking superior this time.

Before I can help myself, my mind starts to spiral. There's a familiar twinge inside my chest, a wound that won't heal, as I replay worst-case scenarios in my head. If I can't get this one tiny thing right, what chance do I have for the rest of the semester and for my dissertation as a whole?

I throw my bag onto the couch and collapse onto it, burying my face in my hands. Tears prick at the corners of my eyes, and

I can't stop them from spilling over. It's pathetic how easily I'm reduced to tears lately.

I'm embarrassed that I let Dr. Khatri down and frustrated at how the meeting went in general. But most of all, I'm angry with myself for not measuring up to my own expectations.

I know I need to do better, to confront my issues head-on, but I don't even know where to start.

And to make matters worse, I still haven't broached the conversation that I need to have with Elio. My mind's a mess, and I can't seem to find the right headspace for it. Or maybe I'm just not ready yet, not when my thoughts are still all tangled up.

I SHUFFLE INTO THE KITCHEN, my body heavy with exhaustion after another sleepless night. The morning sun casts a warm glow over the small dining room, filtering in through the window over the sink.

Lizzie's already dressed to the nines, looking ready to take on the day with her vibrant energy. I slump into a seat across from her, my tired eyes glued to my phone screen. We sit in silence together, and I know her eyes are on me, but I'm too drained to engage in small talk.

As I'm poised to grab some breakfast, she gives me a sly smile. "So, Kaia," she says, raising a mischievous brow. "I've been wondering, how's Holden in bed?"

My heart rate speeds up, and I choke on my coffee. "I'm not sure what you're talking about," I say, feigning innocence.

"Come on." She laughs, eyes twinkling with curiosity. "I know you left the party with him on Saturday night."

Heat rises in my cheeks. "Oh, well, we didn't . . . you know, sleep together."

Her brow raises in disbelief. "You're telling me he came back to our apartment, and you guys didn't hook up?"

"We did . . . other things."

"What kinds of things?" she asks, her interest officially piqued. "Did you go down on him, did he go down on you, what did his dick look like, did he—"

"Jesus Christ, Liz," I chide. "Calm yourself. I'm not telling you any of that."

"What?" She pouts, blinking her big blue eyes up at me. "How unfair. I'd tell you about my nights with Rai if you asked."

I give her an exasperated huff. "That's great, but I'm not going to ask."

"Kaia," she whines, drawing out my name.

"Lizzie, stop. It was a one-night thing, anyway. No use talking about it now."

"One night?" She winces, slumping down into her seat. "Must not have been that good, huh? I knew it—those types of guys are all talk."

"I didn't say it wasn't good."

She perks up. "So it was, then? His dick is huge?"

Blood rushes from my cheeks all the way up to the tips of my ears, and I push up from the table without answering. Lizzie can be so crude sometimes, so blunt, and I don't want to indulge her any longer. At least not at six o'clock in the fucking morning.

Without another word, I head back to my room to get ready for class.

"Wait, Kaia!" she calls, her voice carrying down the hallway. "You can't just leave in the middle of a conversation."

"Bye, Lizzie!" I call over my shoulder, and then I shut

myself inside my room, hoping and praying for a few more minutes of peace.

BY SOME MIRACLE, I managed to make it through the rest of the week without crumbling into a million little pieces. Classes went fine, I was able to rework my research question on my own, and I successfully avoided another mental breakdown.

The only thing I still haven't taken care of is Elio. I messaged him after the whole fiasco on Monday, but he never replied. It's been radio silence from him ever since, and he even skipped out on our second Calc lecture of the week.

It all has me worried sick.

I'm a bundle of nerves waiting to combust. All the momentum I built up on Saturday night has officially evaporated into thin air, like steam fogging up my windows and then suddenly clearing. My one night to reset wasn't enough.

I need a repeat, and I need it stat.

Like clockwork, my thoughts drift back to Holden, who offered himself up on a silver platter to me. But I don't know if it's worth it to screw up our already complicated relationship. So, that leaves me on the hunt for someone else.

The only problem is I don't want a boyfriend. I can barely handle what's on my plate as it is. But maybe Holden's right about one thing; a steady hookup wouldn't be such an awful idea.

It's too bad that finding a trustworthy college guy—who also happens to be up for something casual and consistent—is easier said than done. I have nothing against sleeping around, but having a different guy in my bed every night is not my idea of a good time. I mean, who has the energy for all that?

I just want one person who can satisfy my needs and won't put my health at risk.

As I mull it over, the question lingers: Is Holden fucking Becker really the best option for that?

Perhaps it isn't the most rational decision, but it's undeniably the most convenient one. Against my better judgment, I pick up my phone to text him. Then I change my mind, nearly slamming it back down onto my nightstand.

Then, I pick it back up again. This time, I scroll all the way down to find his contact, bringing up a new message. As my fingers hover over the screen, ready to hit Send, a wave of uncertainty washes over me. I quickly stuff my phone underneath my pillow and shut off my bedside lamp, pinching my eyes closed.

The internal debate rages on, but a part of me knows that going with Holden might just be the solution I need right now. The thought of having someone familiar, someone who understands the pressures of our shared situation, is oddly comforting. And maybe, if I'm lucky enough, this could be the escape I'm desperately seeking.

So thirty seconds later, I dig my phone back out and finally press Send.

KAIA

are you up?

HOLDEN

I'll be there in 20

Less than fifteen minutes pass before I hear a knock. I pause for a long moment, run my hands through my hair, steady myself in front of the hallway mirror. When I finally open the door, Holden's standing there, his dark eyes familiar and intense.

Wordlessly, he steps inside the threshold. As he follows me down the hall and into my bedroom, the fluttering in my stomach grows stronger. We sit down together on the edge of my bed, and I can sense him trying to read my thoughts.

Finally, he breaks the silence with a question. "So, what's up?"

I roll my eyes but can't help the small smile that tugs at my lips. "Well, I did just let you into my apartment in the middle of the night, so I guess it's pretty obvious."

He chuckles, and some of the tension between us dissipates. "Seriously, how have you been holding up? You said we'd talk later, and yet we haven't."

I hesitate, my chest tightening. "I'm still really fucking stressed."

"So, that's why I'm here?" he asks, eyes searching mine. "To help you get unstressed?"

"Yes." I nod slowly, a mix of apprehension and excitement swelling in the pit of my stomach. "And how exactly do you plan on helping me?"

He leans in closer, his breath hot against my skin. "Oh, I have a few ideas," he murmurs, tracing a finger along my jawline.

I shiver, but I don't pull away. Instead, I meet his gaze head-on, trying to gauge his sincerity. "Are you sure about this?" I ask softly. "I mean, I know we've had our moments, but I don't want things to get too complicated."

"I'm the one who practically begged for this, Karras," he says, pinning me with a harsh look. "Besides, if things get complicated, we'll deal with it as it comes."

"Okay." I tilt my head, feeling a small sliver of relief. "Agreeing to this means I'm putting my trust in you. You know that, right?"

"I know." His eyes light up with determination as he flashes me a smile. "And I can promise you, you won't regret it."

He leans in close, the heat radiating off his body, and I catch a faint whiff of peppermint on his breath. Then his lips crash against mine with a sense of urgency, and I eagerly respond, igniting the familiar spark between us.

As we continue to kiss—our lips, tongues, and bodies entwined—his hands slide under my shirt, tracing the curve of my back before he pushes me up to the head of the bed.

With a swift movement, he pulls my pajama bottoms off, and before I can catch my breath, his thick fingers fill me up. I gasp, feeling a wave of pleasure mixed with a slight twinge of pain. I fall forward against his shoulder, biting down hard as he pumps his fingers in and out of me.

"Fuck, baby," he winces. "That hurt."

"I'm sorry," I whimper, my body writhing with pleasure as his fingers curl inside of me. "That caught me off guard."

I tug at the waistband of his sweats, but he shakes his head, denying me access. He continues to fuck his fingers up into me, rubbing his thumb against my clit, and my body arches in response.

"I can't touch you?" I ask, outraged.

"Tonight is just for you, Karras," he says firmly.

"But this *is* for me," I protest, desperate to feel his hard cock in my hands.

"No," he denies me again, and I feel a surge of frustration mixed with excitement. "I'm gonna make you come. At least three times in a row, and then you're gonna go right to sleep like a good fucking girl."

"Fine," I relent, pouting. "I won't touch you, but can you at least take your clothes off for me?"

He smirks, and I can tell he's enjoying my reaction. "Your wish is my command."

As he strips off his clothes, I watch eagerly, trembling with anticipation. I drink up the sight of his naked body before me—his thick corded muscles, the smattering of hair covering his chest, the way his cock sits hard and heavy in between his thick thighs—and nearly combust.

He joins me back onto the bed, eyes locking onto mine. "Are you ready for me?" he asks, voice low and husky.

I nod eagerly, my body pulsing with need. He dives back down between my legs, eager to make good on his promise, and plunges his tongue inside of me, filling me, tasting me. Then for the next hour, he keeps his word, making me come harder than I ever have before.

We're both panting, sweat sticking to our skin, our bodies entangled on my bed. His chest rises and falls in time with mine as we both try to catch our breath. And while he slowly strokes my hair, a low chuckle escapes him.

Despite myself, I smile back, and we lie there in silence for a few moments, basking in the afterglow. But then the drowsiness hits me, my eyelids growing heavy. With a small sigh, he presses a kiss to my temple and says, "Get some sleep, Karras. You look exhausted."

I tuck my chin, already halfway to dreamland. He untangles himself from me and slips out of the bed, rustling around the room as he gets dressed. Before leaving, he comes back over, murmuring, "Sweet dreams," against my forehead.

I wish him a sleepy good night and snuggle deeper under the covers.

Then he tiptoes out of my room and down the hallway. A few moments later, there's the soft click of the door closing behind him. I know he's gone now, but I can't seem to bring myself to care. Instead, I fall into a deep sleep, my mind finally quiet and peaceful for the first time all week.

The next morning, I wake up alone, feeling thoroughly fucked and well rested. A smile creeps onto my face as I move to get up. And there's a little note on my nightstand this time—a few words scribbled onto a pad beside my bed.

*K*

*Sorry for slipping away again, but I had to be up early, and I didn't want to disturb your beauty sleep. Don't worry, I didn't steal any of your hair this time.*

*H*

# Chapter Sixteen

## HOLDEN

I WAKE up to the sound of my phone alarm buzzing beneath me, my heart pounding in my chest and my body aching with a desperate need. After everything, it's hard to believe that Kaia caved so quickly. I know she must have been desperate last night when she texted, and yet, I can't bring myself to care about being her last resort.

The feeling of watching her lose control, and then finally finding some much-needed rest, is worth it all. It's nice knowing I can help her, but I'm not doing this solely out of the selflessness of my heart.

After that first night, I knew I needed to have her again. And again. And again.

I run my tongue over my lips, and I can still taste the sweet, musky flavor of her, feel the way her body quivered under my touch. The thrill of the game we're playing sends shivers down my spine, and I can't help but want more.

With a groan, I shift under the covers, trying to ignore the insistent throbbing between my legs. I know I need to change course, but the memory of her soft skin and the way she begged me for more is too much to ignore. I close my eyes and breathe deeply, the image of her writhing beneath me seared into my mind.

I can't resist the urge any longer, so I fist a hand around my cock and give it a tug, picturing her soft thighs wrapped around my neck. Leaning my head back against the pillow, I stroke myself harder and harder until the pleasure builds and finally crashes over me, leaving me panting and spent.

After a quick rinse in the shower, I move to get dressed for the day, shaking off the memories. As I pull on my shirt, I hear my housemates chatting in the kitchen.

They're blatantly gossiping about where I went last night—which is fair, considering the fact that I took off in the middle of our monthly poker game—and I can tell they're having a field day with it.

Rai flashes me a toothy grin, his eyes sparking with mischief. "Mornin', Becksy. Where'd you disappear to last night?"

It's clear, thanks to Lizzie, that he knows exactly what I've been up to, but he's just waiting for me to admit it to the rest of them. I tense up, hoping my blank expression will mask the truth.

"Just had some stuff to take care of," I respond casually. Heat creeps up my neck, the image of Kaia's bare skin—not to mention the way I just fucked myself to the thought of her—still fresh in my mind.

Will leans forward, eyes glinting with curiosity. "Stuff? Sounds mysterious," he says, and I can practically see the wheels turning in his head. "Is this the same *stuff* you were up to last weekend?"

I roll my eyes. "It's nothing, guys. Just some personal stuff."

They exchange knowing looks but thankfully drop the subject. I don't want to have to explain what's going on with me and Kaia. Not yet, anyway. I need to talk to her first, figure out what the two of us are really doing here.

I let out a sigh of relief as we all pile into my car and head to campus together, making our way to the rink for our game against Trinity. The chatter between the guys is light and playful, but my mind's still reeling.

I can't manage to get the taste of Kaia out of my mouth or the feel of her body writhing beneath me out of my head. It all burns into my skin, branding me with the memory.

As we arrive at the rink, I finally manage to clear my thoughts, focusing instead on the game ahead of us. With each step closer to the ice, I feel the weight of her slowly disappear, replaced by a renewed sense of determination to win.

AFTER CHASING the puck for a couple of hours, I step off the ice, my heart still pounding with the sweet rush of adrenaline. As expected, we absolutely crushed TU, and I revel in the familiar victory that courses through my veins.

The fact that I didn't have to endure my father's incessant commentary on the sidelines is just icing on the cake.

Despite my exhaustion, I agree to tag along with my teammates for a night of bar hopping. We make a quick pit stop at our place and freshen up beforehand.

When we arrive at the Surfbreak, the bar's already swarming with people, and I quickly lose sight of my buddies as they scatter in different directions.

I scan the room, hoping to catch a glimpse of Kaia out here tonight, but she's nowhere to be seen. Naturally, I shouldn't have assumed that Rai would play matchmaker again. Nonetheless, I'm slightly disappointed as I head to the back of the bar solo.

Before I can even take the first sip of my beer, though, a striking redhead approaches me, clad in a dress that could barely pass for a napkin. "Hey there," she croons, sliding onto the stool beside me. "I was at your game tonight. You were amazing out there."

I force a polite smile, hoping she'll take the hint and back off. "Thanks," I mutter, attempting to dissuade her advances.

Unfortunately, my lack of charm must be lost on her because she leans in closer and runs her fingers up my arm. "So, what are you up to after this?" she purrs, her lips strikingly close to my ear.

If this were a few weeks ago, I might've been down. She's smoking hot and clearly not one to play coy. But right now, my thoughts instantly drift to Kaia, and I feel a twinge of guilt.

We're not technically in any sort of relationship, but I'm already loyal to her in a sense. There's no way I could betray that by hooking up with someone else. Not now, not when my mind is still so fucking fixated on the girl.

"Not sure," I say, trying to keep it vague. "I might just head home."

Red doesn't seem to take the hint, though. She persists with her flirtatious banter, and her touch unsettles me. I try to brush her off and focus on the bar, but it seems like every time I glance up, another girl's heading my way, each one more determined than the last. I don't want to be rude, but I also don't want to lead them on.

I'm not interested, and I definitely don't want any whispers of this getting back to Kaia.

As the night drags on, I withdraw further. I nurse my singular drink, trying to blend into the background, hoping the girls will catch on and leave me alone. But they don't. They surround me like moths to a flame, and I grow more and more uneasy.

Enough is enough. I drain the last dregs of my beer, get up, and make my way out of the bar. The other guys can catch their own ride home.

On my way back to the house, I can't help but feel let down. I'd secretly been hoping that Kaia might show up after all, but no such luck. Instead, I spent the night batting off unwanted advances from other girls.

I know, it's not something I have any right to complain about. Because she's not mine, and I'm not technically hers, either.

So when I finally collapse onto my bed at home, I know I need to figure this shit out as soon as possible. Kaia and I need to establish some ground rules, define exactly where she wants this thing to go.

We tried one night to cut the tension, and it didn't fucking work. Now, I'm cool being the guy she calls when she needs her fix, but I need to know exactly where the boundary lies. What's the line, and how do I make sure I don't cross it?

On Monday, I slide into my usual spot in the Calc lecture hall, at the back and across from Kaia. She's sitting in the same place she always does, only this time, Elio's usual seat beside her is empty.

Now that I think about it, he missed out on class last Wednesday, too. If I know Kaia as well as I think I do, then I'm certain she's not taking his absence in stride.

The minute hand on my watch ticks closer and closer to the top of the hour, but still, there's no sign of the kid. I feel a burst of courage, and before I can talk myself out of it, I push out of my seat, making my way toward her.

She looks up, her annoyance clear as she asks, "What are you doing here?"

I raise an unimpressed brow. "I think it's pretty obvious at this point he's not coming. Mind if I sit here?"

Her eyes narrow. "Actually, I'm still saving this seat."

I let out a low chuckle. "You think he's gonna show up?"

"He could."

"And if he does, I'll leave."

She tilts her head with a huff. "Whatever, fine. Just don't distract me, okay?"

I spend the next hour unconsciously pestering her, with the occasional flirtatious comment thrown in for good measure. She keeps telling me to shut up and focus, but I know she's enjoying our little back-and-forth.

"Can you please stop talking to me?" she asks, poorly concealing a smile, her eyes darting back to her desk.

"I'm just trying to make this more interesting," I whisper back with a grin.

"Unlike you, some of us actually have to study for this class."

Leaning back in my chair, I say, "Sorry, this shit's like second nature to me."

"Yeah, go stroke your ego elsewhere."

"Good idea." I toss her another smirk. "Wanna go back to my place?"

"Shh," she quickly chides again, scribbling furiously in her notebook.

This time, I manage to leave her alone for the rest of the hour, saving the conversation for later. When class is finally over, I trail behind her out of the building.

"Karras, wait up," I say. "Why don't we go grab a coffee before my walk-in?"

She gives me a skeptical look. "What, you want to pretend to be friends now? Shoot the shit after class?"

"I don't know. Maybe?" I tilt my head slightly. "Or, you know, maybe I just wanted to hash this shit out with you real quick."

She raises a brow. "Hash what shit out, exactly?"

I take a step closer, lowering my voice. "Well, I did have my face buried between your legs for the last two weekends, so I'm just wondering when or if you wanted that to happen again."

She lets out a displeased groan, shaking her head. "Okay, I'm gonna pretend that you just asked me a normal question for once. You want to define the parameters of our sexual relationship?"

"Wow, you make it sound so sexy."

She gives me a nonplussed look, so I raise a brow, gesturing for her to continue.

"How about I just give you a text or a call when I need to shut off my mind?" she offers. "Something casual, no strings. Otherwise, we keep everything else between us how it's always been. If you're up for that, great. But if you want more, tough luck."

My grin spreads wider. "That sounds like a dream scenario to me."

A warning flickers in her eyes. "Just remember, if you plan to be with anyone else, you need to be really safe. I'm putting my trust in you here."

"No issues there," I say. "Yours is the only pussy I'm interested in at the moment."

She lets out a derisive snort. "You're ridiculous."

I lean in closer, letting my lips brush against her ear. "And you seem to like it well enough."

She shoves me away, but I can tell she's trying to hide another tiny half-smile. "Okay, now leave me alone," she says. "I have somewhere to be."

Without another word, I watch her walk away, her tight little ass swaying in her jeans. I'm already thinking about what I'm going to do to her the next time we're together. It's going to be a long, torturous wait praying for that next call.

But the thought of it coming unannounced—with Kaia ready and waiting for me at the end of it—is more than enough to keep me satisfied in the meantime.

# Chapter Seventeen

KAIA

By the end of the school week, I've grown restless and even more weary.

During a quick break between morning classes, I shoot off a text to Elio before heading over to his apartment. This makes three lectures in a row that he's missed out on, not to mention the silent treatment he's been giving me for the last ten days.

Standing outside his apartment, I fidget with my shirt collar, trying to calm my racing heart. This isn't a conversation that I want to have, but it's one I know I need to.

Steeling my resolve, I carefully push open the front door. I'm immediately hit with the familiar smell of honey lemon and espresso. It's a scent that normally brings me comfort, but right now, it unsettles me.

"El?" I tentatively call out.

"In here," he responds from down the hall, and I make my way toward his bedroom. He's sitting there on the edge of his bed, staring intently at his phone. I take a moment to study him, taking in the bags under his eyes and the general exhaustion etched onto his features.

This isn't going to be easy for either of us.

"Hey," I say softly, trying to keep my voice steady.

He glances up, expression guarded. "What's goin' on, Kai?"

I clear the rasp from my voice, feeling the words stick in my throat. "I just wanted to talk to you about something. Something important."

"I gathered as much from your text." He sets his phone down on the nightstand, giving me his full attention. "So, what is it? You okay?"

"I'm just worried about you, E," I say, scratching nervously at the back of my neck. "You've been skipping classes more often. And you haven't been replying to me all week."

"Just been busy."

I give him a skeptical look. "Okay, well, I just . . . I'm gonna come right out and ask. You aren't using again, are you?"

He flinches at my words, his posture visibly tense. "What are you talking about?"

"Look, I'm not trying to accuse you of anything," I say firmly. "I know work's been really hard on you lately, and I'm just worried about how you're coping."

"Nothing like that's been going on," he assures me, his voice soft and quiet. "You know I'd come to you if I was having problems again."

"Would you, though?" I ask, my tone pointed.

"Is that not what we agreed on?"

"Yeah, of course it is. But after class last Monday, Becker mentioned how strung out you—"

He scoffs, cutting me off. "Wow, I get it now. You're buying into his bullshit?"

Irritation bubbles up inside me. "This has nothing to do with him. I'm worried about you, El. Beck just mentioned that you've been looking more strung out than usual, that's it."

He shakes his head, swiping a ragged hand over his face. "Nothing is wrong, Kaia. I've been missing classes because I'm tired and strung out from work."

Unease settles in the pit of my stomach. "Okay. I'm sorry," I say, trying to keep the frustration out of my tone. "I really wish you didn't have to work so hard."

"It's a job, Kaia," he says sadly. "And I have bills to pay. You think I like doing what I do?"

"I know you don't," I say gently. "And I'm sorry you're in that position. I'm here for you, you know."

Always have been and always will be. It's been this way between us since we were eight years old, when we were just two kids who didn't know any better, forced to be friends through our older siblings. And then, when we were teenagers, we both made decisions that pushed us even closer. The wrong decisions, but they've led us here today—together, at Coastal—exactly where we were meant to be.

"I know. And I'm here for you, too." He flattens his palms over his thighs, his eyes flashing with discomfort. "But I also don't understand this whole thing you have going on with Becker. What happened to you thinking he's just some privileged dickhead?"

"I still think that," I say with a half chuckle. "But he's agreed to help me in a way that you can't."

"Ah. So, it's *just* sex between you guys, then?" he asks, his voice softening slightly.

"Yeah," I confirm with a nod, a small twinge of guilt settling in the depths of my stomach. "Just sex."

Once I make it back to campus, my phone rings in my pocket, signaling an incoming call from Sofia. It's the third time she's attempted to reach me this week. Part of me wants to ignore the call—I have enough going on without having to deal with her right now—but I know she'll just keep trying until I answer.

So, I swipe to accept. "Hey, Sof."

"Hey, you," she chirps back. "How's my favorite little sister doing?"

"I'm doing okay." I resist the urge to wince at her phony term of endearment. "Just busy with school and everything."

"Oh, I bet." There's a pause on the line, and I can almost hear her biting her nails on the other end. "So, listen, I was still thinking about coming to visit you on campus for a little while."

I let out a sigh. "I don't know, Sof. It's kind of a bad time for me right now."

"What do you mean? Are you too busy with classes?"

"Yeah, and I've got a lot of stuff going on outside of school too."

"But it's been ages since we've seen each other," she whines. "I miss you, Kaia."

"I know, and I miss you, too," I say, the lie sitting sour in the back of my throat. "But this just isn't a good time."

"Well, can't you just take a break from studying for a little while to hang out with me?"

I rub at my temples and blow out a hot breath, blood rushing to my head. "It's not just about studying. I've got a lot of stuff going on in my personal life, too, and I don't have the energy to entertain visitors right now."

"Okay, okay," she says, clearly hurt by my dismissal. "I'm sorry, I didn't realize it was such a big deal."

"It's not a big deal, Sof. It's just not a good time."

There's an awkward silence on the line, and I can tell she's trying to think of something else to say. "So, have you talked to Mom and Dad lately?"

My stomach clenches at the mention of our parents. Sofia knows how uncomfortable the topic makes me, but she can't seem to help herself. "No, I haven't talked to them in a while."

"Oh." There's another pause, then, "Well, they're doing

okay, I guess. Mom's been posting a lot of pictures of them on Facebook."

"That's great," I say, pinching my lips into a flat line.

"I think they're planning a trip to Santorini soon. Maybe you should try for a visit over winter break."

"I don't think that's possible. I'm gonna be working on my dissertation even during the break."

"But it would be good for you to spend some time with them, Kaia," she chides in that familiar grating tone. "You never know how much time you have left with them."

My temper flares. "I know that. But it's not like we have some perfect Brady Bunch relationship. They could come visit me in Boyer, too. That is, if they really gave a shit."

"Yeah, as if you'd even let them." She scoffs. "You know, you're letting this wedge between the four of us grow even deeper. It's not healthy."

"This wedge? You mean, the divide that they created, Sof?" I tug at a lock of my hair, painfully hooking it around my index finger. "They moved across the fucking ocean when I was still in high school and left me here to fend for myself."

"That was years ago. Maybe it's time to finally let it go."

"It's not that simple." I sigh, shutting my eyes. "They've hurt me a lot, and I'm not ready to just forgive and forget."

There's a long pause on the line, and I know she's just trying to think of another topic to shift toward. "Fine, enough about them. I've got some other news for you."

"What kind of news?"

"I met someone new," she says, her voice giddy with excitement.

"Alert the presses."

"Oh, just be happy for me, will you?"

"I am happy for you." I release the grip on my hair, continuing my walk through Navy Square. "So, who is he?"

"His name's Andrew," she continues, practically gushing over him. "He's a lawyer, and he's really dedicated to his work and to me. I think he might actually be the one, Kaia."

I can't resist the urge to roll my eyes at her romantic proclamations. My sister's always been so caught up in the idea of love, thinking that every guy she dates is "the one." And hell, maybe they are, at least until she inevitably grows bored of them.

"Uh-huh," I say, trying my best to sound supportive.

"He's taking me to a dinner upstate tonight," she says. "I can't wait. I wish you were here to come with us."

"Yeah, unfortunately, I can't just take off in the middle of the term."

"Oh, right. I forgot you're actually doing something with your life."

"Mhm, and I'm glad you *finally* found someone," I toss back.

"I hope you can meet him soon," she says wistfully, ignoring my not-so-subtle attempt at a jab. "I think you'd really like him. Maybe when you're finally ready for me to visit campus, I can bring Andrew along. And I promise that we won't be in the way. I just want to spend some time with my little sister."

I feel a pang of guilt at her words, knowing that she's likely right. It has been a while since we've seen each other, and I do kind of miss her. Or I miss the idea of her. The relationship we could have had all these years if only things were normal.

"I'll think about it, okay?" I say, doing my best to placate her.

"Okay, fine. But don't think about it too long."

"I won't," I promise, knowing that I probably will.

We say our goodbyes, and I hang up, feeling drained. I hate talking to her because it's like she never bothers to actually listen. She'd rather steamroll right over me with her own agenda.

I let out a sigh, adjusting my hair before heading to my next class, attempting to dispel the negative energy from the conversation. As I make my way, I catch sight of Holden approaching, his hockey bag draped over one shoulder, the sunlight hitting him at the perfect angle.

"Hey, stranger."

"Beck," I say in lieu of a greeting, my pulse hammering at the sight of him.

"How was your day?" he asks as we fall into step, his voice laced with playful sarcasm.

"Oh, you know." I let out a frustrated huff. "Just had a lovely chat with my sister."

He lifts an eyebrow. "That bad, huh?"

"She just doesn't get it," I mutter. "She keeps bugging me about coming to visit campus, which is just not even the realm of something I'm willing to entertain. At least, not right now."

"I get you." He gives me a tight smile, eyes scanning over my face. "I feel the same way every time my dad tells me he's flying over to watch me play. But with him, it's never a fucking question; it's always a demand."

A surprised chuckle escapes me. "Sorry, did you just say he flies over to watch your games?"

He shrugs. "Yeah, he charters a jet over from New York sometimes."

"Oh, right, of course. He charters a jet." I roll my eyes, unable to hide my disbelief. "Very normal."

"What can I say?" He lets out a low, amused breath. "He's a big fucking fan of mine."

"Mhm." I give him a humorless snort, changing the subject. "You know, just so you're aware, I finally confronted Elio. And he's actually doing fine, so we're all good."

"Glad to hear it." His dark eyes lock with mine, fingertips tracing across my upper arm, and heat rises in my cheeks. "So, would you say your stress levels are doin' okay this week, then? No trouble sleeping?"

I work my lower lip between my teeth, craving another quick fix. "I, uh, think I might have a little trouble, actually. Tonight?"

His lips curl into a smirk. "Hm, and I might have a remedy."

"Nine o'clock, Becker. Don't be late."

He leans in close, breath hot against my ear. "Wouldn't fuckin' dream of it."

# Chapter Eighteen

## HOLDEN

I TAKE a brief moment to steady myself as I climb the steps to Kaia's apartment building, pulse racing with anticipation. I'm not sure what it is about being with her, but there's something heavy about it, something different from what I'm used to.

Maybe it's just in the way she moves against me, the way she always pushes back, that makes me feel a little bit more alive.

As I reach her door, I hear the faint sound of music coming from inside. I knock, and a few moments later, Kaia answers, wearing nothing but a tiny pajama set that barely covers her curves. My eyes rake over her body, and my cock hardens in my jeans.

"Hey," I say, stepping inside and closing the door behind me.

"Hey," she parrots back, immediately wrapping her arms around my neck and pulling me in for a kiss.

Apparently, this girl wastes no fucking time.

As our lips meet, that familiar rush of heat and desire courses through my veins. I wrap my arms around her waist, pulling her close, and she moans softly into my mouth.

We break the kiss, and I step back to take in the sight of her again. "You look really fucking good," I say, running my fingers over the silk material of her shorts.

"Figured I'd skip a step," she says, smirking up at me.

I take a deep breath, inhaling the scent of her perfume, something light and floral that always seems to linger around her. "I can't wait to have you again," I say, my voice low and rough.

She takes my hand and leads me over to the couch, where she pulls me down next to her. Then she leans in, her lips brushing against my ear. "This time, I want to take my turn first."

"And what would you like me to do?"

"I want you to sit back and relax," she says, her fingers trailing down my chest. "Just trust me."

I lean back against the couch as her lips meet my neck and let out a low groan. She trails soft kisses down my chest over the fabric of my thin T-shirt, her fingers slipping down my abdomen, and my cock twitches. She reaches for my jeans, undoing them and swiftly pulling them down.

Wordlessly, her slender hand wraps around my dick.

I groan, deep and heavy, as she strokes me, her fingers working expertly over my shaft. "Oh, fuck," I mutter, my hips bucking up into her hand. "I'm gonna come too quickly if you keep doing that."

"Not yet," she whispers. "I have other plans for tonight."

She shifts her focus, precum leaking from my tip as she swirls it around with her thumb. Her lips part, she pitches forward, and then she sucks me into her warm, wet mouth. Deeper and deeper still, until I'm bottoming out in the back of her throat.

And oh God, fucking *hell*, I can't take it anymore.

Her hands return to my chest, tracing the lines of my abs beneath my shirt, and my body responds eagerly. I shift my weight, pulling her onto my lap, lowering my head to capture her lips in a fierce kiss.

Our tongues tangle together—desperate, frenzied. The friction between us shatters me, fractures me, and I know that this time, I'm not going to be able to hold back.

I want her too much. *Need* her too much.

"Fuck, Kaia," I whisper against her mouth. "You're so fucking sexy when you take what you want."

She moans softly, her fingers digging into my skin, and I take that as my cue to continue. I trail my lips down her neck, savoring the taste of her, and her body arches up to meet me.

"God yes, I needed this," I murmur, sliding my hand up her thigh, feeling the warmth and wetness between her legs.

"Me too," she breathes, tangling her fingers into my hair.

I grin against her skin, relishing the feeling of her hands on me. I know that we're both using each other in a way, but in moments like these, it almost feels like something more.

I pull back slightly to look at her, our eyes locked. "You sure about this?"

"I'm sure. I asked you to come over again, didn't I?"

A wide grin spreads across my face. "Yeah, you did. But it doesn't hurt to ask twice."

"Stop being so fucking considerate," she says, grabbing my face and pulling me back in for another kiss.

I lose myself in the feel of her, letting my hands roam over her body, mapping out every inch of her soft skin. As we continue to kiss, touch, savor, that familiar hunger builds inside me, and I know that it won't be long before I lose myself completely.

We break apart only long enough for her to lead me to the bedroom, and I admire the way her hips sway with each step.

These moments between us are fucking radiant, aren't they? But even still, I can't help but want more.

"Get undressed," I order, and she complies without hesitation, shedding her clothes one by one until she's standing there before me, completely bare.

Longing builds with each passing second, and I waste no time in stripping off my own clothes, wanting nothing more than to be inside of her. As I stand there, naked and unashamed, she looks up at me with those big, gorgeous eyes of hers and asks, "Do you have protection?"

I nod, fishing in my pocket to retrieve the condom I always keep on hand. "Of course," I say, ripping open the package and rolling it onto my length. Without another word, I guide her down onto the bed and press against her.

"Tell me you want me, Karras. Beg for it." The words come out low and rough, and she shivers under my touch.

Her eyes widen, and for a moment, she hesitates. But then she leans into me, lips brushing against mine as she whispers back, "I want you, Beck. I need you."

A surge of pride courses through my body at her words. It's been nearly a week since I last made her come, and my desire to have her again, to feel her squirming beneath me, is almost unbearable.

But then, as I lean in closer, a nagging voice in the back of my mind reminds me—she said she doesn't want to cross the line into sex. Not with me, anyway. It's something she proposed, something I've been trying to respect.

"What about your no-sex rule?" I ask, pulling back slightly to look at her.

She rolls her eyes, frustration clear on her face. "Fuck the rule. I need you. Now."

My resolve starts to slip away at her words, but I need more confirmation than that. "Tell me you like me, and I'll consider fucking you."

Her eyes widen. "What?"

"You said you wouldn't have sex with me because we don't like each other. I already admitted that I adore you, so it's your turn to own up." I nudge her shoulder with my nose. "You like me, Karras. And you always fucking have."

"Like you?" She nearly chokes. "You mean, as a person?"

"Sure, as a person." I swipe my thumb over her nipple. "As a friend."

"We're not friends."

"You're right." I let out a humorless chuckle. "I don't often lick my friends' pussies. So yeah, we're a little fucking more than that now, aren't we?"

"Beck."

"Say it, Kaia," I demand, voice ragged. "Or you're gonna end up fucking yourself tonight."

"Fine. Fuck." She pinches her eyes closed, takes a deep breath, then, "Okay, I like you."

My lip quirks. "And?"

"And I always fucking have," she grumbles, yanking my head back down. "Now, stop using your mouth for talking, and let it do what it's best at."

"Always the romantic."

I chuckle as I line myself up, a rush of adrenaline lighting me up from the inside out. This girl always knows exactly how to push my buttons, how to turn me on like no one else, and I'm not complaining.

I shift my weight, pressing her body harder against the mattress, her back arching as she moans against my mouth. Her skin is soft and warm under my fingertips, and I revel in the way her body moves. I can't get enough of her, can't imagine ever getting tired of this feeling.

I run my hand down her body, feeling the smooth curves of her hips and the softness of her inner thighs. She whimpers as I slip a hand back between her legs, my fingers already slick with her arousal.

I break away from her mouth, trailing kisses down her neck and collarbone. "God, you're so fucking ready for me," I murmur, nipping at her skin.

"Shh," she pants, her nails digging into my back.

I slide my hand up to cup her breast, my thumb grazing over her nipple. She gasps, arching her back even more. "So fucking pretty, baby."

"Just fuck me already," she demands, her voice thick with need.

I grin at her impatience and give her what she wants, sliding inside of her slowly. She whimpers, her nails scratching down my back as she arches up to meet my thrusts. I pick up the pace, my hips slamming into hers. We're both panting now, lost in the pleasure of each other's bodies.

I lean down, kissing her deeply as I fuck into her. The feeling of her legs wrapped around me, the way she moans my name with every thrust, it's all too much. I'm fully lost in the moment, lost in her.

She tightens her thighs, pulling me even closer, our bodies moving in sync.

Without warning, I pull out of her, admiring the way she looks as she lies there, flushed and satisfied. But I'm not done yet. I want more. I want to see every inch of her, feel every curve and every tremble.

I tug at her waist, pulling her up onto her hands and knees. "Yeah, I want you like this," I growl, spreading her legs apart.

She whimpers in response, bracing herself against the mattress as I enter her from behind. I grip her hips tightly, my thrusts growing harder and faster with each passing moment.

She's so tight, soaking wet, and it's driving me fucking wild.

I reach around, pressing my fingers against her clit. She moans loudly, head falling forward as I pleasure her in two places at once. Her body shakes with the force of her orgasm, but I don't stop. I keep pounding into her, chasing my own release.

I flip her over onto her back again, her legs wrapping around my waist as I continue to thrust into her. I'm fully immersed in the moment. I can feel myself cresting closer and closer to the edge, the pressure building in the pit of me.

"Fuck yes, Kaia," I groan, finally going over the edge, my body shuddering with pleasure. She comes too, moments behind me, pussy clenching as she cries out my name.

We lie there for a moment, catching our breath. Then I roll off her and pull her impossibly close. "I just can't seem to get enough of you," I rasp, pressing a kiss to her sweat-damp collarbone, tracing it with my lips.

"Yeah," she murmurs back. "I know the feeling."

As I breathe deep, the aftershocks of my orgasm still reverberating throughout my body, I look down at her. She's pinned beneath me, chest heaving as she tries to catch her own breath. The sight of her, blissfully content, only serves to heighten my own pleasure.

I run my hands over her skin, feeling the slickness of sweat and the heat of her body. It's a rush unlike any other, this moment of pure physical connection with another person. And with Kaia, it's somehow even more intense, more explosive than it's ever been.

"Fucking gorgeous," I whisper as I trace her jawline with my thumb.

She smiles up at me, a soft, satisfied expression on her face. "You're not so bad yourself."

I chuckle, the tension in my body finally easing. "Was that a compliment?"

"Believe it or not, I'm capable of those." She exhales a long, slow breath. "Besides, you caught me in a good moment."

We lie there for a while longer, wrapped up in each other's arms, no other words passing between us. It's a strange kind of intimacy, this thing we have going on.

Sure, we agreed to keep things casual, purely physical between us. For Kaia, it's more so transactional, a means to shut off her brain for a little while. Yet, I can't help but recognize that there's something deeper brewing between us.

Something addictive.

But for now, I'm content to appreciate these small moments, in the feeling of her pulse beating against me and the knowledge that—for at least a little while longer—she's mine.

# Chapter Nineteen

## KAIA

I WAKE up to the sound of chirping birds outside my window, their cheerful melody weaving through the late-morning air. As I blink away the haze of sleep, I realize that I'm alone in my bed, the warmth of Holden's body absent from beside me.

I pull the sheets up to my chin, a faint blush creeping across my cheeks. My skin still tingles from his touch, the ghost of his lips on my neck, my collarbone. Every time I close my eyes, I'm transported back to last night, to the way he took control again, the way he made me feel so fucking wanted.

I was fully content beneath him here. Invigorated in a way I haven't been in years.

I can still feel the pressure of his body against mine, the way he moved inside of me, each thrust pushing me closer and closer to the edge.

As I sit up in bed, I'm greeted by the familiar scent of lavender wafting from my bedside diffuser, mingling with the soft murmur of voices from my neighbors beyond the thin walls.

My gaze drifts to another handwritten note and a piece of peppermint candy lying on my nightstand, and a smirk tugs at the corners of my lips as I pick it up. My fingers trace over the slight curves and loops of Holden's neat handwriting:

*K,*

*Gameday. Sorry for leaving before you woke up. I'll be thinking about the sounds you made all day.*

*H*

I shake my head, a bubble of amusement rising in my chest as I fire off a quick text.

KAIA

what's with the candy?

HOLDEN

just something to sweeten your day. besides, it's all I had in my pocket. well, that and another condom but it didn't quite hit the same

KAIA

you really know how to make a girl feel special

HOLDEN

thought you might eat it and think of me. you know, something else to fill your mouth with

KAIA

gross

HOLDEN

you're welcome

I roll my eyes, my lips curving upward despite myself. It's ridiculous how easily he diffuses the tension, how he can dispel all the lingering doubts in a matter of seconds—quiet those nagging fears that always seem to swirl around in my head.

After a quick morning routine, I slowly wake my way into the empty dining room, thankful that I can spend another quiet morning alone. Or, at least, another morning without Lizzie pestering me about Holden's dick size.

As I sip my coffee, the weight of the past week melts away, memories of last night sparking beneath my skin. It's a bittersweet feeling because I know I have my work cut out for me today. And our upcoming advisor meeting looms over me like an ever-present shadow.

But first, I allow myself a few minutes to bask in the afterglow of a night well spent. If I'm correct in my calculations, those seven sweet hours make up the most consecutive sleep I've had since my junior year of high school.

Slowly, the day wears on, and I bury myself in my studies, my eyes scanning the pages of countless academic journals. I scribble notes across the margins of my notebook, but every so often, my thoughts drift back to Holden—to the way he held me, worshipped me, fucked into me, until the sensation of his touch is as tangible as the sun's rays streaming in through my window.

But I can't afford to be distracted for long.

I need to do well on this lit review, to prove to Dr. Khatri that I'm a force to be reckoned with. As the sun finally begins to dip below the horizon, I force myself to set aside everything else and focus on the task at hand.

When I finish up, well into the late evening, the relief is like a soothing balm to my overwrought mind. I know that I'm one step closer to achieving my goals and proving to our advisor—to myself—that I'm capable, credible, and highly competent.

That I'm worth a solid recommendation for Coastal's graduate program.

At the end of the night, as I finally slip back beneath the covers of my bed, the weight of Holden's absence presses down on me, the familiar ache of desire building from within. But it's still not enough for me to text him now—not two nights in a row, at least—begging him to lull me to sleep after a full day at the rink.

He's probably fucking exhausted, working through his own adrenaline crash, and doesn't need to use his free time catering to my needs.

Instead, I'll have to spend another lonely Saturday night fending for myself.

On Monday morning, I step into our Calc class, feeling more than unsettled. I'm not sure what to expect or how to act around Holden now, especially not after the way I begged him to fuck me the last time I saw him.

But what I do know is that, for the last thirty-six hours, it's been nearly impossible to scrub the memory of his touch out of my head.

Thankfully, Elio's back in class today, and I throw myself into our whispered conversations, trying to ignore Holden's presence across the room. But even as I focus on my friend's words—his half-hearted apology for being MIA last week—Holden's gaze burns into me.

It's like he's dropping not-so-subtle hints, trying to ensure I don't forget the way he's claimed my body for the past three weekends in a row. A casual reminder that, beyond the confines of the lecture hall, I belong to him in one way or another.

All week long, he continues to steal glances at me, and I can't deny the slight thrill I feel every time our eyes meet. Nevertheless, I'm also irritated beyond belief. We haven't talked or interacted outside of class since that night, and I'm not so sure that I even want to.

It feels unnatural to avoid him now but even more strange to purposefully seek him out.

By the end of the week, I'm starting to feel restless. Unmoored. I can't stop thinking about having another repeat of Saturday night, but the thought of initiating our time together fills me with dread.

It makes me feel desperate. Clingy. Undesirable, in a way.

Even though I was the one who struck our initial agreement —per his adamant request. I send the signals, and Holden comes calling, ready and willing to serve my needs. Yet, there's still a small, unnerving part of me that wants someone else to do the chasing.

It's not that I'm completely clueless. Or insecure. I know that Holden wants me—he's proven that much by now—but I'm still left wondering how far that desire reaches.

Does he think of me on nights he lies alone in bed? Does he wait and hope for my call? Or am I simply no more than an afterthought—on his mind when I'm in front of him but vanishing like adiabatic fog once I'm gone?

Because for me, that's certainly not the case.

In fact, Holden's been occupying more of my thoughts lately than I'm comfortable with. It's total bullshit, now that I think about it. And exactly the reason I didn't want a boyfriend in the first place.

My focus should be singular—finishing the first half of my dissertation, securing a stellar recommendation from my advisor, and then earning myself a spot in the graduate program of my dreams. I don't have time for anything more, especially not when it comes to placating the golden boy.

Sure, I might like him a little more than I originally wanted to admit. There's something about his presence over the last three years that's been more than a simple annoyance.

As in, I would miss him if he disappeared off the face of the planet. And I'm also grateful for his willingness to help me out now. He's good in bed, and I really fucking like the way he distracts me . . . in a way that no one else seems to be able to.

But that's it. That's all there is to it.

It has to be.

ON FRIDAY MORNING, as class is wrapping up, Holden catches me outside of Weyerhaeuser. He falls into step beside me, his heated gaze sending a pang of unwelcome longing through my body.

"Karras," he drawls, and my heart stutters at the sound of his voice.

Fucking annoying, isn't it?

"Hey," I say, attempting to keep my tone neutral. "What's up?"

He shoves his hands into the pockets of his jeans, rocking back on his heels. "So, the team's traveling out of town this weekend for an away game. Won't be around, just in case you needed me."

I roll my eyes but can't help the tiny smile that tugs at my lips. "Thanks for the heads up."

He looks at me then, his gaze raking over me. "But texting is always an option. And, you know, FaceTime's also a thing," he says, a hint of a smirk playing at the corner of his mouth.

"Right," I mutter, flashing him an unimpressed frown. "I'll be sure to keep that in mind."

His eyes linger on me for a moment longer before he turns to walk away. "See you in class on Monday," he calls over his shoulder.

I watch him go, an uncomfortable mixture of emotions

brewing inside of me—relief that I won't have to worry about initiating things this weekend but disappointment that I won't even have the option.

It's a disturbing thought, honestly, but I'm not so sure how I'm going to make it through an entire weekend without him. I've grown accustomed to his presence in my bed over the last month, and the idea of that has me all worked up.

The rest of the day passes by in a blur of studying, snacking, and mildly panicking. But as the night approaches and I'm left alone in my apartment, I find myself stuck in a familiar predicament.

I mindlessly pick at my hair again, my mind wandering back to all my least favorite places. Ruminating on the worst, darkest thoughts I've ever had, until I have no choice but to think of Holden instead.

I might not enjoy admitting it, but an overwhelming part of me wishes that he was here with me now, shutting off my mind with his touch. The memory of his fingers trailing down my skin, the sound of his voice whispering in my ear, makes my body ache.

It's frustrating, this sudden craving I have for intimacy. With him or with anyone. It makes me feel weak and needy, something that I've always prided myself on not being. But at the same time, there's a warm, soothing comfort in the thought of Holden being beside me.

I can't deny it anymore. The man's certainly not perfect, at least not for me, but he somehow seems to know exactly what I need.

I desperately pull at another strand of hair, letting the pain distract me instead. I shouldn't be focusing on sex with a guy that's not even mine. I have a lit review to finish, another meeting with Dr. Khatri coming up.

But try as I might, I can't help the way my thoughts keep drifting back to that place—to the way he brings me back to life, makes me feel a little more free, for at least a few short hours at a time.

And there's another small, irritating voice in the back of my mind that wonders if maybe there's something more going on between us. But I easily push the thought aside, knowing that it's dangerous territory. I can't afford to get distracted, not now. Not when my future's on the line.

And yet, as I lie in bed alone, unable to sleep, I find myself picturing more than just sex. This time, I imagine his strong arms wrapped around me, comforting me. Holding me until I drift off to sleep and then waking up beside me the next morning.

It helps, at least a little bit, to imagine that I'm not alone in this. That I have someone, someone who might actually *get me*, to help me forget about all my worries.

Even if it only lasts throughout the night.

Even if it's all just a hopeless façade.

# Chapter Twenty

## HOLDEN

We lost our game tonight, our first loss of the season, and I feel like absolute shit.

Now, I'm sitting here alone in a hotel room. Rai's empty bed, my cell phone, and my wounded pride are the only things keeping me company. I hear the distant sounds of laughter and clinking glasses from down the hallway, and it unsettles me.

It's no secret that I take every loss to heart, especially as captain, and the sting of defeat lingers in my bones like an unwelcome guest.

Normally, I'd jump at the opportunity to commiserate with my teammates, to drown my sorrows in booze and the company of my boys. But tonight, I don't feel like it. I don't want to pretend to be okay when I'm not. I don't want to slap on a smile and fake enthusiasm.

I just want to be left alone to wallow in my own self-pity for once.

I'm seated at the edge of my bed, staring blankly at the wall in front of me. The old manual clock hanging above the door ticks away, counting down the minutes until midnight, distracting me from the sounds of murmured voices.

And that's when my mind inevitably drifts to Kaia—the girl with the sharp tongue and those tiny green flecks in her eyes. I wonder how she's doing without me around. Is she out with friends, with Elio, or is she tucked away in her apartment like usual?

The thought of her being with someone else, anyone else, sends a pang of jealousy through me. But I quickly push it aside. I know that we have a simple, cut-and-dry arrangement, and I have no right to feel this way.

It's just sex, after all. Nothing more.

As I run a hand through my hair, I realize how simple it'd be to ease my mind right now. I could just fucking text the girl, couldn't I?

Sighing, I grab my phone, flipping it over before I remember that I shouldn't be the one reaching out to her. It's not part of our deal. And besides, what would I even say?

*"Hey, just checking in to make sure you're not sleeping with someone else while I'm out of town?"*

No, that would be ridiculous. I'm not her boyfriend, and I have no claim over her. She's a grown woman who can do whatever she wants.

Despite telling myself that partial truth, I can't help but feel a sense of possessiveness over her. I don't want anyone else to touch her, to have her moaning the way she does for me. It's a selfish thought, I know, but I can't fucking help it.

I flop back onto the bed, feeling the weight of the loss pressing down on me. It's not just the game we lost tonight, though . . . it's everything.

It's the fact that I'm here, in a hotel room, hundreds of miles away from the one person who makes me feel the most alive—a feeling I don't often experience outside of the rink.

It's the fact that I can't stop thinking about her, even when I know I shouldn't.

I close my eyes, willing myself to fall asleep. Maybe in my dreams, I'll be able to forget about everything else. Or maybe, if

I'm lucky enough, Kaia will be there with me, her soft body pressed against mine, her breath hot on the shell of my ear.

But as the night wears on and the sounds of my teammates' revelry die down, I'm unable to drift off. Sleep usually comes easily to me, but not tonight.

No, my mind is too full with thoughts of Kaia fucking Karras, too consumed with the memory of her body writhing beneath mine—squirming, panting, and breathing out my name.

I know this is pointless. I know I should be focusing on hockey, on my teammates, on winning games, and coming out on top. But at this moment, all I can think about is her.

And so, I lie there in the darkness, my mind a jumbled mess. I don't know what the future holds for the two of us. But what I do know is that, at least for right now, Kaia's all I can fucking think about.

As THE WEEKEND draws to a close, I quickly recover—feeling pretty damn good despite our loss. The team's morale is high, and I'm confident that we'll come back stronger in our next home game.

But even with that part sorted, my mind keeps wandering back to last weekend.

All I can think about is the way it felt to move inside Kaia—to finally fuck her, to own her body, to earn her gasps of pleasure. It's so fucking addictive between us, both inside the bedroom and out, and I don't think I'll ever get enough.

But I can't let myself get caught up in this shit, whether or not I want something more with her . . . or whether or not she'd even dare to entertain the idea. Right now, we've got a good thing going, and I'm content to leave it at that.

The future will take care of itself.

Come Monday, I spot Kaia across the room in our first lecture of the day, sitting in her usual seat beside Elio. At least, he looks to be in good spirits for once. But something's different about her today, something that makes me a little uneasy.

She looks exhausted, drained of energy, like she's barely holding on. I try to catch her eye, but she blatantly avoids me.

As the lecture ends and Elio disappears from sight, I make my way over to her, hoping to check in to see how she's doing. But as I approach, she tenses up like a deer caught in headlights.

"Hey," I say, my voice soft and gentle.

She nods in response, but her body language is tight, defensive.

"You look like shit," I blurt out, cringing at my own words as soon as they leave my mouth.

"Thanks, Beck," she mutters, her voice raspy and hoarse. "That's exactly what I needed to hear."

"No, no, I didn't mean it like that," I backtrack, poorly attempting to fix my mistake. "I just meant that you look like you could use some rest."

"I'm fine," she insists, but I can see the fatigue etched into every line and corner of her face.

"Come on, Karras." I stick my hands in my pockets, restraining myself from running fingers across her flushed skin. "You're sick, aren't you?"

"Barely."

"Let me take some notes for you in our next class," I offer, hoping to ease her burden. "I can cover for you tomorrow too. But you really should go home and get some rest."

"I don't need your help," she snaps back, her hostility catching me off guard.

I hold my hands up in mock defense, brow furrowed. "It was just an offer."

"Well, don't bother," she says, bitterness seeping into her voice. "Let's not pretend like we're anything more than what we actually are."

Her words hit me like a punch to the gut, and I'm left reeling. I'm not sure why it's her first instinct to lash out at me, to always expect the fucking worst.

Honestly, I thought that we were making progress. That we were moving toward something more meaningful—especially after I spent the night inside of her—but it seems like she's content to keep me at arm's length.

"Right, I get it," I say, despite my irritation.

"Great," she says and then turns on her heel to leave.

Jesus Christ. I don't understand why she's running in the other direction, why she won't let me be there for her even in the smallest of ways. But then it dawns on me.

"Are you just being rude because you don't feel good, and it's making you cranky?" I ask, effectively stopping her in her tracks. "Or is this your half-assed attempt to push me away?"

"Excuse me?"

I raise a challenging brow. "You heard me."

"Look, I don't know what you think—"

"What I think is that you're incredibly sick right now. Your immune system's shit because you never fucking sleep properly. I also think that you got even worse sleep this past weekend since I wasn't around. But beyond that, I think you realized that you actually missed me for once, and you really fucking hate it."

She gulps low in her throat. "I don't know what you're talking about."

"You do," I insist.

"No."

"Yes." I lean closer, lowering my voice. "You wish you had me around—to fuck, to fight with, maybe more—and that bothers you."

She reels back. "The things you dream up in that head of yours, Beck."

"It's okay, Kaia, because I'm onto you." I give her a lopsided smile. "Now, get your ass home and rest. Or the next time you come calling for me, I won't answer."

She lets out a humorless snort. "So, you're serving ultimatums now?"

"If it gets you off this campus and into your bed, then yeah, I am."

"Please, you couldn't resist me even if you tried." She breaks out into a horrible coughing fit, her body convulsing with the force of it. Hunching over, she brings a hand up to cover her mouth as tears gather at the corners of her red-rimmed eyes.

"Right now?" I raise a skeptical brow, eyeing her up and down. "I think I could manage it just fine."

She folds her arms across her chest, indignant. "Don't make fun of me when I'm sick."

"Come on, Karras. Go home," I plead, making one last attempt to cajole her. "I'll be by this afternoon with some soup and shit."

"Don't you dare."

"What are you gonna do about it, Sneezy? Fight me?"

"I hate you," she scoffs, but her eyes betray the truth.

"No," I say with a grin. "You don't."

. . .

After finishing my midday lift and afternoon classes, I rush to the store to grab some things for Kaia. I'm worried about her being sick. I know how much it sucks to feel like shit, and I also know that if it were left up to her, she'd never actually take the rest she needs.

When she opens the door, she's wrapped up in a cozy blanket, her nose all sniffly and red.

"Hey," I say, holding up the bag of goodies. "I come bearing gifts."

"You really didn't have to do all of this," she says, her voice softening. "I came home like you said, and I'm already feeling a little better."

"It's no biggie," I reassure her, handing over the bag. "Just some soup and crackers. Pedialyte to keep you hydrated."

She raises a skeptical brow, eyeing what's left in my other hand. "And for some reason, you also brought me an orchid?"

I give her a wide, cheesy grin. "I hear flowers always make girls feel better."

"So, you got me a potted plant."

"Well, I was gonna get you a bouquet of roses," I say with a smirk. "You know, thorns, since you're so damn prickly. But I figured this lasts longer. Besides, I already know you love the color purple."

"And how would you know that?" she asks, surprise coating her tone.

"You used to rock a big purple clip in your hair."

"Freshman year?" she asks, incredulous.

I scratch the back of my neck. "Yeah, I think so."

"I haven't worn my hair up in a claw clip for over two years." She scrunches her nose, sniffling again. "Not since I chopped it all off."

I step forward, taking a strand of her soft, dark hair between my fingers. "I liked that length on you. But this look suits you even better."

She shakes me off, giving me a long, contemplative look before she steps aside. "Look, I know I'm sick, but did you want to come in for a minute?"

I give her a playful grin. "Well, that depends."

"Oh, yeah?" she asks, lifting a brow.

"If I come in, you have to promise me there will be no shenanigans."

"What?" she asks, her eyes widening. "You think I'm gonna try to seduce you in this state?"

A warm chuckle escapes me, but I simply raise my own brow in return, waiting for a real answer.

"Fine, I promise not to try and jump your bones," she finally grumbles. Then she plucks the orchid out of my hand, barely concealing a smile, before leading me into her apartment.

# Chapter Twenty-One

KAIA

No one's ever given me flowers before. Or, I should say—a singular flower.

It's cute, I guess.

And there's a perfect spot for it on the windowsill in my bedroom. It's silly, honestly, that a tiny gesture like this would leave me so fucking giddy inside. It doesn't even mean anything. Holden probably spotted it in the checkout line and then added it to his cart as an afterthought.

Even still, it's nice. Sweet. A thoughtful little get-well-soon gift. And he's right—orchids do last forever, sometimes even up to fifteen years if they're cared for properly. God knows I'll struggle to keep this little guy alive.

But I'm gonna try my best.

As Holden stands in the entryway of my apartment, a wave of uncertainty washes over me. This isn't like me, inviting him inside. It goes against everything I've been trying to maintain between us.

But when I saw the look on his face earlier—the concern etched into his features—and the tiny purple plant in his hand, I couldn't help but give in.

Now, I awkwardly stand in front of him, cradling the orchid in my hands as he raises a questioning brow.

"So?" he asks. "You thinking about moving anytime soon?"

"Yes," I grumble. "I think I'll heat up some soup."

He nods toward the living room. "Take a seat on the couch. I'll do it for you."

"I'm fully capable of using the microwave, Beck."

"Sit," he demands, not backing down, and I begrudgingly comply.

Once the food is warmed up, he joins me on the couch, leaving a safe foot of distance between the two of us. Then he hands over the bowl—carefully wrapped in a dish towel to keep it from burning me—along with a straw cup filled with Pedialyte.

"You don't have to talk," he says, grabbing the remote. "But let's watch something mindless. Just so I know you're not gonna go try to run a marathon or complete your entire dissertation the second I leave."

"You're so bossy," I grumble.

"I thought you liked bossy."

"Only in certain circumstances," I say, my cheeks flushing as I set my bowl on the coffee table.

His grin widens. "Ah, you mean when you have my cock in your mouth."

I sway, clearing my throat before breaking into a mini coughing fit. "Jesus Christ, Becker."

He chuckles. "Sorry, didn't mean to get you so worked up."

I move to shove him, but he grabs my hand, pulling me against him and settling in on the couch. My back is pressed to his front, one arm casually wrapped around my stomach. It's an intimate position, especially for the two of us, but it feels nice.

Comforting.

The air's quiet for a long, drawn-out moment before I eventually say, "Thank you for coming over."

"No problem, Karras. Somebody's gotta make sure you're taking care of yourself."

"I would've asked Elio for help if things really took a turn for the worse. I just . . . he can't really afford to get sick right now."

"Yeah, I guess I'm in the same boat, but my immune system's pretty top-notch," he says. "I'm not too worried about it."

Guilt wriggles in my gut. "You don't have to stay."

"I want to."

I shift my hips, leaning my head against his chest. "Okay."

"But you have to make me a promise first."

"Yeah, and what's that?"

"That you won't come back to class until you're feeling better. And you'll let me take some notes for you," he adds, tugging at a strand of my hair. "I can send you emails after class and bring over any take-home work at the end of the day."

I swallow thickly. "And why would you do that for me?"

He nuzzles his nose against the bridge of my cheek, his voice low and deep as he says, "If it wasn't obvious by now—I kinda give a shit about you, Karras."

I tense up in his arms. "Ah, I see."

"And I think you give a shit about me, too."

"Yeah," I quietly, hesitantly agree. "Yeah, maybe I do."

I'm jolted awake the next morning by the blaring sound of my alarm, disoriented and groggy. Blinking my eyes open, I take a moment to orient myself. Surely but slowly, the events of the previous night filter in.

Holden must've carried me to bed after I drifted off to sleep. I don't recall waking up during the journey from the couch to my bedroom down the hall. So I must've been truly out of it, hopped up on cold medicine or something.

With a yawn, I sit up in bed and stretch, slightly more well rested than yesterday.

There's another note lying beside me, topped with Holden's signature piece of candy. A reluctant smile spreads across my face as I pick it up.

*K,*

*Hope you're feeling better. Did you know that you snore like an old man? Very sexy. Get some rest and I'll check in later.*

*H*

Warmth fills my chest at his thoughtfulness. I never expected him to be so fucking nurturing and caring, especially not when it comes to my health. In fact, I didn't expect him to even notice I was sick in the first place.

I have to admit that it's a welcome surprise.

The rest of the week is spent at home, focusing on recuperating and catching up on classes. Holden took some detailed notes for me, and they're surprisingly meticulous. Well, for him, anyway. For me, they're fairly standard, but I know for a fact that he usually doesn't bother.

As a whole, I'm feeling okay about missing nearly a week's worth of classes. I thought that the stress, the pressure, would weigh me down. But I've been handling the isolation well.

I needed this time holed up alone to actually get better. Usually, when I'm sick, I trek on without any rest, and I never feel fully recovered. Now, with Holden's help, I'm almost back to baseline already.

Unfortunately, the pressure's back on as I prepare for tomorrow's dissertation meeting. In truth, if our situations were reversed, I probably would've taken advantage of his illness to gain an edge.

I don't know what that says about me, exactly, but it's likely not a good thing.

I don't want to come across as this coldhearted, standoffish person. Not when Holden's slowly opening up to me, showing me a different side of himself—a side that I find myself truly connecting to.

It's difficult to admit, but I'm grateful for his ever-growing presence in my life. For the comfort he provided me when I was sick, for the way he refused to let me push him away. It's a strange feeling, but a good one.

I never thought I'd need someone to wait on me, to be a physical and emotional crutch. But maybe it's not such a scary thing to lean on someone else, to let them take care of me in the way Holden so clearly wants to.

FRIDAY FINALLY ARRIVES, and I'm feeling better, ready to face Dr. Khatri and her scrutiny once again. Holden sits across from me, looking composed as ever, but the nerves are churning in my gut.

I've been working my ass off this week at home, trying to make up for my past mistakes and prove myself worthy. But despite my efforts, there's still a little voice in my head whispering that it's not enough.

Dr. Khatri clears her throat, and I sit up straighter in my chair. "Kaia, your revised question is excellent," she says, her eyes meeting mine. "You've taken the feedback and honed in on what's important for your research. I'm impressed."

A wave of pride washes over me, but before I can bask in her praise, she adds, "I assume Holden helped you revise?"

I open my mouth to correct her, but Holden jumps in first. "Actually, this one was all Kaia. By the time I reached out to assist, she'd already figured things out on her own."

"That's good to hear," Dr. Khatri says. "I reviewed the summaries you both sent over, and I can see that you've made some good progress. But Kaia, I think you may be able to eliminate some of the extraneous details from your findings. Holden, if you wouldn't mind sharing some examples with her, that would be a huge help."

"Of course," Holden says.

"Kaia, you'll be able to see how he's written things. It's a little more concise overall. I can give you a copy to look over now, and if Holden's alright with it, you can use that as a reference for your own work."

I tense up, my stomach whirling as I take the papers from her outstretched hand. I can't help but feel embarrassed and inferior again, especially with Holden here to bear witness.

I quickly scan over the pages, reviewing his introductory remarks and summary table. But something's off—the results he included don't match his initial search.

"Sorry," I say. "But I think there might be an error here."

Holden clears his throat. "What do you mean?"

"I mean, there are nearly forty results listed, but only about three-quarters of them are reflected in the summaries."

"Ah, right," Holden says, shifting in his seat. "Well, it's still a rough draft, right?"

"Hm, that's something I didn't take note of during my cursory review." Dr. Khatri quickly scans over the assignment again. "Holden, you're correct that this is a preliminary draft. Unfortunately, you were meant to have all of your results summarized regardless."

"Okay, I can fix that easily," he says with a confident smile. "No problem."

"I'll have to deduct some points for turning in an incomplete assignment, but it shouldn't affect your final grade to a great degree."

"No problem," he says. "I understand."

But as Dr. Khatri looks away, he tosses me a stern look, and I sink down in my seat. The frustration in his brow only serves to tighten the knot in my stomach. It's clear that I've made a mistake here, that I've essentially thrown him under the bus without meaning to.

I try to backtrack, to make it clear that I thought this was a genuine error, but Holden cuts me off with a terse "It's fine, Kaia. I'll fix it later."

I can tell he's hurt, and I don't blame him. Even still, I hate the way it makes me feel like we're suddenly back on opposing ends. Fighting against each other like we always have. But I can't take back what I've just done, and I'm not sure how to make it right.

The meeting ends, and Holden doesn't say another word to me as we pack up our papers, heading out of Dr. Khatri's office. The silence between us is suffocating.

I long to break it, to shout and fight and make him understand that my mistake was an honest one. Sure, he may be reacting exactly the way I would normally, but I've grown to expect more from him—the voice of reason, the one who always has something clever to say.

Instead, I'm left chasing after him now, feeling like I've ruined something fragile.

As he turns the corner, he finally stops and faces me. "What was the point of that?" he asks, voice low and rough.

"I didn't mean to," I say. "I just blurted out the first thing I noticed, I swear."

"You sure you weren't trying to make me look bad on purpose?" he asks, eyes narrowed. "Because you were embarrassed in there for whatever reason? Because you can't take even an ounce of genuine criticism?"

"That's not true," I protest, but he just shakes his head, turning away from me.

"Fuck, I really can't do this right now," he says, glancing at his watch. "I'm sorry, but I've got somewhere to be."

Left standing on the sidewalk, I feel guilty for costing him his grade. Was he trying to take shortcuts all along, or was it a genuine mistake that I brought to light?

Either way, he's partially right. I shouldn't have opened my mouth in the first place, especially not after how helpful he's been this week.

And now that he's left things unresolved, I hate the way I'm feeling—both ashamed and insecure. I don't know if I even have the mental capacity or the emotional bandwidth to deal with this right now.

I'd rather not risk disappointing someone else in my life.

I feel lost as I head back to my apartment. And while I lie in bed later that night, staring at the ceiling, the feeling only grows stronger.

Holden still hasn't returned any of my texts. I know I messed up, but I wish he would talk to me, tell me what I can do to make it right. Or hell, maybe I should just forget this whole thing in the first place, and we can go back to the way we used to be.

Distant rivals. Fairweather acquaintances. Only checking in to throw a quick barb in the other person's direction.

It was easier that way. Cut-and-dry, just how I prefer it to be.

# Chapter Twenty-Two

## HOLDEN

It's been a long, exhausting day. After our meeting this morning, I rushed to our midday practice, and then I had to suffer through PT with Dr. Reynolds. *Again.* She seems to have chilled out after our conversation a few weeks back, but she still insists on keeping me at least once per week.

It's annoying, but it's manageable.

Now, the sun has set, painting the sky in hues of blue, and I'm standing outside Kaia's apartment. She's taking an exceptionally long time to come to the door. So I'm left out here alone, twiddling my thumbs like some sort of clingy asshole.

When she finally opens the door to greet me, there are worry lines etched onto her forehead. I know I was harsh with her earlier, lashing out without waiting for an actual explanation.

But I'm here now, ready and willing to make amends.

"Hey," I say, the weight of the day sitting heavily on my spine.

"Hey," she says, her voice small. "You done ignoring me now?"

"I wasn't." I stifle a grin, shaking my head at her blunt accusation. "I've been really fucking busy, and I didn't have time to hash this out with you properly."

She purses her lips. "You sure about that?"

"Yes, and I'm sorry if I made it seem otherwise," I say,

running my fingertips along her forearm. "But I'm here now, and I want to talk."

She shakes me off, wordlessly turning on her heel, and I take that as my cue to follow her inside. I carefully settle in beside her on the couch, and the tension between us starts to ease.

"Look, Beck," she starts, pressing her palms flat against her thighs. "I'm genuinely sorry for costing you points today. I know it may not seem like it, but I wasn't trying to tattle."

"I believe you."

She raises a brow. "You do?"

"Knowing you, you'd actually admit to being vindictive. And to be honest, I just didn't have time to finish the assignment," I say with a shrug. "I figured it wasn't that big of a deal."

She scoffs, rubbing an irritated hand across her brow. "So, it wasn't even a genuine mistake?"

"I mean, it's a fucking rough draft. I thought no one would notice."

She tilts her head back with a sigh. "Becker . . ."

"Come on, Karras." I wrap my fingers around her knee with a gentle squeeze. "Not everyone can be as perfect as you are."

"Apparently, you're more than perfect," she says, waving a flippant hand. "If Dr. Khatri asks you to help me one more time, I think I'm gonna lose my ever-loving mind."

My lips curl in a smirk. "That really bothers you, huh?"

"It's basically a scene straight out of my fucking nightmares."

"Wow, the drama."

"Hey." She swats me on the arm, laughter spilling free. "You were the one bringing the drama today, not me."

"I know, and I feel like shit about it. I shouldn't have lashed out at you like that."

She swallows, her gaze softening. "You swear you weren't ignoring me on purpose? Trying to give me a taste of my own medicine?"

"That was just a lucky little side effect." I tap my fingers against her thigh. "Feels pretty shitty, doesn't it?"

"Yeah, it does."

"I'm sorry, baby," I say, rubbing my thumb in small circles on her inner thigh.

She rolls her eyes, shifts her body closer against my touch. "Not your baby."

"You are when we're alone."

"Whatever," she grumbles.

"Speaking of, you finally feeling better?"

"Yeah." She hesitates for a long moment, clears her throat, glances to a blank spot on the wall behind me, then, "Thank you again for all your help."

"I know it must've hurt you to say that."

She chuckles, something soft and sweet. "It really did."

"You know, I wouldn't have been so tied up if it weren't for Harper keeping me late again. She's been doing it all season."

"Ah."

I narrow my eyes in suspicion. "Do you happen to know anything about that?"

She winces, awkwardly avoiding eye contact. "What makes you ask?"

"Kaia," I say, my voice stern. "I need to know."

"Okay, okay," she says, holding up her hands in surrender. "It was Elio. He may have asked Harper to go hard on you."

"I fucking knew it."

"She's such a sweet person, though. I'm sure she was just exaggerating the sessions the tiniest little bit. Don't blame it all on her."

Honestly, it's not the biggest deal in the world. She gave me the help I needed and caused me a minor annoyance along the way. I'll survive, but I still want to make Kaia squirm a little.

"No, I don't," I say, voice dropping low. "I blame it on you."

"But it wasn't even my idea. If you're gonna blame anyone, blame Elio."

"He was acting on your behalf, I'm sure." I squeeze her knee again, slowly working my way up her thigh. "You love to sabotage me."

Her eyes narrow. "Didn't we just agree that was an accident?"

"Today, maybe, but what about all the times before that?"

"Statute of limitations."

"I don't think so." The corner of my mouth curls. "I think you still deserve to be punished."

"Oh," she murmurs, gulping low in her throat.

Without another word, she pushes up from the couch, bolting down the hallway. It's difficult not to smile as I watch her run, her poorly concealed laughter echoing around the apartment.

I easily catch up to her in the bedroom, tackling her onto the bed and pinning her to the mattress, shoving both hands above her head. "You're not getting away that easily," I say, grinning down at her.

"Please, no," she says, still laughing. This time, it's full, unbridled, a small symphony of giggles that escape her until she's pink in the face. "I'm too fragile for your punishment."

"You asked for it." I lean down to kiss her neck, nuzzling my nose into the crook and nipping at her soft skin.

She arches into me, and I release her hands. She tangles them into my hair as I kiss my way across her face. The taste of her is like honey on my lips, sweet and addictive. Heat radiates off her in waves, and it only ignites the flames burning within me.

I need her, need this, need us.

I tug at her shirt, desperate to feel her bare skin against mine, and she eagerly complies, shedding it off in one swift movement. She's beautiful, always has been, with curves in all my favorite places.

I kiss my way down her chest, reveling in the softness of her skin, the scent of her lavender bodywash. My hands wander down to her hips, pulling her closer to me. She moans softly, fingers digging into my shoulders as we slowly work the rest of our clothing off.

I take my time exploring her body this time, trailing kisses down the curve of her waist, over the swell of her hips, and back up again. She arches into me, a sweet sound escaping her as my tongue flicks against her nipple.

The way she moves beneath me is mesmerizing, every little sigh and moan driving me wild with need. I'm not sure how much longer we spend like this, tracing the curves and edges of each other's skin, but time slips away as the room grows darker.

And when I finally push inside her, it's pure fucking bliss. Perfect. Complete. I know this isn't what we agreed on, but it's what we were meant for—two halves of a dysfunctional whole.

I said before that I was content to leave things how they are, but I'm realizing that's a bald-faced lie. I'm so fucking far from being content. The truth is, I want this girl for a million other reasons than what she can do for me in the bedroom.

I want to wake up with her in the mornings and not have to worry about whether or not I crossed a line. I want to take care of her when she's sick and not have to practically force her into letting me. I want to fight with her and not have to fear that she'll never speak to me again.

I want security. Trust. To be the one person she comes to when she's in need. But for the first time in weeks, I'm not so sure the two of us are on the same page.

I WAKE up in the middle of the night in Kaia's bed, stretching my limbs out, the warmth of her sheets tangled around my body. Her head's nestled against my chest, and the sweet, steady rhythm of her breathing lulls me back into a peaceful state.

I lie there for a while, admiring the delicate curve of her hips and the way her hair spills across my skin. It's like a waterfall of dark silk. The soft light of the moon casts a gentle glow across the room, illuminating her features.

I'm not sure why, but last night felt more intense between us, more passionate, and it feels really fucking good to wake up with her in my arms. Reluctantly, I move to disentangle myself. But in my haste, Kaia stirs, her eyes fluttering open.

"Stay," she whispers, a drowsy smile spreading across her face.

So I do. I stay wrapped up in her embrace until the morning light comes, until she kicks me out with a half-hearted chuckle and a swift pat on the ass.

Driving back home, I can't shake the confusion that lingers in my chest. What happened last night between us? Was it just another casual hookup for her, or was there something more there?

I know what I'm feeling now, and it's like a revelation, a sudden understanding of something that's been there all along. Something hidden beneath the surface. It's become crystal fucking clear to me that I'm falling for her, that I want more than just a casual hookup or some insignificant fling.

But even as I revel in this, I can't help my apprehension.

As much as I pride myself on understanding her, Kaia's mind's still a mystery to me sometimes, her emotions locked up like a vault. But with each passing day, I'm beginning to see glimpses of the real her, the one behind the carefully constructed façade.

And I'm falling deeper and deeper every damn day, despite the fear that she might never let me in fully.

As soon as I step inside our house, I find Rai lounging on the couch with the TV blaring in the background. He looks up at me with a self-satisfied grin, like he's been waiting for me to come home all morning.

"Hey, man," I greet him, plopping down beside him on the couch. "Hypothetically speaking, what does it mean if a girl you've been sleeping with suddenly asks you to stay the night?"

He looks up at me, a mischievous glint in his eye. "It depends."

"On what?"

"On whether or not the girl in question is Kaia Karras," he says, a smirk spreading across his annoying face.

"Rai, you don't need to use the girl's full name," I say, rolling my eyes. "She's not a fucking celebrity."

"She is in this house," he retorts, not missing a beat.

"My god, man."

"Okay, so that answers my question." He flicks the TV off, turning to face me full-on. "As for yours, the answer's simple, Becksy."

My interest's officially piqued. "Elaborate."

"She's starting to like you for more than just the hanky-panky," he says, waggling his eyebrows.

"Jesus, where'd you even pick that up? The retirement home?"

"Sorry, let me try that again," he says, fully beaming now. "She likes you for more than just a good ol' dicking down."

"Okay, I'm out of here." I snort, ignoring his mumbled protests as I make my way up the stairs.

Now, with Rai's words swirling around inside my head, my thoughts are fully consumed. For too long, I've been in denial about my true feelings for Kaia. But now, I know it's time to confront them head-on.

Is it possible that she's starting to feel the same, or am I just imagining things?

I nearly miss my door as I stumble inside my room, collapsing onto the bed. This past week has been a whirlwind of taking care of Kaia, doubling up on notes, and pushing through our grueling practice schedule.

And now, the weight of it all has finally caught up to me.

# Chapter Twenty-Three

KAIA

After watching Holden leave this morning, I curled up in bed well into the midmorning. For me, it's a luxury I don't often allow. And now, hours later, I'm still sitting here smiling at nothing, mindlessly kicking my feet, cheeks heating at the thought of waking up beside him again.

But that's when it hits me. Like a ton of bricks. Like a train that just ran me over. Like a goddamn hurricane.

I have a crush. An actual, bona fide crush on Holden Becker.

I mean, it's not like I didn't know I was attracted to him before. But this is different. This is like, butterflies in my stomach, heart racing, can't stop thinking about him kind of crush. And it's freaking me out.

I mean, sure, he's ridiculously good-looking. And he's great in bed. But it's more than that. It's the way his laughter hits me right in the fucking chest. The way he touches me, soft and gentle when I need it and rough when I don't. The way he leaves me those goofy little notes in the morning before he sneaks out.

This is bad. Really bad. I don't do crushes. The last couple of guys I've dated have been a complete nonissue, mostly because I didn't actually give a shit about them. Being with them never carried the risk of real distraction.

But this is uncharted territory for me.

Maybe it's just a fluke. Maybe I'm just overthinking things like usual. But then I remember the way I asked him to stay the night, the way he held me, comforted me this past week. And when we woke up together, I didn't want him to leave.

Fucking hell. I really, genuinely like the guy, don't I?

I groan, throwing myself back onto the bed. This is not how things are supposed to be. I'm supposed to be the one in control, the one who doesn't catch feelings. But here I am, falling head first for the golden boy, with his warm, brown eyes and the whitest fucking smile I've ever seen.

It's like I'm in high school all over again, awkward and nervous and hoping he likes me back. It's silly, really, considering the fact that his dick was inside me just a few hours ago.

I huff a frustrated sigh, burying my face in a pillow.

The rest of the day is a flurry of trying to shut him out of my brain. I distract myself with laundry, cleaning, and reorganizing my bookshelf. But no matter what I do, I can't shake the thought of him. Every time I catch myself humming, dancing, daydreaming, I force myself to snap out of it.

I can't let this thing between us consume any more of my time.

But then, just as I'm starting to feel like maybe I can handle this newfound infatuation, my phone lights up with a text.

HOLDEN

hey, we're having people over after the game tonight. wanna come by?

My stomach flutters at the thought of seeing him again so soon, but I know I can't give in. This isn't what we agreed upon. In fact, it's far from it. I need to create some semblance of distance between us while I still can.

KAIA

sorry, can't make it

HOLDEN

oh, okay. that's too bad. was hoping to see you tonight

I can practically hear the disappointment dripping from his words, and it sends a pang of guilt straight to my gut. I'm sure he's well aware that I'll be sitting at home doing nothing instead.

KAIA

maybe next time

HOLDEN

sure thing

I toss my phone onto the bed with a sigh. It's like I'm stuck in this purgatory of emotions, torn between my head and my heart. My head's telling me to stay away, to protect myself from the distraction. But my heart's begging me to take a chance, to see where this thing between us could really go.

And as the day turns into night, I end up back in my bed, staring at the ceiling, wondering what the hell I'm going to do about all of this. I can't deny the way he makes me feel, the way he brings out a different side of me, but I also can't ignore the fear that comes with letting my guard down.

I work to collect myself, trying to calm my racing heart. But as much as I try to push him away, Holden's like a moth to a flame, drawing me in, tempting me with his golden light.

It's ridiculous, really. I'm acting like a lovesick teenager. But I can't fucking help it. The boy has wedged his way so far under my skin, and now I'm not so sure I want him to leave.

I pinch my eyes shut, rubbing at my temples. The thought

of spending another night alone, drowning in my own thoughts, feels unbearable. So before I can second-guess myself, I grab my phone and type out a quick message.

KAIA

hey, changed my mind. if you still want me to come, then I'd love to

When there's no immediate response, I grow restless. Impatient. I check my phone every few minutes, hoping for a simple affirmation from him. But as the night continues to wear on, it becomes clear that he's not going to text me back in time.

Despite my better judgment, I throw on some new clothes, grab my keys, and head out the front door.

It's nearly ten o'clock by the time I arrive at his place, my heartbeat pulsing in my eardrums as the Uber pulls up. It's quiet tonight. A few cars are parked haphazardly on the curb, but it's clear that this party's much more subdued than the last one.

As I step out of the car, I can barely make out the sounds of laughter and music drifting through the air. But it's more than enough to make my stomach do backflips. I'm still waiting for a response to my text, but I'm hoping that he'll be glad to see me anyway.

I make my way to the entrance, up the creepy statued stairway, and knock on the front door. Of course, Rai's there to greet me with that goofy grin of his.

"Kaia! You're here!"

"I am," I say, trying to conceal the uncertainty in my voice.

"No Liz tonight?" he asks, hopeful as he glances past me.

"I think she's out with friends somewhere," I say, a pang of sorrow hitting me directly in the chest. I'm not sure when she decided to move on, but I don't think she's too interested in Rai these days. Maybe she never really was. "Sorry, she's been pretty distant lately. I barely get to see her myself."

"No worries," he says, pulling me in for a quick hug. "Honestly, I wasn't sure you'd show up, either. Becksy made it sound like you were a no-show."

"Yeah, my schedule cleared up."

Once Rai ushers me inside, I quickly glance around the room, searching for any sign of Holden. But he's nowhere to be found.

"Feel free to make yourself at home," Rai says, gesturing to the rest of the partygoers. As expected, I don't recognize any of them.

"Is Holden around here somewhere, or is he upstairs?" I ask.

"I think he's in the kitchen or maybe out back somewhere."

I make my way to the dining area first, but when I turn the corner, Holden's there leaning against the countertop, his arm perched halfway around some girl. He's not exactly touching her, but they're standing awfully close, laughing and chatting in a way that makes my heart sink.

I try to slip away unnoticed, but Holden catches sight of me just as I'm making my escape. "Kaia?" he calls, following after me. We nearly make it all the way back to the front porch before he catches up, gently grasping my wrist and spinning me around to face him.

"What are you doing?" I ask, my voice trembling.

"What do you mean?" There's confusion in his eyes. "I thought you weren't coming."

I cross my arms tightly over my chest. "Yeah, well, it looked like you were doing just fine without me here."

"That's what this is?" His brows shoot up. "You're seriously jealous of me talking to some random girl for, like, thirty seconds?"

"No, you can do whatever you want," I say, working to keep the hurt from my voice.

"Kaia, come on." He takes a step closer, presses a hand to my shoulder. "You know me better than that."

"Do I?" I ask, looking up at him. "We never made any promises to each other. We agreed to keep things casual, remember?"

"Kaia," he murmurs again, low and soft this time.

"What?"

"That girl in there is my teammate's girlfriend. And I don't give two shits about her."

"Oh."

"But I *do* care about you, and I'm glad you showed up tonight after all. I wanted to talk to you."

"About what?"

"I had this whole speech planned, actually," he says. "And then when you said you weren't coming, I kinda threw it all out the window."

"Oh God, is this some sort of breakup speech?" I ask, panic wriggling in the pit of my stomach. "Because you know we're not even really together, right?"

"But that's the thing. We could be."

I rear back. "What?"

"I think about you when we're apart. All the goddamn time." He brushes a strand of hair behind my ear, cupping my jaw. "Do you think about me?"

"Beck . . ."

"Just answer the question."

"Yeah, I think about you," I say softly, flushing at the admission.

He smiles, and it's the kind of smile that makes my knees weak. "Good to know."

"Is that all?" I ask, struggling to keep my emotions in check.

"No." He takes a step closer, tips my chin up with his thumb. "I've been thinking, and I want more for us. I think we're already headed in that direction, but I want to make things crystal fucking clear. I want you, Kaia. And it's for more than just sex, or . . . for good banter when I'm bored. Do you feel the same?"

I swallow hard, heart pounding in my ears. "Y-you know it wouldn't work between us, though."

"It would," he insists.

"But I'm . . . me, and you're you, and we just, we argue too much."

"It doesn't matter," he says, his voice soft but firm.

"It does."

He shakes his head. "You'd be bored if we didn't."

"You're the one who'll get bored of me."

His expression softens. "Is that what you think?"

"I'm not always this . . . *fun*," I say sarcastically, tears pricking at the corners of my eyes. "I mean, the challenge is the fun part for you, right? And I'm really more of a homebody myself. I basically only have one friend, and I'm pretty screwed up in the head. I mean, God, I can barely shut off my fucking brain most of the time. I overthink everything. And also, you were right before—I do take every tiny piece of criticism to heart. I'm not some happy-go-lucky little sweetheart. I can't be that girl even if I wanted to be."

"You think I don't know this already?"

"You might think you do, but whatever you think you know, I'm worse," I say, my voice breaking.

"There's nothing fucking wrong with you, Kaia," he says fiercely, pulling me even closer. "All that shit you just listed—it's what makes you human. Uniquely fucking perfect. I don't like you in *spite* of who you are. I like every little piece that makes you whole. I'm not getting bored of you, ever, so don't even let your mind take you there."

"Are you sure?" I ask, desperately in need of affirmation.

"If that's what's holding you back from giving this, *us*, a real shot, then let it be known—there's not a world in which I do better than you. I want you, Kaia, every conceivable part of you. Tell me you want me, too."

"I . . . I don't even know what to say," I admit, overwhelmed.

"Try that again," he says, our eyes locked.

"Fuck. Okay, yes. I want you back, so badly," I confess, my voice raw with unfiltered emotion. "I think of you when we're not together, all the fucking time. And I don't even know if I can pinpoint when it shifted from something physical to something more. But I don't want to lose you. I can't even make myself picture it."

His eyes light up, sparkling in the dim light. "I was hoping you might say that."

"So, what does this mean?"

"It means that you and I are gonna be together. Just us." His hand moves to caress the back of my neck, pulling me against him. "And we're giving this thing a real shot from now on."

"You mean, like an experiment?"

"Hell no."

"So we're *together*, together?"

He breaks out into a wide grin, fingers curling up into the soft hair at the nape of my neck. "I'm not speaking in riddles here, Karras."

"So, you and I are gonna go on dates? And . . . be nice to each other in public from now on?"

"If you can manage to tolerate it." He bumps his nose against my cheek. "The second part's still up for negotiation, though."

I let out a shaky breath, the weight of my uncertainty finally lifting. "Okay."

"Okay," he echoes, a soft, gentle reassurance. And then he pulls me in for a long, all-encompassing kiss—one that nearly makes my heart stop.

# Chapter Twenty-Four

HOLDEN

My heart pounds in my chest as I lead Kaia up to my bedroom. I'm so fucking happy right now; I can't even make an attempt to contain it. I don't want to be downstairs for another second longer—not surrounded by my teammates or my friends. I'd rather be alone with Kaia, basking in the fact that she's finally fucking mine.

To my surprise, she's agreed to give us a real shot. And right now, I feel an inescapable pull toward her, this urge to be closer, to hold her, to please her.

I can't wait anymore. I need her now.

Once we're safely tucked inside my room, I grab her wrist and guide her over to the bed. Her hands shake as she reaches for me, pulling me into a deep kiss. She's so fucking soft, so warm, and a scorching heat builds between us as our bodies entwine.

I spin her around, gently pushing her onto her back before me. A groan escapes me as she scoots toward the head of my bed. This is the first time I've had her here, in my room, ready and willing to let me fuck her.

The only other time she was up here, the idea seemed like a far-off possibility. Something I could've only imagined in my wildest fucking fantasies. But now, it's reality. This girl is mine, and I'm gonna make damn sure she doesn't forget it.

"Take your skirt off," I say.

Her eyes widen for a fraction of a second and then slowly darken with desire.

She's in her element here, with me, more than willing to listen to my commands. She likes it when I take control, that much has been established. And as for me, the whole idea of her bending to my will suits me just fucking fine.

When she doesn't immediately comply, I try again. "Take off your fucking skirt, baby."

She lifts her hips, gently tugging it down her waist, exposing the tiny scrap of her soft purple panties. My cock jerks in my pants, blood rushing to it so quickly that I feel lightheaded.

"Shirt," I murmur next.

There's a twinkle in her eyes now. She licks her lips, working her shirt up and over her head, exposing her naked chest to me. Apparently, she decided to forego a bra tonight. So it's just her soft, plump breasts and those little, rosy nipples that sit so fucking pretty.

"Fuck," I rasp, dying to get my hands on her now. She's splayed out in front of me, completely naked except for her panties. And God, I really want to taste her.

"Spread your legs for me."

Her thighs part immediately, but I don't miss the irritated eye roll she gives me. My lips curl in amusement. Unable to wait any longer, I join her on the bed. She reaches for me, sliding her hands up and underneath my shirt. Together, we push it the rest of the way off.

Using my thumb, I bring her panties to the side and plunge two fingers deep inside of her, gently curling them against her inner walls. She's already dripping wet, desire pooling between her legs.

"It's so fucking easy to turn you on. You're a little slut for me, aren't you, Karras?"

"Shut up," she mutters, whimpering as I fuck my fingers into her at a faster pace.

I pump them in and out, rapidly, deeply until she's a squirming mess beneath me. Then I press one palm flat against her lower stomach, curling my fingers up to meet the pressure. She moans so fucking loudly that it makes me proud.

"Don't come," I order.

"What?"

"I said, don't fucking come."

"Please, Beck, I need to."

I dip my head down to lick her, pressing my tongue flat against her clit. Slowly, I take it between my lips and suck—small, light, and fluttery, still pumping in and out at a dangerous tempo. She's fully shaking now, fingers digging into my scalp as she presses my mouth impossibly close.

Her pussy, so fucking wet and swollen now, drips like honey onto my tongue.

"You can come now, baby," I say.

"Oh, God." At my words, she breaks like a fucking floodgate, bucking against my tongue, clenching so impossibly tight around my fingers. I can't take it for another second longer. I want—no, I fucking *need*—to feel this sensation around my cock.

As she rides out her orgasm, I quickly undress, grab her hips, and align our bodies.

"You good with this?" I ask, tensing as she grabs hold of my ass.

"Mhm, please. I'm protected." She's still moaning even now, whimpering against me as I slide inside of her, the aftershocks playing out their sweet melody against me.

Fuck, fuck, fuck. I can't manage to control myself. I pump haphazardly in and out of her, fucking her so frantically that I can no longer tell where I end and she begins.

Our breaths come in ragged gasps, our bodies slick with sweat as we give ourselves over to the moment. The world around us fades, our universe shrinking, confining to the intimate space between us.

And when I finally spill inside her, I'm beyond dizzy.

We kiss again, slow and soft, our bodies pressed together as I run my hands through her damp hair. My heart races, the adrenaline pumping through my veins. It feels unbelievable to finally have her like this—fully and unrestrained.

"Kaia," I say, struggling to catch my breath. "You're staying the night, the whole night, with me. And tomorrow, I'm taking you on a date."

She nods, a tiny smile playing at the corners of her lips. "Yeah, alright."

I WAKE up beside her the next morning, my heart feeling lighter than it has in a long time. I can't resist smiling as I watch her sleep, her dark hair splayed out on the pillow, lips slightly parted.

I've never felt this way about anyone before, and the thought of that is terrifying.

But it's also exhilarating, knowing how much I want her—to hold her, to be with her, to go through this phase of life with her by my side. And it feels really fucking good to know we're on the same page now.

I gently shake her awake, and she opens her eyes, smiling up at me. "Good morning, baby," I say, pressing a kiss to her temple.

"Good morning." She stretches like a cat, curling into a ball at my side, and then nuzzling up against my neck. "So, what's the plan for today?"

"I thought we could go see the lighthouse at Bluewater Cape," I say, combing my fingers through her hair. "It's only about a half-hour drive from Amber Isle."

"I haven't been there in years," she says, her voice lighting up. "I used to beg my parents to take us when Sof and I were younger."

"Yeah, I stumbled upon it freshman year when I was at Lookout Point. I spotted it from the car, and then I went back there on my own the next weekend. The views from the top are fucking incredible."

She pulls back, waggles her brows. "Lookout Point, huh?"

I run a ragged hand through my hair, a wide grin pulling at my lips. We're in bed together the morning after we decided to give things a real shot, and she's teasing me about going to a notorious make-out spot. This is better, lighter and sweeter, than anything I could've imagined for us.

"Oh, come on," I tease. "Didn't you grow up in Boyer?"

"And?"

"I'm sure even the illustrious Kaia Karras has been to Lookout Point a time or two."

"Yeah, when I was, like, sixteen and still trying to hide from my aunt."

"Your aunt?"

"Yeah, Thalia," she says, her tone melancholy. "I lived with her for a few years, just so I could finish up high school here. My parents moved to Greece after Sof graduated, and I was kinda backed into a corner."

"Ah, okay. So, you haven't been back to Bluewater since you were a kid?"

"Nope." She gives me the tiniest hint of a smile. "But, you know, I do have a lot of homework to catch up on still and—"

"Karras, come on." I take her chin in my hands, tilting her gaze up to meet mine. "You can take one day off."

"A whole day?"

"Give me at least the rest of the morning." I press a kiss to her forehead. "I'll make you lunch and drop you back off when we're done, okay?"

"Yeah, okay."

Once I'm ready, I swing by Kaia's apartment so she can do the same. Then we hop back into my car. On the short drive over, she points out the exit for her old house and opens up a little bit more about her aunt.

Apparently, the two of them were never quite close, not until Thalia became her last resort. Kaia says she enjoyed their time living together, but they haven't kept in touch nearly as much since she went off to Coastal.

As we make our way up the lighthouse, we continue our conversation, and I find myself opening up to her as well. I tell her about my dad, his affair, and the mandatory monthly dinners he forces me to attend. And she tells me about her strained relationship with her parents and her sister, who she's been avoiding for a while now.

"You know," she says. "I might finally let Sof come visit me in a couple of weeks, just to get her off my back. But I may need you around as a buffer."

"You got it," I say without hesitation. "And in return, you can be mine the next time my dad comes into town."

As we reach the summit, I feel lighter somehow. Weightless. The view from up here is nothing short of breathtaking, the sky painted with hues of red and orange as the sun rises over the water.

It's fucking golden up here. Iridescent.

The ocean stretches out before us, vast and unending, and for a moment, it feels like we're the only two people in the world. I turn to Kaia, noticing the way the morning light enhances her sharp features. The wind catches her hair, sending dark strands of it flying around her face.

It's a moment I'm committing to memory, filing away in my bank of Kaia.

"You know," I say, wrapping my arm around her waist and pulling her against me. "I've had a thing for you pretty much since the second I laid eyes on you."

"Oh, yeah?" She snorts. "You couldn't have made that any less clear."

"What do you mean? I was always finding some excuse to talk to you."

"To poke at me, maybe," she counters, tensing in my arms. "Or to throw some arrogant commentary my way."

I let out a soft chuckle. "Like what?"

"Let's see, do you remember the first thing you ever said to me?"

"Uh . . ." I rack my brain, running my hands over her chilled arms. "I asked about you applying to the Biomed program?"

"No, I actually heard that *you* were applying first. And, um, I thought you were kinda cute. So after class, I came up to you, told you I was gunning for the same thing."

"The suspense is killing me here, Karras."

She leans her head back against my chest. "You really don't know, do you?"

"Nope."

"You said, 'Should be pretty easy for you,'" she mocks in a grating voice. "'You've got the whole *Women in STEM* thing going on. They'll probably accept you into the program no matter the prereqs.'"

"Oh, Jesus," I groan. "Baby Beck really fucked that one up, didn't he?"

"You could say that."

"Honestly, Kaia, I was intimidated to speak to you back then. And, I have to admit, I was jealous of your relationship with Elio, even though I had no reason to be."

"Jealous? We barely even knew each other."

"In my dreams, we knew each other quite well." That earns me a laugh. "I definitely don't think of you that way, just so you know. Or any woman, for that matter. You were accepted into our major because of your own merit. I mean, God, you're the hardest worker I know."

She nudges me with her elbow. "Yeah, and how'd you get in, then?"

"Well, some of us don't have to try to be the best. We just are."

"See, there's that telltale arrogance of yours."

"I never denied I had an ego. But I will say, I think you took this confirmation bias a little too seriously," I say, laughing.

"What do you mean?"

"Seeking out information to match what you already thought about me, like a dogpile. Every little thing I said or did just gave you more ammunition."

"Yeah, in a way, I guess." She lets out a soft breath. "But you also did it on purpose. At least, some of the time, right?"

"Yeah, Karras, teasing you has always been my favorite hobby."

I slowly thread my fingers through hers, running my thumb along her lifeline, and it feels more intimate than anything we've done before. Despite our history, I'm so fucking thankful that she's given us a real chance.

I press a kiss to her crown, hold her against me, and make a silent promise here and now: I'll do everything in my power not to screw this up.

# Chapter Twenty-Five

KAIA

On Monday morning, I make a plan to meet Elio for coffee before class. We haven't seen each other nearly as often as we used to—to study, to hang out, to chat and spiral about all the nonsense going on in our lives.

And I still feel kind of shitty about our last real conversation. I accused him of slipping back into old habits, but the truth is he's just exhausted from working his ass off. Plus, I also need to tell him about me and Holden . . . before he works it out for himself.

I arrive at the coffee shop early, nerves bubbling in my stomach. As I approach, I notice that he's brought Bentley along, and he's found a spot for us all to sit outside in the warm morning breeze.

He greets me with a quick hello and then dips inside to order our coffees—two Americanos, black. I reach under the table to scratch Bentley's ear, relishing in the feel of his soft fur beneath my fingertips. He looks up at me with his big, brown eyes, and it's impossible not to smile.

He's such a good dog, so full of boundless love and energy. I'm happy that El decided to give him a chance, and I'm hoping that it'll be good for both of them.

As I wait for him to return, I take in my surroundings—the quaint, little blue door of the café and the aroma of freshly brewed coffee wafting through the air. One of my favorite smells. It's the middle of fall now, and the air is crisp yet somehow gentle on my skin.

I close my eyes, focusing on the sun's warm rays on my face, the cool air on my arms, and the sounds of seagulls in the distance. It's a peaceful oasis in the midst of life's chaos.

Finally, Elio emerges from inside, a steaming cup of coffee in each hand. As he sets them down on the table, Bentley tries to hop up onto his lap, tail wagging furiously.

"Sorry, I couldn't resist bringing him." He gives me a sheepish grin, ushering the dog back to the ground. "He loves car rides, and I didn't want to leave him alone this morning. I'll drop him back off before class."

"No worries. I'm glad you did." I square my shoulders, steeling myself for the ensuing conversation. "El, there's actually something I need to talk to you about."

He sets down his coffee, giving me his full attention. "Let me guess—you're either screwing Becker on the regular now, or you decided to actually date the guy."

"Wow." I let out a derisive huff. "Subtlety is not your strong suit."

"Kai." He raises a brow, urging me to continue.

"Yeah, we're dating." I press my palms to my cheeks, attempting to hide the rising heat. "How'd you know?"

"I figured it would happen sooner or later." He leisurely sips on his coffee, kicking his feet onto the extra seat beside me. "You guys have always had this weird tension, no matter how much you insisted that he's a bag of dicks."

"I mean, he's still kind of a dick sometimes," I admit, voice soaking in unexpected tenderness. "But I guess he's my dick now."

He groans, a hand on his face. "Oh, please spare me the details."

"He's a good guy, E. I think I may have misjudged him a little bit, and he's been there for me lately."

"As long as you're happy."

"Also . . . I confessed that you sicced Harper on him. And he's not too happy about it."

"Shit, Kaia." He sits up straighter in his seat, worry lines etched into his forehead. "Is he gonna try and get her in trouble with the team?"

"No, I told him it was all our fault. Well, actually, I tried to place most of the blame on you."

He rolls his eyes. "Nice."

"It was *your* idea. And *your* family member."

"I was acting mostly on your behalf."

A chuckle escapes me at the irony. "That's what Beck said."

"I guess we do have something in common, then."

I give him a sharp look, suppressing a grin. "You guys better not try and gang up on me now."

"Please, I don't see the two of us splitting an ice cream cone anytime soon."

"You never know," I say, shooting him a sly glance. "I could find out his favorite flavor for you."

He gives me a humorless snort. "I think I'll survive without that knowledge."

"So, how's work going?" I ask, deflecting the conversation away from me and my current relationship status. "Any better this last couple of weeks?"

"Not really," he says with a pinched look on his face. "I'm always exhausted after a big weekend, and I'm overwhelmed with juggling Bentley and school. It's really fucking hard not to skip class every day."

"That sounds like a lot to deal with, E." I give him a reassuring look, reaching across the table to pat the top of his hand. "I'm sorry."

His voice tightens. "I just don't know how I'm going to keep up."

"Could you maybe ask Luca for a loan?" I ask, already knowing the answer to my question.

He's too stubborn and strong-willed to ask his family for any more money, especially his older brother. The two of us are similar that way. Except, his decision is for more noble reasons. Borrowing money from his siblings was a mistake he made in the past, when he was buried in the depths of his addiction. But for me, it's more so due to the principle of the matter.

My parents already pay my tuition and board—they make enough money for it not to hurt their bank accounts—but I refuse to ask for anything more than necessities. I already feel indebted to them in a big way. And in no uncertain terms, they've made it clear that I'm not topping their priority list.

"I'm not asking my family for money ever again," he says, giving me a tight smile. "You know that."

I let it go, and we quietly finish our coffee, the silence filled only by the sounds of Bentley panting at our feet. Then I hop into the back of his car—because apparently, the dog needs to ride shotgun—and we drop him off before heading back to campus.

My heart races, breath catching in my throat as we make our way through the quad. My palms are damp with sweat, and my stomach's churning. It's over-the-top, I know, but today's the first day I'll see Holden since we made our decision.

We're officially dating now. It's new, exciting, and kind of strange. A feeling that'll take some time to get used to.

As we enter the classroom, my gaze immediately gravitates toward his usual seat. He's sitting there across from me, his eyes glued to his phone. I huff out a breath as I sit down beside Elio, trying to ignore the thumping in my chest.

Before I manage to get myself situated, Holden glances up, and our eyes meet. A tender smile spreads across my face, and I give him the two-finger wave. In response, he shoots me a sly grin and a wink that makes my cheeks flush with heat.

I like the way it feels, though, all fluttery and nice. So, as the lecture drones on, I can't resist sneaking tiny glimpses of him. I try to be subtle, turning my head just enough to catch his gaze without drawing attention from Elio or our professor.

It's a game we're playing, a dance of stolen looks and secret smiles. And for once, I allow myself to fucking revel in it.

Once classes end for the day, I head back to my apartment to get some work done. I'm attempting to finish the rest of October's assignments so I can put my full effort into graduate school applications.

As I sit at my cluttered desk, surrounded by stacks of paper and scattered pens, my phone vibrates loudly beside me. I glance over to find Sofia's name flashing on the screen. Hesitant to take the call and break my concentration, I weigh my options before deciding to pick up.

"Hey, Sof," I answer, propping the phone against my ear.

"Hi," she says, her voice chipper. "How's it going?"

"It's fine. Just working on some school stuff. What about you?"

"I'm good, thanks for asking." She quickly changes course. "So, listen. Andrew and I are coming to Boyer this weekend. I want to show him my hometown. So, if you can spare like one night to have dinner with us, then that would be appreciated."

I hesitate for a moment, unsure of how to broach the

subject. Holden and I have only been seeing each other for a few weeks now—a few *days*, to be more accurate—and I don't know if I'm ready to introduce him to my family yet.

But he did agree to be my buffer, and this would be the perfect opportunity for it.

"Actually, yeah, that could work out," I say, my voice filled with trepidation. "I've . . . been seeing someone, and it would be a good chance for you to meet him."

"Really? Who is he?"

"His name's Holden." I sigh, noting the absolute shock in her voice. "He's a hockey player, and he's in my major. We've known each other for a while now, but things have just started to become more serious."

"Oh, wow." Her voice drips with sarcasm. "An athlete, huh?"

"And what's that supposed to mean?" I scoff, tapping my pen against the desk in front of me. "You know, your first two serious boyfriends are both pro athletes now."

"Exactly." She draws out the word, overenunciating the consonants, and it grates on my fucking brain. "And things didn't work out with us for a reason."

"Didn't *you* dump both of them?"

"Yeah, because football was always going to be more important than our relationship."

I blow out a heated breath and set my pen down, running a few strands of hair through my fingers. "Well, Holden and I both have our own stuff going on. Different hobbies and interests. It doesn't bother me that hockey's practically his life."

"You may say that now, but just keep in mind that things can change after college."

"Thanks for the advice," I say, allowing my bitterness to

seep through. "We just started dating, though. I don't think I need to worry about this right now."

"Just keep an open mind, Kai. You know I've already been there."

"It sounds like you're the one who's not keeping an open mind," I mumble under my breath.

"Sorry, what was that?"

"Nothing." I pick at my split ends, tossing the little pieces of hair into my trash can. "Why don't you just text me your plans for the weekend, and I'll come up with a schedule to work around it?"

"Sounds good. Oh, and Kai?" she adds before hanging up. "I'm really excited to see you."

A pang of guilt consumes me as I process my sister's words, and my heart aches with a familiar pain. Sure, she can be condescending and overly critical, but she's still my sister. And it seems like she's at least trying to make amends, to repair our relationship.

I should extend the olive branch and let bygones be bygones. But the thought of spending a whole weekend with her and her newest boyfriend has me drained already.

I absentmindedly twirl a strand of hair around my finger, and before I know it, the simple action escalates into a fixation. An obsession. I move from picking at my split ends to pulling out my hair, strand by strand, from the root.

It hurts, and it's an unnerving distraction, but it also silences my mind.

When I find a drop of blood underneath my fingernails, I know I need to search for a different escape. I can't focus on my work anymore, so I pull up Holden's contact and send him a desperate text.

KAIA

you busy?

HOLDEN

I can be there in an hour?

KAIA

any sooner?

HOLDEN

45 minutes, tops

you need a distraction??

KAIA

I just need you

# Chapter Twenty-Six

HOLDEN

I PULL up to Kaia's apartment, a surge of emotions hitting me. It's an unusual blend of apprehension and eagerness, a coil that pulls tight in my gut. I know that she's been dealing with a lot of stress lately, and I want to offer her some sort of comfort, a sanctuary amidst the turbulence in her life.

But as soon as I walk through the front door, she throws herself at me, her lips already searching for mine. She said earlier that she needs me, not just as a distraction but maybe as something more. And God, do I want to be that guy for her.

So I slow her down with a soft kiss, sweeping my hand into her hair before holding her at arm's length. "Whoa there, tiger," I tease with a grin. "As much as I like kissing you, we should probably talk first."

"So, no sex, then?" she asks, the mischievous glint in her eyes making me laugh. "I could just go down on you if you wanted?"

"Not right now." I shake my head with a groan, silently cursing myself before guiding her over to the couch. Yeah, of course I want to fuck her, but I'm trying to prove that I have more to offer here. "I want to figure out what's going on inside that big brain of yours."

She gives me a tiny smile. "Yeah, okay. Let's *talk*, then."

We sit side by side, and I take notice of her warmth, her sweet smell, the softness of her skin as I wrap an arm around her. She snuggles closer, seeking comfort and reassurance in my embrace. The silence between us is comfortable, filled with the sound of her breathing and the steady rhythm of my heartbeat.

It's nice to be here with her like this—no pressure, no expectations.

I take a quick glance around the apartment before I ask, "Where's Lizzie tonight?"

"Honestly, I've barely seen her these last few weeks." She glances down at her hands, fidgeting with her fingers. "She's started hanging out with the football guys. And since then, she's been completely MIA."

My brow lifts. "Poor Rai Rai."

"Yeah, did he really like her, then?"

"I think so, but I'm sure he'll get over it. He's not too short on options himself."

It's true. Rai's always been popular with women. It's his ability to instantly joke around, to actually listen, and to make people feel comfortable in his presence. He's a giant goofball, sure, but he's also one of the best guys I know.

"That's good."

There's a moment of silence between us before I cut to the chase. "So, you want to tell me what's bothering you?"

"Everything, I think." She sinks against me. "I finally agreed to let Sof visit this weekend, and she wants to meet you. She's bringing her new boyfriend along, too. Some lawyer dude. And honestly, I know it sounds silly, but she drives me up a fucking wall every time we talk. I know I just need to tune her out, but being around her makes me feel itchy and nervous and . . . basically ready to erupt at any second."

I take her hand in mine, rubbing my thumb over the back of it. "Have you guys always had a shitty relationship?"

"Yeah, it started when I was really young. She's five years

older than me, so I think by the time I came along, she was just used to being the only child."

"Ah, I can relate to that a little bit. My younger brother's a menace."

"See, but I was never like that." She lets out a bitter laugh. "She insisted that I was a spoiled fucking brat all my life. I'm nearly one hundred percent sure that I was the product of an accident, and my parents have never treated me quite the same as they do her. It's basically like I'm second-best at everything. Like they threw all of their attention and love at Sofia and didn't have any left to spare me."

Damn. The thought of that hits me hard—the idea of Kaia growing up with the belief that her parents didn't care about her. It's both infuriating and heartbreaking.

"That sounds really tough."

"It was, but I've learned to compartmentalize over the years. Sof is really close with them still, and she's always pressuring me to make amends. But she doesn't get it because she hasn't been treated the way I have." Her gaze drifts down, the flecks of gold in her eyes muted and dull. "She thinks I'm being overdramatic."

"I can tell that you're not. And you know, just because someone's your blood, your family, it doesn't automatically mean you have to put up with them."

She glances up at me, a small, sympathetic smile on her face. "You put up with your parents' bullshit, though."

"Hardly." I let out a rueful chuckle. "I do the bare minimum just to keep my dad happy, and my mom's a good person anyway. She's always been really loving. I just hate what they've done to each other."

"I mean, your dad's actions also affect you." She reaches up, affectionately pushing my hair back, fingertips caressing the side of my face. "You've had to grow up around this really shitty example of love."

"Yeah, I guess so." I swallow, thick and heavy. "I mean, I get why she stays. She doesn't want to give up the comfort of the life she has, and she's shackled by this false image they project."

Her brow furrows. "What do you mean?"

"Like, they have to be picture-fucking-perfect all the time. My dad wants people to think that Becker and Slate is this little homegrown law firm. A generational, family-run establishment with traditional values," I say in a mocking voice. "My mom plays right into it. She makes herself small so that he can look bigger in front of all of his clients and colleagues. I hate it."

Her nose wrinkles. "If it's so important to him, why hasn't he pressured you into following in his footsteps?"

"He's tried, for years. But he's letting me pursue my own passions, which I'm thankful for. He knows I'm not interested in being a lawyer. They would push my younger brother, Harris, into it, but he's kind of a fuckup himself. I'm the golden boy in their eyes."

"Ah, I see." She taps the end of my nose. "You're their little sunshine, aren't you?"

"Yeah, in a way." I stifle a snort. "Fuck the pressure of it all, though."

She nudges me with her elbow. "And what's Harris done to earn the illustrious title of *fuckup*?"

"You may have noticed that my family has their fair share of money."

Her eyes light up in amusement. "Hard to miss."

"Right, well, my brother's only a couple of years younger than me. He's got his trust fund and an allowance, and he also doesn't go to college." I cup my hand around her knee, gently squeezing. "While I'm spending my money on tuition, he's spending it on girls and booze and drugs."

"Ah."

"Yeah, he just doesn't have a care in the world." A sharp edge creeps into my tone, betraying my frustration. "He'd probably be content to just fuck it all away on useless shit."

She tenses up, and I have the sudden urge to backtrack.

"So, he has an addiction?" she asks.

"I don't think so." I work to neutralize my tone. "It's more so recreational. He's put together in front of my parents, but behind closed doors, he's partying hard."

"Are you at all worried about him?"

Before I can help it, bitterness creeps up inside of me, like a vine twisting around my heart. I know she's comparing Harris' situation to her best friend's, but it's not the same. Harris doesn't care about anyone other than himself.

"Sometimes," I say, attempting to remain indifferent. "But I've got so much of my own shit going on. I just need him to take care of himself, you know?"

"Yeah." Her voice is soft, a quiet whisper in the small space between us. "So, you two obviously aren't close, then?"

"We just have different goals, lifestyles." I let out a sharp exhale. "I wish the best for him, though."

"Hmm," she hums, quiet and tense in my arms now.

"You okay?"

She gives me a tiny nod and a fleeting half-smile. "Yeah."

"You know I'll be here for you this weekend, right?" I smooth a hand over her hair, tucking it behind her ear. In the process, I expose a tiny patch that's missing at the top of her head and make a mental note to ask her about it later. "We can fight your sister together."

Her expression softens as she looks up at me. "Thanks, Beck," she says quietly.

We sit there in comfortable silence for a few more minutes, just holding each other, our breathing in sync. Her body relaxes into mine, and I can sense the tension slowly leaving her. I run my fingers through her hair, tracing soothing circles on her back with my other hand.

After a while, I stand up and offer my hand. "Come on," I say, gently tugging her toward me. "Let's do something to occupy your mind."

She joins me, and we spend the rest of the evening together, watching movies and cooking dinner. It's not the grandest of gestures, but it's enough to remind her that she's not alone, that I'm here for her in more than just a physical way.

As the night grows late, I walk her to her bedroom, tucking her in with a gentle kiss to her forehead. She tightens her grip on my hand as I move to leave, and her eyes search mine, silently pleading with me to stay.

Without hesitation, I nod and shed my clothes, climbing into bed beside her. She snuggles into my chest, her warm breath tickling my skin, and I wrap my arms around her, holding her close.

We lie there in the darkness, the only sound the soft hum of the air-conditioning and her bedside diffuser. My fingers trace lazy patterns across her back as she slowly drifts off to sleep. It feels good to be here for her, to protect her from the demons that plague her mind.

I press a soft kiss to her temple and whisper, "Sleep well, pretty girl. I'll still be here in the morning."

She nuzzles into my neck, her body heat radiating into me, and I feel her breaths slow and deepen as she drifts off to sleep.

I lie there for a while, listening to the quiet sounds around us, enjoying the way her body presses against mine. It's moments like these that make me feel like I may be able to break through her impenetrable walls. That it's worth it to put my time and effort into something that's uncertain, that's hard, that's risky.

I want this girl. I want her in all the ways that matter. I want to be the one she turns to when she's feeling down, the one she laughs with, the one she dreams with. The one she trusts with every tiny secret and insecurity.

I close my eyes, my own body relaxing as I let myself get lost in the rhythm of her breathing. But even in this moment of quiet peace, it's difficult not to think about the challenges that lay ahead for us. Of the upcoming visit from her sister and the anxiety it's already causing her.

I know I'll have to be there for her in a different way, not just as a comfort but as a shield from whatever mayhem might arise. But I'm ready for it. I'm ready to show her that I'm not just a guy who's in this for a good time—for the sex, for the novelty, for the fun of it all—but someone who's in it for the long haul.

Eventually, I drift off to sleep, my fingers curled tightly around her hip, indulging in the sweet lavender scent that's starting to feel a lot like coming home.

# Chapter Twenty-Seven

KAIA

THIS PAST WEEK has flown by, a whirlwind of endless nights and lazy mornings that all blend together into one.

Holden's become a regular presence in my life, coming over every evening to spend our nights talking, occasionally bickering, and studying for hours. We've reached a level of comfort where silence is louder than words.

Most nights, we explore each other's bodies until we're completely sated, but it's not always about sex. Sometimes we just lie there, enjoying the warmth and the closeness. It's like we're discovering each other in a new way, exploring every nook and cranny, every inch of each other's skin.

It's intimate and sweet and exactly what I need right now.

As I walk Holden to the door again this morning, my heart swells with happiness. It's funny how just a week ago, I was convinced that I didn't want a relationship, that I was content with simply hooking up behind closed doors.

But now, being with him feels like the most natural thing in the world. He's become my safe haven, my lighthouse in the storm.

After kissing him goodbye, I barely make it two steps back down the hall when Lizzie appears in her doorway, arms crossed tightly over her chest. It startles me, rattles me a little, because I didn't even realize she was home.

"Kaia, we need to talk," she says, her tone cold.

I give her an odd look, raising a brow. "Okay?"

"Look, I understand that you want to spend time with Holden. Who wouldn't, right?" She gives me an overtly fake laugh, one that grates on my patience. "But he's been staying over every night, and that's not fair to me. He's practically living here rent-free."

I reel back at the accusation. "He isn't living here, Liz. He's just staying the night. And it's not like he's causing any problems."

She shakes her head, lips pressed together in a flat line. "He's using our utilities, taking up space in our apartment, and I never agreed to have a third roommate. I think it's only fair that you start paying extra rent to cover the costs."

My irritation rises, but I force myself to stay calm. "He isn't using that much of our resources. He doesn't even shower here. I don't see how me paying extra rent is justified."

She sighs, twirling a strand of hair between her fingers. "This is our home, and I have a right to feel comfortable here. I didn't sign up to share this space with the guy you're fucking. I don't think it's unreasonable to ask for some compensation."

I grit my teeth and take a deep breath, attempting to push down the anger that threatens to bubble up. "It's been a *week*, Liz. And you're acting like he's some sort of freeloader. He's not even here during the day, and he doesn't interfere with your life whatsoever. So why should I pay more?"

"Because it's the principle of the matter," she says, her voice raising slightly. "If you don't start paying extra rent, then I don't see any reason why I should continue to pay the same amount as you. It's just not fair."

I let out a frustrated groan. "You're blowing this way out of proportion. It's not like he's moving in permanently or anything. And you're barely ever home as it is. I didn't even realize you knew he was coming around."

"That's not the point." She narrows her eyes at me. "The fact remains that he's here almost every night, and I'm not okay with that. I don't think it's too much to ask you to contribute a little more to cover the costs. *Holden Becker* can afford it, I'm sure."

I stare at her, trying to come up with a solution that will satisfy both of us. After a moment, I let out a defeated sigh, unable to keep the sarcasm from my tone. "Fine, you want me to ask him to make the check out to you directly?"

A wry smile forms on her lips, and a scoff escapes her as she says, "I just want things to be fair for both of us."

"You know," I say, ticking each finger off as I list her expenses. "I've paid for your groceries, your Ubers, our cleaning service, your drinks when we've been out before. And I don't understand where this is coming from. Are *you* paying portions of the rent when you stay over at a guy's house?"

"No, because I'm not just at *one* guy's house."

"Liz . . ."

"What?" she spits out, her posture defensive now. "You gonna judge me for that, too?"

I throw my hands up in exasperation. "You know what, let's just forget it. I'll stay over at Holden's place from now on."

"Whatever."

"Yeah, whatever," I parrot back.

Sure, Lizzie and I have had our differences in the past, but I was hopeful that we were making progress toward a better relationship. I guess things haven't changed as much as I thought. I understand that we may not be BFFs, but I still value our living arrangement.

I find comfort in having my own space, with my own sleep

aids and well-established routine. But I'm willing to make an exception and spend the night at Holden's place instead, especially if it means avoiding any future conflicts. I'd rather not fight over useless shit like this.

It spikes the anxiety, the compulsions, that I'm already struggling to keep at bay.

LATER THAT NIGHT, as Holden and I head inside a local diner —an old Boyer haunt—my heart is pounding. I'm jittery, my foot tapping up and down, stomach full of knots. I've been so distracted by my nerves that the two of us barely spoke a word to each other during the entire drive here.

I'm anxious about this dinner, about seeing Sofia again and introducing her to Holden. She's always been so critical of my choices and my life, and I don't want her to judge him too harshly.

We slide into a booth side by side, waiting for them to arrive. I lean against Holden's bicep and breathe deeply, but my legs are still shaking. He places a comforting hand over my knee.

"Hey," he whispers in my ear, his voice low.

"Hey," I breathe back.

"What's going on in that head of yours?"

"Don't want to talk about it," I murmur, immediately changing the subject. "But . . . there is something else I need to talk to you about."

"Go on."

"I spoke to Lizzie this morning. Since you've been staying the night, she wants you to pay a portion of our rent."

He leans back in the booth, slinging a casual arm over my shoulder. "Huh."

"Isn't that fucking ridiculous?" I lean my head against his arm. "I told her I'd just stay over at your house instead."

"Well, how much is your rent?"

I cock my head to the side, giving him a quizzical look. "Eighteen hundred bucks a month, why?"

"I could just pay the whole thing. Get her off your back."

"Stop."

He shoots me a mischievous smile. "I'd love to be your sugar daddy, Karras."

"Oh, gross," I groan, unable to suppress a full-body shudder.

Just then, our guests of honor stroll inside. Sofia's dressed in an expensive outfit, her dark waves styled to perfection, and Andrew's there beside her in a tailored suit. They both look out of place in this small, homestyle diner, but they don't seem to notice or care about it.

They make their way over to us, fake smiles plastered on both their faces. "Hey, you two," Sofia greets us, her voice sickly sweet.

"Hey," I say, trying to keep my tone light. Carefree. I need to approach this with an open mind, after all. To make an effort toward reconciliation.

Andrew slides into the booth across from us without so much as a word, his eyes scanning the menu. "So, what's good here?" he asks, tone dismissive.

Holden and I share an incredulous look, and I almost let out a full-bodied laugh. Somehow, I manage to restrain myself, and we roll ahead with our introductions. After placing our orders, Sofia turns her attention to Holden.

"So, Kaia tells me you're a hockey player," she says.

Holden flashes his signature smile, a grin that could light up the entire room. "That's right."

She cocks her head, feigning innocent curiosity. "So what is it that your parents do?"

"My father's a partner at Becker and Slate."

Andrew snorts. "Ah, so a real job, then?" he mutters under his breath.

Holden bristles at the comment. "Hockey's a real job, and I fucking love it."

Sofia raises a skeptical brow. "But don't you think you could be doing something more stable? Something more . . . practical, like working at your father's firm?"

"I'm doing what makes me happy," Holden says. "Isn't that what's most important?"

"But what happens when you get injured?" Andrew chimes in. "You'll be out of a job with nothing to fall back on."

"I have a backup plan," Holden says coolly, narrowing his eyes. "Kaia and I share the same major, actually. And I've been looking into the possibility of biomedical research. I could use my degree to help people in a different way than my dad does."

Sofia looks impressed. "That sounds like a solid plan."

"Sounds like a pipe dream to me," Andrew says dismissively. "I mean, what's the likelihood of that actually happening?"

"I have faith in myself and my abilities," Holden says firmly, working to keep his jaw from clenching.

"Still seems like a lot of uncertainty." Andrew scoffs, his tone petulant. "At least I know where my future's headed. My father has connections at Piper and Ellis, you know?"

Holden rolls his eyes. "Good for you. I don't see how your father's connections are relevant to this conversation."

"At least I'm not wasting the privilege I've been given," Andrew snaps.

Oh, Jesus Christ, I can't take this anymore. "Can we please change the subject?" I say, my voice sharp.

Sofia tilts her perfect little head. "Why? Is our discussion bothering you, Kai?"

"Yes," I snap. "It's bothering both of us. Holden's hockey career is important to him, and it's not something to be made fun of."

Holden squeezes my hand under the table, a small smile playing at the corners of his lips. "That's my girl," he says, voice low, an endearment meant just for me.

Sofia and Andrew exchange an irritated look, but thankfully, they drop the subject before my sister can resort to her favorite insult. It's good for everyone involved because her calling me a brat again certainly would've thrown me over the edge.

The rest of the dinner is awkward, with Andrew mostly talking about himself and his upcoming career prospects. But Holden doesn't let it get to him. He knows that he's on the right path for himself, even if it's not the most traditional.

Instead of engaging further, he sneaks his hand under the table to rub my knee. His fingers slowly work their way higher and higher, brushing my dress to the side as they dance toward my inner thigh.

I gasp, poorly attempting to disguise it with a cough, and nudge him with my elbow. But as he continues to rub circles against me there, my breathing turns shallow. I work hard to tune out the two assholes across from me, focusing instead on the sensation of Holden's hands on my skin.

His fingers reach the fabric of my panties, and he pauses when I involuntarily clamp my legs together. I glance over, making eye contact, and give him the tiniest nod of encouragement.

If my sister and her boyfriend can't show us their basic respect, then they certainly haven't earned ours in return.

With my consent, he moves full steam ahead, sliding his fingers up and into my panties. I'm soaking wet for him like I always am. And the smirk on his lips, the sparkle of mischief in his eyes, has my pussy clenching around nothing.

I'm at a public diner—sitting across the booth from my nearly estranged sister—and I want Holden's fingers to fill me up. But instead, he works his thumb over my clit, pressing and rolling it between the rough pads of his fingertips.

It feels so good, so fucking dirty, that I can't stay quiet for much longer. I need him too badly. All of him.

"Sorry," I finally speak up. "We're gonna have to cut this night short. Holden has a big game in the morning, but it was *so* nice chatting with you two."

I awkwardly shift in my seat, sliding my dress back into place before I bolt up from our table. It's difficult, but I manage to ignore Sofia's protests while we slip away.

The cool night air wraps around us as we burst out of the diner, our laughter finally spilling free. We hop over the passenger side doors of Holden's convertible, like two criminals on the run, and the engine quickly roars to life. I feel giddy, ridiculous even, as we speed out of the parking lot and onto the open roads of Boyer.

And while we're driving back to his place—the wind whipping through my hair, his hand up my dress again—I realize that I feel more alive, more awake, than I have in years.

# Chapter Twenty-Eight

HOLDEN

I'M STRUGGLING to wake up, contemplating my will to crawl out of bed and fulfill my captainly duties, as my thoughts drift back to this past weekend. I've been replaying the moments in my head, savoring the memories like a favorite meal.

The highlight of them all, though, was when Kaia stood up for me in front of her sister. It's a moment I didn't expect, and it's left me with an overwhelming sense of pride. I assumed I'd be the one shielding her on Friday night, but for a moment, she became my protector.

I know it wasn't easy for her, but she did it anyway, and that speaks volumes about the relationship we're building. While things are still new between us, this was the reciprocity I'd been hoping for all along.

Until now, I've been the one pushing for her to give me a chance, providing comfort and security when she needs it. But this time, she was the one who stepped up, who guarded me against the judgment and criticism threatening to weigh me down.

And then, I got to be the guy she laughed with afterward—the guy she stayed in bed with late into the next morning—until I inevitably had to drag myself back to the rink.

It's not just about this one moment, though. In general, there's a level of connection between us that I never thought I'd find, especially not during my college hockey career. And it's one I'm learning to cherish more every day.

I'm struck by how lucky I am to have found her.

She's strong, intelligent, and fiercely loyal. She has this carefully concealed inner light—secret sunlight for a soul—and she's not afraid to stand up for what she believes in. Despite our differences, I couldn't have asked for someone better suited for me.

With a contented sigh, I roll over and grab my phone, scrolling through my emails as I shake away the grogginess. I'm expecting to see a reminder for our meeting with Dr. Khatri this week, but instead, I come across something unexpected. An email from her, addressed to both me and Kaia.

I sit up in bed and open it, still half asleep but curious.

***From:*** *maya.khatri@coastal.edu*
***To:*** *holden.becker@coastal.edu*
***Subject:*** *DU Symposium*
*Good morning,*
*I hope this email finds you both well. In lieu of our scheduled dissertation meeting this week, I would like to extend an invitation for you both to attend a biomedical research symposium at Dayton University this weekend, beginning Saturday evening and running into the following afternoon. I believe it will be a valuable opportunity for you both to learn about the latest advancements in your field and network with other professionals.*
*Please let me know if you're able to attend, and I will send over the necessary information.*
*Best regards,*
*Maya Khatri, Ph.D.*

Well, shit. Dayton U is nearly a two-hour drive from here, and I have a game on Saturday afternoon. It should end early enough for us to drive up afterward, but I'll be cutting things close either way. Still, I want to make a good impression on our advisor.

At this point, she's the judge, jury, and executioner of our future here at Coastal. The person who decides if we've earned the right to graduate or not. And the fact that she's inviting us both to tag along with her is a huge honor.

I shoot off a quick text to Kaia, and she immediately confirms her interest in attending. So, that means I'm gonna make it happen one way or another.

As I text her back, telling her that we're on for this weekend, there's a twinge of disappointment that she's not here with me right now. She left halfway through the night last night, restless and unsettled, and I don't blame her. Sleep's always been hard for her to come by, and she was just getting used to me invading her routine at home in her own familiar environment.

I wish I could've gone back to her apartment with her, but I didn't want to cause any more drama between her and Liz. Although, I was halfway serious in my offer to pay their rent. I wouldn't mind spending my trust fund on the girl who's steadily consuming my every thought.

My girl. The same girl whose pussy I'm eating on a near-daily basis.

Speaking of which, I can still smell her lingering scent on my pillow. The sweet smell of her bodywash and the faint hint of essential oil that always clings to her skin. It's intoxicating.

A familiar heat rises in my body, and fuck, I'm hard again just thinking about her.

I picture her lying next to me, her head resting on my chest, my fingers dancing across the lines of her collarbone. By now, I've fully memorized the feel of her skin, soft and warm, and the way she always nuzzles her face into the crook of my neck.

My hand drifts down to the growing bulge in my boxers, and I close my eyes, relishing the sensation of my fingers tracing the outline of my cock. It's only been a few hours since she left, and I can still taste her on my lips, the way her tongue twines with mine as she arches into me.

Goddammit.

I can't obsess over being inside of Kaia right now. I have practice in a few minutes, and I still need to wake up the fucking sideline squad down the hall. So I force myself to pull my hand away, trying to ignore the throbbing ache in my groin.

Trust me, it's not easy.

This girl's always had a way of getting under my skin, of making me want all the things I shouldn't—of making me want *everything*—as long as it's with her.

SATURDAY, post-game and adrenaline still pumping, I swing by Kaia's place to pick her up. As she steps out of her apartment building, I can't resist admiring how stunning she is. Her hair's styled in loose waves that frame her face perfectly, and she's wearing a simple dress that hugs her curves in all my favorite places.

She's the epitome of perfection, and she's all mine.

We make our way to my car, and I open the door for her like the fucking gentleman I am. I watch as she slides into the passenger seat, the skirt of her dress riding up a little. I gulp in a breath to center myself before closing the door and hustling over to the driver's side.

Our ride there is filled with easy conversation and cozy

silences, and before I know it, we're pulling up to the hotel I booked for us. We have just enough time to set down our bags, grab a drink of water, and check our hair in the mirror before heading over to the Dayton Institute of Medicine.

As we make the short drive over, my nerves edge their way to the surface. I'm not usually one to stress over shit like this, but I want to make a good impression this weekend. Not just for myself but for Kaia, too.

I turn to her in the parking lot before we head in, placing a firm hand on her shaking knee.

"Before we go inside," I say, giving her a quick little squeeze, "I have something I need to say to you."

She gives me a tight smile, cocking her to the side. "You're freaking me out here, Beck."

"No need to spiral." I give her a reassuring smile. "I just want you to know that this isn't a competition for me."

"What?"

"This. Tonight. This whole weekend." I tap my thumb against her inner thigh, swirling it in small little circles. "Despite whatever thoughts are brewing in that beautiful brain of yours, none of this is a competition between us. Sure, I'd like to make a good impression on our advisor, but that's never going to come at your expense. You got that?"

"Got it." She swallows, thick and heavy, before her expression turns rueful. "So, you're saying you don't want me to throw you to the wolves in front of our professor and all her colleagues?"

The corner of my mouth quirks. "If you think you could manage it, that would be swell."

"Don't worry, Beck." She smooths out the nonexistent wrinkles in her dress. "I don't need to tear you down to build myself up."

"Because you think I'll fumble on my own?"

"No, I know you won't." Her voice dips, a disingenuous sweetness to her tone. "We can both shine this weekend. But I also won't apologize if I naturally shine brighter."

"So happy you're willing to share the stage with me, Karras."

"Anything for you, Becker."

I shake my head, amused, as I hop out of the car. When I open up the passenger-side door and offer my hand to her, she quickly declines, reminding me to be professional in front of our advisor.

She's right, anyway. We probably shouldn't be caught kissing in front of Dr. Khatri, especially not during a networking event.

Instead, we walk side by side, a safe distance apart from one another as we head to the entrance of the DIM building. It doesn't take long for us to spot our advisor, and she greets us with a welcoming smile.

"I'm so glad you could both make it," Dr. Khatri says warmly, ushering us both inside.

Amidst the sterile halls, the air crackles with anticipation. Researchers, entrepreneurs, and fellow students flock inside, eager to exchange ideas and make connections. In the lobby, the three of us search for our name tags and quickly secure them into place.

Thankfully, there isn't too much going on tonight outside of this. It's meant to be a mixer and networking event, while the real breakout sessions and keynote speakers take place tomorrow.

As we roam around the room, Dr. Khatri first introduces us to a fellow professor, Dr. Thiel, who's working on neuro stim research for veterans with PTSD. It's right up our alley, meshing with both Kaia's and my dissertation topics, and we're both hooked on the work he's doing.

We're quickly engrossed in the conversation, and I sense Kaia's excitement bubbling over. She's always been so passionate about academia, research, and the field of biomedicine as a whole; it's great to see her connect with someone who shares that same mindset.

The night goes on, and we're introduced to a handful of other researchers and academics—true visionaries who are changing the world through their work. Kaia is a star—of course she is—engaging effortlessly in conversation and exuding confidence.

It's sexy as hell, and I'm brimming with pride as I watch her shine. She was right, after all. The girl's a real fucking natural.

Eventually, the event winds down, and we reconvene with Dr. Khatri. The three of us make a plan for tomorrow's sessions before Kaia and I head to the hotel together.

Once we're tucked back into our room, the weariness in Kaia's eyes is visible, but it's mixed with a fire that I know all too well.

"So, you can probably tell that I loved that," she says, kicking off her shoes and collapsing onto the bed.

I join her there, wrapping my arm around her as she snuggles into my side. "Yeah, and I'm so proud of you, baby. You were incredible tonight."

She smiles, a faint blush coloring her cheeks. "Thanks, Beck. You did good, too."

"Ah, another compliment from Kaia."

"Hey, I compliment you sometimes."

"Sure you do," I tease, curling my finger underneath the strap of her dress. "With a thinly veiled insult thrown in for good measure."

"You can take it."

"That I can," I murmur, tracing a tiny star-shaped pattern against her bare shoulder.

"Hey, Beck . . . this isn't weird, right?"

"*This*, what?" I ask, brows knitted in confusion.

"Us, here, going to research symposiums together." Avoiding my gaze, she rolls onto her back beside me and stares up at the ceiling. "Sharing a hotel room. Complimenting each other and genuinely meaning it."

I chuckle softly. "I sure fucking hope not, considering the fact that you're my girlfriend and all."

Her eyes widen, and she visibly stiffens. "Your . . ."

"Girlfriend." My lip lifts in amusement. "Right, you can say the word."

"I-I didn't realize I was your girlfriend."

"We're dating exclusively, sleeping together nearly every night, yet for some reason, you didn't think you were my girlfriend?"

"Well, you never actually asked!"

"Karras, come on." I give her a sideways glance, stunned by her denial. "I didn't think I needed to."

She abruptly sits up on the bed, crossing her arms over her chest with an exasperated huff. "If you want me to be your girlfriend, then you have to ask me properly."

"Okay." My lip curls up into a smirk. She's trying so hard to be serious right now, but the way she crosses her arms over her chest and purses her lips just makes her look even more adorable. A hint of a smile tugs at the corners of her mouth, and it only serves to make me grin wider. "Kaia, *baby*, will you please be my girlfriend?"

"No," she says simply, settling back onto the bed.

My brows shoot up. "Excuse me?"

"Ask me again later." She tilts her chin, glancing away from me in a shoddy attempt to hide her smile. "Ask me again when it's not an afterthought."

"Impossible. Fucking. Girl."

I shift my body, hovering over her as I secure her wrists above her head. Then, I tickle her sides until she's giggling uncontrollably, her cheeks flushing with heat. She flails her legs, attempting to kick me in the nuts, but I threaten to stick my tongue in her ear if she doesn't stop.

Her laughter quickly devolves into a high-pitched series of shrieks, and they may be shrill and piercing, but damn do I love the sound of them anyway.

Honestly, I'm just happy she can finally let her guard down like this. And even happier that I get to be the one to make her feel this way—joyful, carefree, and fully fucking alive.

# Chapter Twenty-Nine

KAIA

THE NEXT MORNING, Holden and I lazily crawl out of bed, our limbs tangled together beneath the sheets. We spend some time under the hot spray of the shower, finding new ways to tease each other until we're both satisfied.

And as we finish getting ready, I'm all sorts of happy inside —enveloped in my little cocoon—warm and content with the golden boy beside me. I've grown attached to these little moments with him. The pockets of time where we can be completely ourselves, free from the confines of our daily lives.

Once we're dressed, we head out to the car and drive back to Dayton. We make small talk along the way, but our minds are preoccupied. My nerves bubble up to the surface as we get closer to the symposium, and I'm fully fidgeting in my seat by the time we arrive.

Holden's hand finds mine, giving it a gentle squeeze, and a sense of calm washes over me. Despite being in my element here, surrounded by peers and researchers who share my same interests, that familiar anxiety gnaws at me. I'm overwhelmed by the prospect of attending sessions, making connections, and impressing our advisor all at the same time.

"You good, Karras?" Holden asks, his voice low and laced with concern.

"Yeah, I'm good." I nod, attempting a smile. "Just a little nervous, I guess."

He offers me another comforting squeeze. "You're gonna do great," he says. "Remember, there's no pressure today. This is just a chance to network, to see how things will go for us come spring term. When we're ready for it."

He brushes the side of his hand against mine as we walk, bumping our hips together, and the physical touch serves as a welcome distraction, grounding me.

After a few minutes of searching, we meet up with Dr. Khatri, and she informs us of her plan. We've been advised to select separate sessions so that we can all regroup and debrief at the end of the day.

Once we make it inside, I'm struck by the sheer size of the place. People of all ages and backgrounds, each with a sense of purpose, fill every nook and cranny. I didn't notice it last night, but this building is both huge and immaculate.

The main floor's a bit sterile—cold and impersonal. But upstairs, there are these large glass walls on either side that let in all the natural light. It's modern, sleek, and open. The most striking feature, though, are the blown glass pieces suspended from the high ceilings.

It's beautiful up here, ornate, a space you could truly get lost in.

Dayton's a top-notch research university and extremely well-funded, so it makes sense that their facilities are state-of-the-art. I'd venture to say that it's even nicer than what Coastal has to offer.

After we're done admiring the architecture, Holden and I officially part ways. Per Dr. Khatri's recommendation, we've chosen different sessions to attend throughout the day, with a midday catch-up during lunch.

As I settle into my first one, I'm instantly intimidated. The speaker shares groundbreaking discoveries in telesurgery, where doctors have the ability to control robots from remote facilities. As I listen along, jotting down a few notes, I'm in awe of their wealth of knowledge.

It's fascinating, but it's also daunting as hell.

After the session ends, I gravitate toward a group of undergrads, eavesdropping as they discuss their grad school plans. They all appear to be fourth-year students here at Dayton, and they've mentioned applying to at least a dozen different schools each.

By the sounds of it, they're all determined to cast a wide net.

At this point, I've mostly committed myself to Coastal's program. I don't want to put all my eggs into one basket, per se, but it's always been my top choice. I've never wanted to live too far away from Boyer, and there are only a handful of other schools where I could picture myself attending.

The thought of being denied entrance, though, is terrifying. I don't even know how to conceptualize my life elsewhere. Not only would I have to get used to someplace new, but I'd also have to endure all the stresses of starting grad school along with it.

As I exit the room, my original confidence wavers, and I'm left questioning things. Attempting to ignore it, I head to the next session, a talk about transdermal patches that sparks my interest.

But despite my best efforts, thoughts of inadequacy linger in my mind.

During the lunch recess, when I reunite with Holden, he instantly notices something's wrong. He takes my hand, guiding me to a quiet corner away from the bustling crowds.

"Hey," he says gently, "What's going on?"

I inhale a deep breath, attempting to articulate my feelings without sounding completely unhinged. "I don't really know," I admit, my voice quivering. "I think that being here has just made me feel very underprepared."

He wraps an arm around me, and I lean into his comforting embrace. "Hey," he says, tipping my chin. "You're gonna do great things, baby. And besides, we're all just here to learn and grow. There's no need to compare ourselves to anyone else."

"Yeah, I guess you're right," I mumble against his chest.

He pulls back, takes my hand again, and says, "Come on, let's go get some lunch and regroup."

We make our way to the buffet table to grab some food, and finally, I unwind. Holden listens intently as I ramble on about my applications, offering support and encouragement where he can. I allow myself to relax in his presence for a moment, feeling a little more like myself already by the time we finish lunch.

The rest of the symposium is a blur of lectures and presentations, and with my nerves at bay, I can fully focus on the content. I take copious notes, determined to absorb as much information as possible.

During my last session of the day, I find myself sitting beside the same group of undergrads from earlier. They're discussing their application process, and I try to tune them out at first, but their conversation's too interesting to ignore.

"Have you guys applied to Coastal yet?" one of them asks, and my ears perk up.

"Yeah, I submitted for early decision last week," another says, sounding confident. "I'd been working on my personal statement for months, and I had solid recs from our department heads."

"Same here," a third student chimes in. "I studied for the GRE for months, and now I'm just waiting on scores. I feel like I've done everything I can to prepare."

The first student shakes their head. "I still need to retake the GRE. I'm really fucking nervous about it."

"Don't be," the second student reassures them. "Just give yourself plenty of time to study and take a few more practice exams. You'll do fine."

As I listen in, a knot forms in my stomach. I've been so consumed with my dissertation—and my newfound relationship with Holden—that I haven't dedicated as much time to this as I should have.

And now, I feel so fucking far behind.

"Yeah, I've got a spreadsheet going of every school in the states," the first student continues. "Their deadlines, what materials I need to submit for each one. I've been researching the directors of each program and tailoring my application and essays to fit them."

Oh God. My heart fully plummets into my stomach. I haven't started a spreadsheet, let alone tailored my applications to each individual school board.

Their conversation ends, and my self-assurance slips away with it. I thought I had everything under control, but hearing them talk about how much work they've done and how prepared they are makes me feel like a complete failure.

As I make my way back to the main area, I'm on the verge of a thought spiral. How am I going to compete with students who have spent months preparing, specially tailoring their applications, and have already submitted for early decision?

There's still a fucking month left until the deadline, and I've barely worked up the courage to ask Dr. Khatri for a letter.

At this rate, how can I even hope to compete?

No matter what I do, I can't shake off this feeling of inadequacy, of being so far behind. The rest of the symposium flies by, but I can't concentrate on anything. All I can think about is how underprepared I am for the next step in my academic journey.

And by the time I've conferred back with Holden and our advisor, I'm ready and waiting to get the hell out of this place. I need to spiral and panic alone, at home, in the comfort of my own bedroom.

I'M quiet on the drive home, all two hours spent in silence with Holden attempting to break through my shell.

I'll talk to him about it eventually, I swear, but I need a little more time to get my head together first. I'm afraid I'll lash out if he asks me even one wrong question, and I don't want to do that to him.

I can only hope he's willing to grant me the time and space to calm myself down, to work out how I'm feeling, and to come to him when I'm ready.

He pulls into a spot in front of my apartment and cuts the engine, running a hand through his hair before he turns to me. "Want me to come up?" he asks.

"I think I just need to spend some time by myself tonight. If I can just, like, make a couple of spreadsheets and a detailed timeline, then I'll feel a little bit better."

"You don't want to talk anything out?" he offers, his dark gaze locked on mine. "I could help you prep."

"For things like this, I work better alone. But thank you."

He leans over the center console for a kiss, but I can't bring myself to return it. I duck my chin at the last second, unwilling to drag him into my headspace right now. I can see the hurt in his eyes, but I don't know what else to say.

It's not his fault; it's mine. It's hard enough to let him in on a regular day, but when I'm feeling like this, it seems impossible.

"I get it," he says softly, leaning back into his seat. "Just . . . text me later if you need anything, okay?"

I nod, my throat tight with emotion. "Okay. I will."

He gives me a small smile before reaching over to squeeze my shoulder. "Take care of yourself, Karras."

I grab my bag and get out of the car, trying to push down the guilt in my chest. As I walk up the stairs to my apartment, I pause at the threshold, trying to steady myself. I know I need to focus on my future, on making sure I'm on the right track and doing everything I can to achieve my goals.

Once inside, I head straight to my desk, pull out my laptop, and dive into my work. I need to keep my hands busy, to focus on something other than the mess that's going on inside my head. But as I write, my thoughts keep drifting back to Holden.

I can't ignore the way my heart aches at the thought of pulling back from him, even just the tiniest bit, but I know it's probably what's best. At least for right now. We can still be together, but I can spend less time focused on him—on us—at least until the application cycle ends.

I work into the night, my mind and my body running on adrenaline. I'm pushing myself to the limit, trying to do everything in my power to get ahead. But the more I work, the more I feel like I'm falling behind. The more I try to push my thoughts away, the louder they become.

As I finally lie down in bed, exhausted and drained but unable to sleep, I feel like I'm in a worse place than when I started. My thoughts are a jumbled mess, and I can't seem to get them in order. I close my eyes, trying to push everything to the back of my mind, but it's no use.

The worries and doubts that I've been quelling come crashing in, and I'm stuck in the same old spiral, uncertain of how to stay afloat.

# Chapter Thirty

## HOLDEN

The air between Kaia and me is heavy, laden with an unspoken tension that's been building since we came back from the symposium. It's been three days already, and I feel like there's something more behind her distance than just jitters about graduate school.

All last week, our nights were spent curled together in bed. But since then, we've barely talked, let alone seen each other outside of classes. It's as if she's purposefully avoiding me now, pushing me away, and I can't understand the reason.

I've made multiple attempts to coax her into sharing her thoughts, to confide in me about whatever else is troubling her, but she's unyielding. She either shuts down completely or dismisses my concerns as if they're no big deal.

I'm not used to feeling this way—anxious, unsettled, confused about where we stand. I usually take things as they come and go with the flow, but now I'm in full-on worry mode.

Did I do something wrong? Is she grappling with an issue that I'm not aware of? Or is this really just a minor setback for her—for us?

I'm wary of prying or pushing her too much, but maintaining the façade that everything's fine is growing increasingly difficult.

It's only been a few days, and I miss her—the feeling of her body pressed against me, the taste of her lips, the sound of her sweet, hard-earned laughter. I miss the way her hazel eyes spark when she's excited about something, the way she scrunches her nose when she's deep in thought, and the warmth of her hand as it fits perfectly into mine.

I miss the conversations we've shared late into the night, discussing everything from our dreams and aspirations to the trivial, everyday moments that make up our lives.

I miss the way she challenges me, pushing me back when I piss her off.

The more time we spend apart, the more I realize how integral Kaia's become to my daily life. But it feels like she's suddenly slipping through my fingers, and I don't know how to hold on to her right now.

I try to focus on other things, like hockey and my classes, but she's always at the back of my mind. I catch myself daydreaming about the future we could share together, and then I remember how distant she's been, and it feels like a punch to the gut.

I already can't bear the thought of losing her, but fixing what's broken seems impossible if she refuses to communicate. All I can do is continue to practice patience and cling to the hope that, eventually, she'll let me all the way in.

Fully and without question.

WITH KAIA ON MY MIND, it's difficult to fully immerse myself in anything else. But life keeps moving, and so do I. The hockey season's in full swing, and I'm doing my best to stay focused on our practices, trying not to let my worries affect my performance on the ice.

My roommates and I are keeping our spirits up as the holiday season approaches. Will's going home for Thanksgiving, but Rai, Bodie, and I have decided to stay on campus. We're making the most of it by hosting our own Friendsgiving at the house.

We've invited a few of our other teammates who couldn't make it back home, and I've extended an invitation to Kaia. I know she won't be seeing her family this year, so I thought it would be the perfect opportunity for her to take a break from her work and join us.

But, as expected, she declined the invitation, explaining that she plans to use the two days off school to finish her assignments and focus in on her applications. I'm disappointed, but I understand her need to prioritize her work.

By the time Thursday rolls around, the house is bustling with activity. With Will already gone, Rai, Bodie, and I divide up the cooking duties and get to work. Rai Rai's in charge of the turkey, Bodie takes on the sides, and I'm tasked with making the desserts.

The kitchen is a whirlwind of chopping, mixing, and laughter as we each work on our respective dishes.

As the hours pass, our feast officially comes together. The mouthwatering smell of turkey roasting in the oven fills the air while various pots and pans bubble away on the stovetop. I'm busy whipping up a pumpkin pie—Mom's old recipe—and a batch of chocolate chip cookies, the sweet scents mingling with the savory ones.

Finally, our teammates arrive, each one bringing a dish or a case of beer to contribute. I keep glancing at my phone, half expecting Kaia to change her mind and text me that she's on her way. But my phone remains silent, and I do my best to shake off my disappointment and focus on the friends who've already shown up.

As the day wears on, we all gather around our makeshift

dining table, which is really just a couple of beer pong centerfolds pushed together and covered with a festive tablecloth. We all raise a toast to friendship and good food before diving into the meal.

As we sit around the table, enjoying the fruits of our labor, Rai launches into some goofy story about a family vacation.

"Okay, so you guys won't believe what happened on our trip to Disney a couple of years ago," he begins, his eyes sparkling with mischief. I already know where this story is going, and it's not exactly mealtime appropriate, but I'm content to let the man do his thing.

"My parents, my little sister Maya, and I were all super excited. But on our very first day there, my dad insists that we have to try every single ride, no matter how long the lines are. He's determined to get his money's worth, you know? And of course, my little sister's all on board with that idea. She's a total adrenaline junkie, even at ten years old."

Rai pauses for dramatic effect before carrying on. "Now, my mom gets motion sickness pretty easily, so she's a bit reluctant. But my dad and Maya somehow manage to convince her. And that's when things start to go downhill."

We chuckle, anticipating what's coming next.

"First, we get stuck on It's a Small World for nearly an hour," he says, shaking his head. "You know that song? It just keeps playing over and over and over. By the time we finally get off the ride, we're all ready to lose our minds."

He goes on, mimicking the repetitive tune, and the guys burst into laughter.

"But that's not even the worst part," he continues, grinning. "Later that day, we decide to tackle Space Mountain, and my mom's already looking a bit green around the gills. We try to convince her to sit this one out, but she insists on going with us. Big mistake."

The rest of the guys lean in closer, captivated by his story. I know what's coming next, and I'm tempted to tell him to save it for after dinner, but I don't want to interrupt his flow.

"We're all strapped into our seats, hurtling through space at breakneck speeds, and then it happens. My mom starts throwing up—and I mean, like, projectile vomiting—right in the middle of the ride."

The guys erupt into laughter as Rai gesticulates wildly, illustrating the chaos of the situation. "My poor dad ends up with puke all over his Mickey Mouse ears, and Maya's screaming her head off. And me? I'm just trying not to add to the mess by laughing too hard."

As Rai finishes his story, everyone's in stitches, but I'm still disturbed by him bringing up puke in the midst of our meal. Bodie reaches over to swat Rai in the back of the head. And as Rai sputters forward, choking on his turkey leg, I officially join in on the laughter.

It feels really good to let loose like this—carefree, warm, and content with all my friends—but I can't help but wish that Kaia was here to join in on the fun.

I know she has her reasons for staying home, but I'm still worried about the ever-growing distance between us. And as I help Rai and Bodie clean up the remnants of our feast, I make another silent promise to myself: I'll find a way to bridge this gap, this rift that keeps widening, no matter what.

I ROLL out of bed the next morning, still full and content from the day before. But now it's game day, and there's a familiar mix of nerves and excitement welling up inside me. Unfortunately, there's something else brewing beneath the surface, too.

My dad's flying in for tonight's game, and it's difficult not to feel a bit on edge.

Our relationship has always been complicated, to put it mildly. And I'm sick of my stomach dropping whenever his name lights up my phone. We haven't even so much as spoken since his last visit, and now he's dropped a voicemail overnight, informing me that he'll be showing up in a few hours. A little post-Thanksgiving treat for me, I guess.

It's in moments like these that I wish Kaia were here to help ease the tension.

Other than our few classes together, we still haven't connected this week. I know she's been swamped with her own work. But tonight's game's important to me, and I want her there.

I want to see her in the stands, wearing my jersey, cheering me on like the other girlfriends do for my teammates.

It's not only about her being present—it's about having her as a part of my life, a part of this world that I'm so passionate about. I know that she appreciates and supports me, but having her physically there, sharing in the excitement and the tension of the game, would mean more than I can put into words.

I've already imagined her there in the stands, her eyes locked on me, following my every move. I want her to see me thrive in my element and recognize all the hard work I put in over the course of my life.

I've envisioned her waiting for me after the game, her arms open, ready to embrace me and tell me how proud she is, regardless of the outcome. And it would only be a couple of hours out of her night. We could be a united front against my dad, and I know that it would make all the difference.

Centering myself, I grab my phone and send her a text, hoping she'll make an exception for me just this once.

HOLDEN

hey baby, I know you're busy, but I want you to come to my game tonight. my dad's gonna be there. I can have tickets for you at will call, and I've got a jersey sitting here with your name on it

I hit Send and wait, my heart hammering in my chest. I know it might be a long shot, but I hope she'll see how much this means to me and decide to come anyway.

After what feels like an eternity, her reply comes through, and my heart sinks as I read it.

KAIA

hey, I'm really sorry, but I just can't make it tonight. I've got so much work to do, and I need to focus on these applications still. I hope you understand, and I promise I'll be cheering you on from home

good luck tonight, though! you're gonna do great

I stare at the screen, feeling a mixture of disappointment and frustration. I understand that she's busy and that her future's important, but I'm still hurt by it. She won't even take a couple of hours to support me when I need her the most.

I type out a quick reply, fighting to keep my emotions in check.

HOLDEN

it's okay. I understand. good luck with your work

I miss you

KAIA

miss you too!

As I set my phone down, I try to brush off the disappointment and focus on the game. I have a job to do tonight, a team that's relying on me, and I can't let my feelings about Kaia or my dad get in the way.

# Chapter Thirty-One

KAIA

It's Friday night, and I can't stop obsessing.

I've gone the entire week without spending any extra time with Holden, and as a result, I haven't slept at all. I feel terrible about not going to his game tonight, but I can't bring myself to stop working on my applications. I've nearly completed every piece now, and I've even added an additional ten schools to my roster.

Once we return from Thanksgiving break, I plan to ask Dr. Khatri, along with one of my other professors, for their letters of recommendation.

I think back to how I spent yesterday, sitting in my apartment—alone—eating microwaved popcorn and drinking an old, flat Diet Coke I found in the back of the fridge. I wish I could've just been normal and gone over to Holden's get-together, but I couldn't muster the strength to make myself.

He even offered to drop off food for me last night, but I was worried that if I saw him, I would have a complete and total breakdown and never be able to regain my focus.

I glance over at the orchid on my windowsill, and I see that it's wilting. The pretty lavender petals have faded, tinging an ugly brown at the tips, the stems already dying off. I've been overwatering it, and it's only freaking me out more.

I feel like my relationship—despite its freshness—is already hanging in the balance. And I know it's all my fault. Tears prick at the corners of my eyes, welling up slowly until they spill over my cheeks and down onto my notebook.

I'm so tired, but there's nothing I can do about it. I can't stop ruminating, and I've been picking at my hair so much that my scalp is bleeding again. The symptoms of my compulsions have become more noticeable than ever.

It's something I've gained control over throughout the years, but when my anxiety flares, it picks back up again. I used to pull from spots all over, but now it's centralized to one smaller location at the top of my head. There's a bald patch there, and every time it starts to grow in, I just can't help myself —I pluck all the tiny hairs away.

And now, over this past week, the spot has only grown in size. The stress I'm feeling has pushed me to my limits, and my subconscious coping mechanism has taken full control.

I'm worried that it will get just as bad as it used to be. And then, I won't be able to hide it anymore. That's why I chopped all my hair off after freshman year. With less hair, there's less to pick, and pull, and fidget with.

Inevitably, I feel self-conscious whenever I see it in the mirror. Even though I try to hide it as best as I can, I know the missing patch is there, serving as a constant reminder of my struggles.

It's something I've tried to keep hidden from Holden, but it's getting harder and harder to do so. I'm sure he's noticed despite my efforts, anyway.

I truly wish I could stop, but it's like an itch I can't resist scratching—a cruel affliction, taking away not only my hair but also my confidence and sense of self-control.

I want to be able to share this part of myself with him, to let him know what's really going on inside my head, but I'm scared of what he might think. Will he see me as damaged, as weak?

When all I want to do is project strength.

Now, with so little sleep all week and all the underlying stress, I've completely lost my focus. I'm sitting at my desk, staring blankly at my laptop, but my mind keeps drifting back to Holden.

I imagine him at the rink, the determination in his eyes as he skates, the sound of the puck as it slides across the ice. I think of how proud he must feel when he scores a goal and how much I wish I could be there to share that moment with him.

I close my laptop, doomed by the realization that I'm not getting anything done, and lean back in my chair. A heavy sigh escapes me. I know I need to find a way to strike a balance between my academics, my relationship, and my nagging compulsions, but I'm struggling to figure out how.

I push myself up and walk over to the window, looking down at the dark empty parking lot. Holden's on campus, playing his heart out, and I'm not there to see it. The thought of him looking up into the stands—wishing I was there—only to find an empty seat where I should be, eats me up inside.

I wish I could just be a normal fucking girlfriend for once.

I wrap my arms around myself, the weight of my exhaustion and guilt washing over me. I know I can't keep going like this, but I'm at a loss for how to change my situation.

All I can do now is hope that I'll find a way to make things right eventually—later on, when I'm done with all this shit.

Hours later, in the middle of the night, I'm still plagued by the same horrible feeling inside. My mind's racing, and I'm losing it.

I'm struggling with old, long-forgotten thoughts . . . like maybe I could take something—just this one time—to help me focus and get through my work. I know I could probably head to the nearest campus library and find a couple of students who could supply me.

But I'm also terrified about falling back into old habits.

I remember the person I used to be, the person I fought so hard to leave behind, and I don't want to go back to that dark place. My hands are shaking as I battle with the decision, bearing the weight of my exhaustion and the temptation of the quick fix that Adderall could provide.

In a moment of desperation, I pick up the phone and dial Elio's number. I need support, and I know he'll understand what I'm going through. The phone rings a couple of times before he answers, his voice groggy but concerned.

"Kai, what's going on? It's the middle of the night."

"I'm really struggling right now." I swallow a shaky breath, fighting back even more tears. "I've been thinking about taking something, just to help me get through this work. And I'm scared."

There's a brief pause, and then Elio's voice comes through the line, steady and reassuring. "I'll be there soon. I'm gonna help you get through the night, okay? You don't have to do this alone."

My heart swells with gratitude, and there's a small flicker of hope amidst the chaos in my mind. "Thank you, El. I really appreciate it."

Within half an hour, Elio's knocking at my door. He looks tired but determined, and he pulls me into a tight hug as soon as I let him in. We sit down on my couch, and he starts talking to me, asking about my week, distracting me.

As we chat, some of the tension in my body eases, little by little.

Elio makes us both some coffee, black and extra hot, and then we spend the rest of the night working through my personal statement together. He offers a fresh perspective and helps me with some of the more difficult parts, and I make quick progress.

As we finish up the last bit, I shut down my laptop and tuck everything away into color-coordinated files. We head back to my bedroom, settling onto the edge of my mattress, and Elio breaks the silence.

"So, how are things going with the golden boy?" he asks, eyes filled with genuine curiosity.

I know he's still wary about my newfound relationship, but it's nice that he's taking an interest regardless. His concern wraps around me like a cozy sweater, relieving some of the burden I've been shouldering.

"It's been . . . complicated lately." I blow out a breath, looking down at my hands. "I've been so wrapped up in all this shit that I've been pulling away. But when we do get time together, it's really great. He's been so supportive and patient with me."

He raises a skeptical eyebrow. "But you still haven't talked to him about all this stuff? I mean, more than just the usual Kaia Karras meltdowns. But the pills, the picking?"

"No, I haven't," I admit, feeling a blend of remorse and apprehension.

"You don't trust him with it yet?"

"It's not that. I trust him, but I just don't want him to see me any differently."

"And he hasn't pushed you about it?"

"No. If anything, he's been giving me exactly what I need—space and time to figure my shit out." I feel grateful for Holden's understanding but also guilty for not opening up to him yet.

"Well, I'm glad he's at least treating you right. Not that I'm not happy to be here for you, but I'd imagine he'd want to know what's going on, too."

"I know." My voice shakes a little. "You're right. And I'll tell him, but I just needed someone tonight who's been there."

"I know exactly what you mean."

"It's hard, right? Opening up to someone new about all this?"

"Yeah, I wouldn't really know, considering the fact that I haven't mentioned it outside my own family, rehab, and therapy."

"No?"

"You're the only one I know who really gets it."

"Yeah, it's the same for me. A part of me worries that Beck will have a hard time understanding. He has a shit relationship with his brother, who's apparently big into partying himself. And then, you know, he's made a comment or two about you using."

"You're worried he'll lump you in with the rest of us tragic lost souls?"

I laugh, a playful smirk crossing my lips. "You know, I actually think you and Beck might get along better than we thought," I say, swatting him on the arm. "You're both snarky assholes, so you're perfect for each other."

He feigns offense, placing a hand over his heart. "Me? An asshole? Wounded, Kaia. Truly wounded."

We both let out a chuckle, nearly delirious with sleep deprivation at this point.

But even still, it feels good to share a laugh with my best friend. It reminds me that, despite everything that's been going on, I still have a few good people in my corner—people who truly care about me and want to see me happy.

As our laughter subsides and we settle back into the silence, I realize how lucky I am that he showed up tonight. He's been there for me a lot over the years, both as a friend and as a sober companion.

In the past, we've taken turns. Sometimes I need him more, and then other times, he needs me. It just so happens to be my turn this time. Plus, it's comforting to know that I can still lean on him, even as my relationship with Holden continues to evolve and grow.

By the time the clock strikes four in the morning, our eyelids have grown heavy, and our bodies are finally giving in to the exhaustion. Elio glances at the floor, preparing to craft a makeshift bed for himself.

"I'll sleep here," he says, already gathering some blankets and a spare pillow.

I shake my head, fighting back a yawn. "Come on, we've shared a bed before," I remind him.

There's no reason to make him sleep on the floor when there's plenty of space beside me. I've known the guy since primary school, and we've had plenty of sleepovers in the past. This is no different.

He hesitates for a moment before giving me a tired nod. "Alright," he agrees, abandoning the blankets.

We both make our way to my bed, pulling back the covers and climbing in. It's cozy and warm, a stark contrast to the cold floor he was prepared to sleep on.

We lie down, our backs facing each other, maintaining a respectful distance. And although we're far from touching, it's comforting to know that he's there. He's a steady presence, someone to help me resist the temptation that's clawed its way inside my head.

And when I finally drift off to sleep, I'm comforted by the tiny, temporary slice of peace he's granted me.

# Chapter Thirty-Two

## HOLDEN

I WAKE up in a cold sweat, the numbers on the clock flashing 6:15 a.m. It's unusually early for me on a weekend morning, especially considering the game last night. My father, who for some unknown reason decided to stay overnight, asked me to join him for breakfast at his hotel.

I'm not sure why, but the sense of urgency in his voice left me uneasy. My phone lies next to me, still no message from Kaia this morning. I texted her after the game, but she never replied. It worries me a little bit, but I figure she finally got some much-needed rest, and for that, I'm thankful.

I groggily roll out of bed, throw on some clothes, and brush my teeth. The mirror reflects a tired, worried face staring back at me. I wish I could just go back to bed, but my father insists on this meeting.

I check my phone one last time, hoping Kaia has woken up by now, but still nothing. With a deep breath, I leave my room and make my way to the hotel.

As I walk into the breakfast area, I see my father sitting at a table, looking somehow more human than he usually does. I approach cautiously, and as I near, he stands up and embraces me in a hug.

It's unexpected, to say the least, and I can't resist tensing up.

"Good morning, Holden," he says, his voice shaky.

"What's going on, Dad?"

"Well, for one, your mother's leaving me," he chokes out, eyes welling up.

A storm of emotions rages inside me—shock, confusion, and, eventually, anger. My fists clench as I stare back at him. "Why the hell are you crying, then?" I spit out. "This has been a long time coming, you know? Not to mention, it's your fault."

"You think I don't already know that?" He sighs, accepting the blame. "You're young, son. You might understand things differently once you've been with the same woman for twenty-four years."

"You're wrong," I retort, my blood boiling, voice shaking with anger. "I know how to appreciate a good thing when I have it."

My father stares at me for a long moment, then nods. "I'm leaving the house to your mother, and she'll get her fair share of alimony," he says simply. "That should be enough to comfort and provide for her for the rest of her life."

"Yeah, well, some people care about more than just money, Dad," I snap, my vision blurring.

"Save me the speech."

The rest of our shoddy attempt at a meal passes in strained silence, each of us lost in our own thoughts. My father's actions have finally shattered our family, and I can't help but feel betrayed.

My mind inevitably drifts to Kaia and how I can't imagine myself ever growing tired of her. I know I'm not destined to become like my father. But still, the thought of going down that same road terrifies me.

As we leave the hotel, my father hugs me once more. It's stiff, unnatural, and I have to resist the urge to flinch away. "I'm sorry, Holden," he whispers, his voice barely audible now.

I don't know what to say to that, so I offer a dismissive wave of my hand, my heart heavy with conflicting emotions—remorse for my father's actions and pride for my mother's courage.

We go our separate ways, and I'm uncertain of what the future will hold for our family and for me.

I shoot off a quick text to my mom, congratulating her on finally taking the leap. Lord knows what the catalyst was in making her decision, but I guess she's realized that there are more important things in this life than maintaining a perfect image.

And then, I decide to call my girl, desperately needing her to ground me in the midst of this whirlwind. I dial her number, eager to hear her soothing voice and confide in her. But with each ring of the phone, my stomach clenches tighter, a growing sense of agitation settling over me.

The line continues to ring until it connects to the all-too-familiar sounds of her voicemail box. My heart sinks, weighed down by disappointment and the realization that the person I need most right now remains out of reach.

SITTING in my car in the parking lot of the hotel, I lean my head back against the seat, my body tense with apprehension. The entire situation feels like a storm cloud hovering above me, ready to unleash its fury. My stomach churns, and I struggle to contain the wave of nausea threatening to overwhelm me.

As I sit here, lost in thought, my phone suddenly dings with a text, and I perk up the tiniest bit, hoping it's finally Kaia replying to me. But instead, it's a message from my mom.

She tells me she wants to see me soon and hopes I can fly home during the winter break to spend some time with her. At least, before the divorce proceedings get underway. My heart aches for her, and I can't even begin to imagine how she's coping with all of this.

Moments later, another text comes in. This time, it's from Harris, asking if I've heard about Mom and Dad. I ignore the message, not wanting to deal with talking to my brother right now.

The only person I want to see, the one person I think could truly help me through this, is Kaia.

I mull it over for a while longer, hesitant to disturb her if she's genuinely asleep in her apartment, but eventually, I decide to throw caution to the wind and head over anyway. The need to see her and find solace in her presence trumps my hesitation.

I park my car and walk up to her door, my heart pounding with every step. But when I knock, Lizzie answers, looking awkward and put out.

"Hey, is Kaia home?" I ask, failing at my attempts to sound casual.

She hesitates, clearly wary about letting me in. She looks over her shoulder and then back at me before finally rolling her eyes.

"Screw it," she mutters, stepping aside and allowing me to enter. "She's in her room."

I make my way down the hallway, and as I push open her bedroom door, my heart lodges itself into my throat. There, curled up in bed, is my girlfriend lying beside another man. A thousand thoughts race through my brain, and a sharp pain sears through my gut. But as I take in the scene more closely, I notice they're both clothed, barely touching.

Fucking hell.

I highly doubt Kaia would even have the capacity to cheat

on me. And I'm also aware that she and Elio have always just been close friends. But seeing them together like this, when I needed her to be there for me, is an unbearable feeling.

I thought she needed space and time to work through her stress and anxiety alone, so I've been granting her that, but it's clear now that she needed someone to be there for her last night. And that person, sadly, wasn't me.

With a surge of emotion, I slam the door shut, marching back through the apartment, unable to handle this right now. But Kaia—clearly woken up by my fit of irritation—chases after me. Her hair is wild, and her eyes are still groggy with sleep.

"Beck, wait," she calls out, her voice thick with concern and confusion.

I hesitate, torn between the desire to confront her and the need to distance myself from the hurt. But as she reaches me, her eyes filled with a mix of worry and sincerity, I'm unable to turn away.

"Please, Beck," she pleads, her voice cracking, "can I just explain?"

My chest is tight, my heart heavy. I'm still seconds away from walking out her front door when a small voice inside me convinces me to stay. This deserves a real conversation, and I refuse to let her off the hook so easily.

"Look, I'm kinda going through some shit right now, and this is the last thing I needed to deal with," I say, my voice shaking slightly.

"What do you mean?"

"You know what?" I say, exasperated. "Never mind. I thought I could do this with you, I really did. But I just can't."

Her eyes widen as she runs a ragged hand through her hair. "So, that's it, then? We're done?"

"No, we're not fucking done. I'm not breaking up with you, Karras."

She worries her teeth over her bottom lip, shoulders slumping. "You're not?"

"No," I say firmly. "I really, really like you. Do you know that? And all I fucking want is to be there for you. Your person—the one you come to when you're in need, the one you call in the middle of the night when you can't sleep. And I thought that's where we were headed, together. But somehow, you've defaulted to pushing me away while letting Elio in. And I'm starting to think that it will always be that way."

"I don't want it to be that way, though." She reaches for me, but I step back, evading her touch. "I want to let you in."

"Then why don't you?" I ask, exasperated.

She sighs, long and heavy. "Because it's hard."

"It's hard." I let out a humorless snort. "Come on, Karras. That's not a reason. I know for a fact that you can do hard things. You're the hardest worker I know, after all."

"Maybe I'm just not used to all this." Her voice cracks. "Feeling this way about someone. Maybe I'm just scared."

"Of what? I told you I want you just as you are."

She stares down at the floor, avoiding my gaze as she mumbles, "I know, but that was before."

"Fuck, Kaia," I rasp, unable to keep my emotions in check. "You've been treating this relationship like we're living on a fault line, ready to destruct at a moment's notice. It doesn't make me feel very good, especially when I've done nothing but try and stick beside you. So if you're looking for an out from me, I'm not gonna give you one."

"I don't want an out," she promises, eyes pleading.

"It sure as hell seems like it. I was willing to give you more time and space if that's what you really needed, but seeing Elio in your bed this morning, well . . . it shows me that you *did* need someone to be there for you after all. Unfortunately, that person wasn't me."

"I'm sorry, Holden, about calling him instead of you." Her eyes fill with remorse. "But I do need you, too. You know I do."

"Too little, too late for that," I snap, my frustration boiling up to the surface. "And you know what else? I fucking needed you too. Last night. This morning. I got a bomb dropped on me by my dad, and you were the first fucking person I wanted to come to about it."

"Oh Beck, what happened?"

"It's not even worth it." I blow out an impatient breath. "When you're ready for me to be there for you—fully—then maybe I'll let you return the favor."

"Holden," she whispers, voice breaking.

"Goodbye, Kaia. Have a nice morning with your friend."

I turn my back on her, my chest tightening with disappointment. With one hand on the doorknob, I fight the urge to turn around and try to fix things—right here and now—but I know that it won't be fruitful.

We're still learning how to navigate each other's emotions and boundaries, and she needs to understand the importance of her actions. We can't grow together if she's constantly pushing me away.

As I step out of the apartment and the door closes behind me, I pause to collect my composure, trying to remain steady. It's a bump in the road for us, I tell myself, not the end of the world. We've only just started this journey together, and there are bound to be obstacles along the way.

But an even bigger part of me still wonders if she'll ever truly let me in.

Doubts creep their way inside my head, making me question if we can overcome this hurdle. But the memories of the last few months—more accurately, the last few *years*—keep me hoping that maybe we can work through this after all.

For now, though, I think I need to take some space of my own.

# Chapter Thirty-Three

KAIA

THE SOUND of the front door closing reverberates through the apartment, each fading footstep a painful reminder of the distance growing between us. The weight of what just happened is pressing, and I feel like I've failed both of us.

I make a half-assed attempt to collect myself, my heart flittering in my chest as I make my way back to my room. Elio's sitting there on the edge of my bed, his hair and clothing ruffled from sleep. His dark eyes fill with concern as he rubs at the back of his neck, clearly having overheard our conversation.

"Shit, Kai. I'm sorry."

I sink down onto the bed beside him, my voice barely a whisper. "It's not your fault, E. It's mine. I should've just been more open with him from the start."

His gaze softens, and he nudges my shoulder. "You were just trying to protect yourself. There's nothing wrong with that."

"But I hurt him in the process," I say, blowing out a breath. "And now he's going through something, and I can't even be there for him."

He squeezes my upper arm, trying to offer some comfort. "You can still be there for him, Kai. But maybe he just needs some time to process everything."

"I know." I rub at my temples. "I just . . . I'm scared. I messed up, and now I don't know if I can fix it."

"You're stronger than you think," he tells me, his voice warm and reassuring. "Just give him some space, and let him know you're there for him when he's ready."

"Yeah, okay." I wipe my eyes, pressing my palms together to calm myself. "I just hope it's not too late."

He pats my hand before standing up. "It won't be. He clearly gives a shit about you. And you obviously like him too much to let it end like this."

"Yeah, I do." I offer him a small smile, grateful for his presence and support. "And, um, thanks again for being here for me last night, despite the shitstorm we woke up to this morning."

The corner of his mouth lifts. "I got you. That's what friends are for, right?"

With that, he leaves the room, giving me some time alone to gather my thoughts. And as I sit here, I contemplate the possibility of losing Holden for good. The idea makes my skin crawl, and I know I need to do something to make it right. To fix this rift, this divide, that I created between us—sooner rather than later.

I spend the rest of the day fully lost in my head, as per usual, my heart heavy with regret. I keep replaying our conversation, wishing I could have found a way to make him stay. To be there for him the way he's been there for me these last few months.

I should've just gone to his fucking game last night, and then maybe none of this would've ever happened. I could've controlled myself for a little while longer, just until I was able to muster up the courage to open up to him.

But most of all, I wish could've just been the person he needed right from the start.

Somehow, I manage to make it through the rest of the day without completely falling apart. But by the time the moon hangs in the sky, I'm compelled to send him a text. My hands shake as I type out the words, pulse racing in my throat.

KAIA

hey, just wanted to let you know that I'm ready to talk whenever you are. I want to let you in, and I want you to know I'm here for you too

I hold my breath as I wait for his reply, my nerves on edge. After what feels like forever, my phone buzzes with a new message, and I'm torn between relief and dread as I read his response.

HOLDEN

I appreciate that. I think it would be best if we take the week just to let things settle, and then we can talk

I let out a slow exhale, forcing myself to calm the fuck down. It's not the response I was hoping for, but it's better than nothing. At least he's willing to talk eventually, and that gives me the tiniest shred of hope.

KAIA

I understand, talk later. miss you <3

HOLDEN

me too

As the week progresses, I obsess over what's happening with Holden. I wish I knew what was going on with him and his family, what was causing him so much pain. But I also understand that he needs space, and I respect that.

He sure as hell gave me mine when I needed him to.

Despite my growing concern for him, I know I need to keep moving forward. So, with a heavy heart, I focus on securing those letters of recommendation. They're the final pieces I need for my applications, and the thought of having everything complete—and having Holden by my side again—is a bittersweet dream.

The two of us barely speak during the school week, and I feel his absence like a physical weight. We still share classes, but our once easy banter—and all of our stolen glances—have been erased. I try to concentrate on my studies, but my thoughts are consumed with how much I miss him.

How much I've grown to need him by my side.

As the week draws to a close, I'm constantly thinking about how to mend our relationship. My heart aches with the desire to be there for him, to support him through whatever he's dealing with.

But I also know I need to be patient.

On Friday morning, I receive another text from him, and it sends my brain into overdrive.

HOLDEN

hey baby, just wanted to let you know I'll be out of town for another away game this weekend. but I'll be back on sunday, and we can talk then

The familiar endearment warms me up, offering another small glimmer of hope. Now, I'm determined to seize the opportunity he's given me. To find a way to show him how much I truly do care.

I want to be there for him this weekend, to cheer him on from the sidelines and prove that I'm committed to showing my support, even if it comes a little too late.

But to make this happen, I'll need some help, and that

means reaching out to Lizzie. Our relationship has been strained lately, to say the least, with her acting so distant and cold. Not only has she been weird about Holden staying the night, but she intentionally let him walk into my room without any warning.

The whole situation was definitely my fault, I'll admit that, but she didn't need to contribute to it either. Still, she's my only connection to Rai, who I'm counting on to help me now.

Squaring my shoulders, I shoot off a text, asking her for Rai's number. To my surprise, she responds almost immediately. No questions asked. I thank her, relieved that she's willing to help me out despite our recent tensions.

With Rai's number in hand, I work up the courage to contact him. He's undoubtedly warm and receptive, even going so far as to sneak a jersey for me to wear—Becker #16 flashing across the back in big, bold letters.

My heart swells with gratitude, and I feel like this might be a turning point for us. A chance to show Holden that I'm here for him, that I'm finally ready to go full-in.

I ARRIVE in Hanford a few hours before their first game starts—a small town with quaint charm, surrounded by miles of empty countryside. Then I book a room at the Harmony, a hotel just a couple of blocks from the Hawkes' ice rink, wanting to give Holden his space in case he still needs it.

My stomach is officially twisted up like a pretzel. I've never been to a hockey game before, let alone an away game—one that takes place miles and miles away from our home rink at Coastal.

As the game time approaches, I slip into my loaner jersey and head toward the rink, taking slow breaths to calm my nerves. I know this is the right thing to do, but I'm still slightly terrified about Holden's reaction.

The rink's bustling with energy when I arrive, fans from both teams clad in their respective colors, eagerly chatting about the upcoming match. I make my way to the stands, filing into the sparse student section.

There aren't many die-hard Coastal fans that will make the trek all the way out to Hanford, but there are still a few students scattered amongst family members and other close friends.

As the teams take to the ice for their warm-ups, my eyes search for Holden. When I spot the number on his back, a rush of warmth floods through me, despite the chilly bite in the air. He's focused, gliding effortlessly on the ice, every movement filled with grace and power.

I'm so impressed by him—his skill, his athleticism, his dedication to the team. All of it makes me so fucking proud, and it also makes me wish I had been here for him from the start.

The game starts with a burst of wild energy, and I cheer loudly for Holden and his team, my eyes glued to the rink. I don't even really know what I'm supposed to be looking for, but I can feel the adrenaline all around me, the excitement coursing through each of the players.

As the first period progresses, I know Holden's in top form. He skates with precision and determination, his eyes locked on the puck as he maneuvers around the opposing players.

About halfway through the game, during an intermission between periods, Rai points me out in the stands. I watch, shaking in my boots, as Holden's gaze follows his friend's finger. And when our eyes finally meet, I can see the happiness that overwhelms him in spades.

A broad, genuine smile lights up his face, and it melts the

ice inside my chest. He skates right up to the glass that separates us and waves enthusiastically, brown eyes sparkling.

I wave back, my cheeks burning as I return his smile. The joy I see on his face is contagious, and a wave of optimism floods through me. Before he heads out to the locker room, he mouths, "That's my girl," and my heart swells.

The rest of the game is a whirlwind of action, my eyes never leaving Holden as he leads his team. He has all the confidence and skill of a true captain, and it's sexy as hell to watch him out there, dominating on the ice.

As the game reaches its final moments, the score is tied, and the atmosphere in the rink is charged with tension. Every person in the stands holds their breath, anticipating the outcome.

Coastal gains possession of the puck, and with a burst of speed, they launch into a well-executed attack. Holden, at the center of it all, glides across the ice with grace. He weaves through the opposing players, his eyes locked on the goal. And as he approaches the net, he expertly maneuvers the puck, feinting left before quickly switching to the right.

The goalie's caught off guard, and in a flash, Holden takes his shot.

The puck soars through the air, hitting the back of the net with a satisfying thud. The small crowd around me erupts into thunderous cheers, and I can't resist joining in, my heart brimming with pride and admiration for my guy.

As the final buzzer sounds and the players celebrate their hard-fought victory, I know that I made the right decision in coming to Hanford.

. . .

After the game, I wait outside the locker room, fidgeting nervously as I anticipate our first real interaction since last weekend. The thought of facing him now—and finally having our talk—fills me with apprehension.

The door to the locker room finally opens, and Holden emerges, still clad in his gear, his golden hair damp from exertion. When he sees me, his face lights up, and he walks over to me with purpose.

"Karras," he says, amusement lacing his tone. "Who would've thought I'd find you roughing it in Hanford."

I breathe a sigh of relief, lips curling into a smile. "I'm willing to make exceptions for you."

"Well, I'm honored." He chuckles, rubbing the back of his neck. "I have to say, it's a nice surprise to see you here."

"I figured someone needed to keep an eye on you this weekend, make sure you didn't get too full of yourself after winning another game."

He laughs, eyes sparking with interest. "Oh, so you're just here to keep me grounded, huh?"

"Among other things," I tease, raising a brow.

He smirks and leans in a little closer, his voice dropping to a conspiratorial whisper. "You know, I scored that last goal for you, baby. I hope you were paying attention."

My cheeks flush, but I manage to maintain my composure. "Trying to impress me, Beck?"

"You know I always am."

# Chapter Thirty-Four

HOLDEN

As I MAKE my way back to the team bus, I'm practically skipping in my fucking shoes. Kaia came to watch me play, and seeing her in the stands was like living out a fantasy I'd had for years.

I can't stop thinking about how gorgeous she looked in my jersey, how good she smelled in my arms, and how glad I am that she's here tonight, in the flesh.

I text her the details of our hotel, making sure she cancels her room at the Harmony. She's staying with me tonight, no question about that. She told me that she booked somewhere else just in case I still needed space. But I'm all fucking good on that front.

I'm more than ready to be close to her again.

Before I board the bus, I field a few more press questions, my mind only half-focused on the task. All I can think about is Kaia and the mixture of anticipation, relief, and lingering hurt swirling inside me.

The high of winning the game only fuels my desire for her, and I wish I could take her back to my hotel room and make her mine again in every way possible. But I know we need to talk first.

We can't keep on sweeping everything under the rug, as tempting as it may be.

Deep down, I'm still really fucking hurt by the way she

sought someone else out to fix her problems. And I've been reeling from the news about my parents all week. I wanted so badly to forget all about it and break down, go to her, and let her comfort me.

But in the end, I thought that space would be best for both of us. Some distance from the situation to get our heads on straight.

Really, it wasn't a test, but I wanted to see if Kaia would come after me—if she would fight for me just the tiniest bit—so that I would know, once and for all, where she really stands. Or if she would just let this singular fight, this one rocky path between us, create a deeper divide.

So the fact that she's here now trumps everything. It feels so fucking good to see her. And the way we could slip back into our old habits, our old banter so easily, lets me know that everything's gonna be just fine.

As I take my seat on the bus, I can barely contain my bliss. I glance around at my teammates, who are all celebrating our win. I make a half-hearted attempt to join in, but my thoughts keep drifting back to Kaia and how she's here, in Hanford, just for me.

The bus ride to the hotel takes fucking forever, my impatience to hold her growing with each passing mile. But when my phone buzzes with another text, I grin to myself as I read her words.

KAIA

waiting for you in our room <3

My pulse pounds in my throat as the bus finally pulls up to our hotel. I jump out of my seat and hurry inside, my mind focused on one thing: getting to Kaia as quickly as possible.

But before I can make it that far, I locate Rai and inform

him that he's been evicted for the night. He gives me a knowing smirk but doesn't protest, instead heading off to find another teammate to crash with.

Once he's gone, I practically sprint the rest of the way to my room. As I open the door, I'm greeted by the sight of Kaia, sitting on the bed, her pretty eyes lighting up when she sees me.

And in that moment, everything else fades away. All the hurt, the distance, the uncertainty. All that matters is that she's here, and we're together. And I know, deep in my bones, that we'll be able to work through whatever secrets she's been keeping.

"Hey," I manage to say, my voice sounding breathless from the jitters coursing through me.

"Hey," she parrots, a tentative smile gracing her lips, and it feels like the sun breaking through storm clouds.

I close the door behind me and walk over to the bed, taking a seat beside her. Our eyes lock, and for a moment, we drink each other in, appreciating the simple fact that we're sharing the same space again.

"So," I start, my voice a little steadier now. "I guess we should talk."

"Yeah, we should," she says, holding my gaze. "Beck, I'm so sorry. I know I've been pushing you away, and I feel really shitty about it. You didn't deserve it, and you don't deserve the way I've been treating you."

I don't say anything, but my expression softens. She's being open, vulnerable, and that's all I've ever wanted from her.

"I've been scared," she continues, her voice barely above a whisper. "Scared of getting hurt, scared that you'd look at me differently. But I realize now that by pushing you away, little by little, I've only made that more likely."

"I just don't understand why," I say, my voice heavy with

emotion. "I've been nothing but supportive of you, Kaia. I told you I want to be there for you. That I adore you, that all your flaws are what make you whole."

"I know," she admits with a heavy sigh. "And I promise you, I'm going to let you in. I want you to be the person I turn to, the one I lean on. And I want to be that person for you, too."

I look at her for a long moment, then take her hand in mine. "You know, I don't mind you leaning on your friend for support. I know you two have a lot of history, but I just want to be looped in. Part of it all. I don't want to feel like an outsider in my own relationship."

"You're right, Beck. I know you're right. And you should know, the reason that I called Elio is because we made a promise to each other a long time ago."

"What kind of promise?"

"We're . . . he's kind of like my sober companion, in a way. My accountability check."

"Oh, okay." My brow furrows, and my brain flits into overdrive, attempting to make sense of what she's saying. "Wait, you're sober? But I've seen you drink before."

"It's pills, actually—Adderall—that's the issue. It got really bad a few years ago, to the point where I couldn't do anything without them. It fucked with my sleep, and I'm still reeling from it all. Elio was the one who helped me get clean, and we made a pact: if either of us starts to lose control, we call the other. He's the one who made me realize I needed to get my life together in the first place, back when he went off to rehab."

"Wow, okay." I nod, finally understanding the depth of their connection. "I'm sorry, Kaia. I really had no idea. I shouldn't have made those comments about him using again, at least not so flippantly. If I'd known your history, I would've gone about it differently."

"But you didn't, and that's on me. I was worried about how you'd react, especially knowing your brother's situation."

"In my mind, that's completely different." Guilt gnaws at me, bringing to mind all the insensitive remarks I've incidentally made. "I know you, Kaia, and I know you don't ever choose to take the easy way out."

"Thank you for saying that." She squeezes my hand, giving me a tiny sad smile. "You should also know that Elio's been there for me more times than I can count, and I've done the same for him. But that's all it is, Beck. Just support, because we understand that part of each other in a way that not many people do. But that doesn't mean I should've left you in the dark, either."

"Well, I'm glad you're telling me now."

My chest swells with understanding and appreciation for what she's endured, for her resilience all these years. I realize that beneath the façade of strength, she was silently grappling with her struggles all this time, and it only deepens my admiration for her.

"There's something else, too. I have this . . . habit." She hesitates for a moment, hands shaking. "When I'm stressed or anxious, which is basically all the time, I . . . I pull my hair out. Sometimes in chunks, sometimes in little pieces. I have this spot, right here." She moves her hair to the side, showing me the missing patch I noticed a few weeks prior. "It's been getting worse lately. And I'm not doing a very good job at hiding it anymore."

I rub my thumb across her palm, my heart aching for her. "Kaia, you don't have to hide anything from me. We all have our struggles, our insecurities. It doesn't make me think of you any differently, make me want you any less."

She sniffles, tears welling in her eyes. "I just didn't want you to see this side of me, I guess. All the broken parts that I'm still trying to put back together."

"I get that. But Kaia, I don't need you to be perfect. All I want from you is your trust."

"And you have it. Do I have yours?"

"You do."

We sit in silence for a moment, letting the weight of her confessions settle around us. And then, with a shaky breath, I decide it's time for me to be honest, too.

"You know, I came to you last weekend to talk about my parents," I say, my voice cracking. "My mom finally asked for a divorce, and my dad just dropped it on me out of the blue on Saturday morning. I . . . I didn't know how to handle it, and I guess that's why I was so quick to latch onto the idea of giving us some space. I just . . . I wanted to know that you were going to fight for me, for us, even when things got hard."

She wipes a tear from my cheek. "I'm so sorry, Beck. I had no idea. I should've been there for you from the start."

"You're here now," I say, offering her a small smile. "And that's what matters."

"How are you doing?"

"Not great," I admit, my voice barely audible. "I've been trying to put on a brave face, but it's been eating me up inside. On the one hand, I've known this was coming for a long time. Hell, I wanted it to happen. God knows my dad doesn't deserve her loyalty, but it still doesn't change the fact that his decisions have officially torn our family apart."

"It's really awful what he's done."

"Yeah, it is."

I lean into Kaia, burying my nose in the crook of her neck and breathing in her comforting scent. It's a small gesture, but it helps to ground me in the moment, reminding me that she's here with me now, that we're facing these obstacles together.

In a single fluid motion, I scoop her up into my arms and carry her over to the head of the bed, her body fitting perfectly against mine. As I gently lay her down on the soft mattress, she looks up at me with a warm, reassuring smile.

It makes me feel good, like everything's right again in the world.

We lie down, our bodies flush, and a sense of relief floods through me. The weight of our secrets has been lifted, and we've come out on the other side stronger for it.

It's not going to be easy, and there will undoubtedly be challenges ahead, but I know in the end that we're going to be okay. Because we're in this together now.

And as we both drift off to sleep, Kaia's hands, her body, her soul intertwined with mine, I know that we'll tackle whatever comes our way, side by side, using trust and open communication as our foundation.

# Chapter Thirty-Five

KAIA

We head back to campus after our little weekend getaway in Hanford, recharged and rejuvenated.

Sneaking around in Holden's hotel room to dodge his coach —undoubtedly snuggled up together—put the easygoing thrill back into our relationship. Plus, cheering him on again during Saturday's game, where his team clinched another victory, was exhilarating.

It's like the challenges of the past few weeks have finally dissolved, leaving us with a fresh sense of clarity and a stronger bond in our relationship.

Now that I've submitted all my applications and secured those letters of rec, I can finally breathe again. I'm less stressed and more self-assured in my abilities than I have been in a very long time.

Holden and I have one last meeting with Dr. Khatri before winter break hits, and I'm a little sentimental about it all. It's incredible how far we've both come since we first started working with her, together and individually.

As we sit down in her office, she greets us with a warm smile. "Kaia, Holden, it's been a pleasure working with you this semester. I'm impressed by the progress you've made, and I'm looking forward to seeing what you accomplish next term."

"Thank you," I say, grinning in return. "We couldn't have done it without your guidance."

Holden chimes in, his voice filled with gratitude. "Yeah, you've been an incredible mentor to us. We really appreciate everything you've done."

She spends the next hour going over our plans for the spring semester, discussing the research we'll be conducting and the goals we've set for ourselves. As our meeting draws to a close, she leans back in her chair and gives us a thoughtful look.

"I have an opportunity for one of you that I'd like to discuss," she says, her voice measured. "When we return from the break, I'll be giving a series of lectures to a junior-level class, and I'd like someone to assist me with them. It's a great chance to gain some teaching experience and work closely with me on a professional level."

Holden and I exchange glances, both of us intrigued by the prospect.

Dr. Khatri continues. "I trust that both of you are more than capable of handling this responsibility. However, I understand that you also have your own commitments and priorities, so I'll leave the decision up to you. Take some time to discuss it amongst yourselves, and let me know your decision when we reconvene after the break."

The offer hangs in the air between us, tempting us with a chance for some friendly competition.

"Thank you," I say, attempting to keep my eagerness at bay. "We'll definitely discuss it and let you know our decision."

"Excellent." She stands, ushering us out of the room. "I have no doubt that whichever one of you takes the opportunity will do an exceptional job. I look forward to working with you."

As we exit her office, excitement builds inside of me. The moment the door closes behind us and we make it out of earshot, I flip around to face Holden.

"I'm doing the lectures," I say, narrowing my eyes.

"Hey now, you heard the woman." He shakes his head, giving me an arrogant smirk. "We need to make a decision about this, together, fair and square."

I lower my voice as we make our way out to the quad. "Okay, how about this? I give you a blowjob, and you let me do the lectures."

"Karras," he says with a low chuckle. "I could get you to suck me off anytime I wanted. Think of something else."

"Fine, you want competition? I'll beat you in any game of your choice, just no sports."

He tilts his head, considering. "Do I have a second to think on it?"

"I'll give you five minutes. I'd take you back to my apartment, and we could settle this right now, but I'm afraid Lizzie would have a conundrum."

"Oh, come on." He gives me a wry smile. "I think I can handle Liz."

"You think so, huh?"

"Yeah, you should let me talk to her."

I raise a brow, both hands planted on my hips. "And what are you gonna say to her?"

"Take me back to your place, and you can find out."

"Be my guest, then," I say, and his grin only widens at the idea of a challenge.

Holden and I walk back to my apartment, hand in hand, ready to face whatever attitude Lizzie has in store for us. As we enter the living room, her gaze narrows, and she immediately grabs her things, preparing to make a hasty retreat to her room.

But Holden stops her in her tracks. "Lizzie, can I talk to you for a minute?"

She looks surprised but hesitates nonetheless, her arms crossed defensively. "What do you want to talk about?"

He straightens his posture, choosing his words carefully. "Look, I know you're not comfortable with me being here for whatever reason."

"No, it's not that, Holden," she cuts him off, her tone defensive. "I honestly don't mind you being here at all."

"Oh really? I must have misread the situation, then," he says, a hint of sarcasm in his tone.

She sighs, frustration evident. "It's not *you*. It's just the fact that we basically have a third roommate now. Kaia already had Elio over all the time, and now she's brought you into the mix. I just didn't expect this to happen when I took her to that party at your house, or I wouldn't have done it in the first place."

A slow smile spreads across Holden's face. "Ah, so I have you to thank for bringing Kaia to me."

"I guess you could say that," she mutters.

"Then how about I write you a check for all your contributions? A little something to help your pain and suffering for the next few months of me sticking around. Would five K be fair?"

Her eyes widen in disbelief. "Oh, um, I wouldn't ask you to—"

"How about I double it, then?" he interrupts, the shit-eating grin never leaving his face. "I can leave the check on the counter before I head out tomorrow."

"Um, I suppose I won't argue with that," she stammers, taken aback. "But, er, is there a reason that you're both so opposed to staying at your house instead?"

Holden gives her a devilish grin, wrapping me up in his strong arms. "See, the thing is I'd really like to fuck my girl in the comfort of her own bedroom from now on. If that's okay with you, Liz."

"Whatever," she groans, rolling her eyes before sauntering her way down the hall.

I lean my head back against Holden's chest, blinking up at him, laughter bubbling up inside me. "What the hell, Beck? Did you seriously just bribe my roommate with ten grand?"

"Yeah, well, it's my dad's money anyway. Not like I did anything to earn it."

"Still a waste."

He chuckles, a playful twinkle in his gaze. "It's not a waste if it makes you happy."

"You're ridiculous, you know that?"

"But you like me anyway," he retorts, pulling me close and pressing a tender kiss to my forehead.

I sigh, leaning into his embrace. "Yeah, I really do."

With Lizzie's bullshit officially out of the way, we head into my bedroom, the door closing softly behind us. The competitive banter from earlier still lingers in the air, but there's a newfound sense of peace between us.

Spending that much money to get Lizzie out of our hair is outrageous, there's no denying that, but it's also sort of sweet. And I'm feeling unexpectedly sentimental about it. I mean, it's nice to know how far he's willing to go just to make me smile.

We sit on the edge of my bed, our thighs brushing against one another. He leans in slowly, his gaze flickering around my face, and I catch my breath as our lips meet in a soft, tender kiss.

When we pull away, our foreheads touch, and an unstoppable smile spreads across my face. Holden twirls a strand of my hair between his fingers, his hand gently smoothing across the top of my head.

"You know," I say, "if you were expecting me to be one of

those girls who tell you not to spend your money on them, then it's not gonna happen."

"Wasn't expecting anything like that," he says with a sly grin. "I know you better by now."

"Good. Because I like gifts, and you can afford it."

"That I can, Karras."

He stands and walks over to the window, reaching for the curtains to draw them open. Panicking, I rush over and place my body in front of him like a human shield, my hands covering his as they grip the fabric.

He glances down at me, confusion etched into his brow. "What's the matter?"

"Nothing," I rush out, my hastiness breeding suspicion.

"Are you secretly a little vampire, just hiding away from the light?"

"No, it's not that." I stiffen, trying to brush off his teasing. "I just think it's better in the dark."

"Now, that's a bald-faced lie if I ever heard one."

"Fine." I sigh, reluctantly stepping aside. "You can open them if you must."

As he pulls the curtains back, my poor, little orchid comes fully into view, its petals wilting and dying away. I feel a blush creep up my neck, embarrassed by its sad state.

"I, uh, accidentally overwatered it," I admit, misery seeping through my tone.

"It's alright, baby." He runs his fingers across the wilted petals, snapping off a dead stem. "It's just a plant."

"No, but it's a symbolic plant," I insist.

"Symbolic of what?"

"Er, it's the first and only time someone's ever given me a flower, and I really wanted to keep it alive as long as possible."

He chuckles with a little shake of his head, his dimples

making an appearance as he pulls me closer. "You're thinking too much into it, Kaia. I'll get you another orchid. I'll get you fifty orchids, or tulips, or daisies, or whatever fucking flowers you want."

"Shut up," I say, laughter bubbling up in my chest as I swat at his arm. "I know I'm being dramatic, but I felt like it was important."

"I'm being serious," he insists. "We've just made it clear that you like gifts, and I like giving them. So you better expect me to give you so many fucking flowers that you're gonna be drowning in them."

He grins down at me, his dark eyes full of affection, and I wrap my arms around his waist, walking us backward until I'm able to push him onto my bed.

"You always know how to sweet-talk me," I tease, settling myself on top of him.

"It's my new favorite thing."

He winks at me, his hands gently resting on my waist, thumbs tracing small circles against my skin. Slowly, his hands glide over the curve of my hips, fingertips teasing their way across my body until they reach my ass. With a playful smile, he gives me a firm squeeze, making me squirm against him.

His touch is both delicate and playful, tender and teasing, a perfect reflection of our newfound dynamic.

"So, have you decided what you want to do for this competition of ours?" I ask, my curiosity piqued, eager to know his plans.

"Yeah, I have." He nudges my cheek with the bridge of his nose. "But I'm gonna take you back to Bluewater Cape this weekend, and I'll tell you then."

"Wow, I think the anticipation might kill me."

"I'm sure you'll be fine." He presses me even closer, his hips slotting into the perfect space against mine.

"Anything specific I need to do to prepare?"

"Not that I can think of," he says, his voice husky as he grips my chin, pulling me in for another passionate kiss, one hand still firmly grasped onto my ass. When he finally pulls back, he looks into my eyes and says, "Just be ready for anything, baby."

# Chapter Thirty-Six

HOLDEN

I'VE PLANNED the entire day for us out at the cape, ensuring that everything will be absolutely perfect. I've been wanting to take her back to the lighthouse for ages, not just for the nostalgia factor but also because it's the place where she first opened up to me.

The place where I felt the tiniest crack in her armor and started to work my way inside.

I pack snacks and blankets, making sure we have enough to keep us comfortable throughout the day. Once everything is ready, I pick her up from her apartment, and we set off to Bluewater together.

As we drive, she leans over to sneak a peek at the contents of our bag. I swat her hand away, grinning over at her. "You'll see soon enough."

She huffs but settles back into her seat, a teasing smile dancing on her lips. "You're enjoying this way too much."

I chuckle. "You have no idea."

When we arrive, her pretty eyes light up, shimmering in the sunlight like flecks of gold on the beachfront. We make our way to the lighthouse, the brisk air hitting us as we walk. I wrap an arm around her, pulling her close to rub some warmth back into her body.

Once we reach the top, I lay out the blankets and unpack

our snacks—some peppermint candy for me, Cheetos and popcorn for my girl.

She takes a seat beside me, her eyes twinkling with curiosity. "So, what's the big plan for today?"

I pull out a deck of cards, a smirk spreading across my face. "We're going to play a few rounds of blackjack."

She raises a curious brow. "Really? Why?"

"Because," I say, shuffling the deck. "It's what I was playing when you first decided to give me another shot. I left in the middle of my monthly poker game with the boys and booked it over to your apartment. Since then, I haven't been able to get the taste of you, the feel of you, out of my fucking head. It's only fair you play against me now."

She laughs, a warm sound that echoes in the empty room. "Okay, Becker. You're on."

We dive into the game, our competitive spirits going head-to-head with each passing round. There's a stack of chips between us, and the game is surprisingly even. But as time continues to pass, we become more immersed in the contest, each determined to outwit the other.

"Hit me," she says, her eyes locked on mine, daring me to beat her in this round.

I draw a card and place it in front of her. "You sure about that? Looks like you might bust."

She smirks back at me, undeterred. "I like to live on the edge."

As the game continues, our playful teasing escalates. Every winning hand is accompanied by a suggestive comment or lingering touch.

"Feeling confident, are we?" I ask, noticing her stack of chips growing.

She leans in, lips brushing against my ear. "Oh, I already know I can beat you."

Her breath sends shivers down my spine, and I lick my lips, grinning at her version of smack talk. "We'll see about that."

We play on, the sun setting outside the lighthouse windows, casting a warm, orange glow over the space between us. Our rivalry never fades, but the only thing I can think about is how good this all feels—to be with her here, carefree and so fucking happy.

During a brief break between games, I pull her into my arms, our bodies pressed together as we share a soft, lingering kiss.

"I'm really glad we did this," I murmur against her lips.

"Me too," she whispers, her eyes filled with warmth.

As the daylight continues to fade away, our competition reaches its peak. Kaia stretches her arms above her head, lips curling up as an idea forms in her mind. "Why don't we up the stakes, Beck? Let's switch to strip poker."

I raise both brows, momentarily taken aback by her suggestion. "As much as I'd love that, it's really fucking cold out here, baby."

"Oh, come on," she teases, poking me in the chest. "Are you chicken or something?"

I stare at her for a moment, and then I blow out a long, relenting breath. "Alright, fine. Strip poker it is."

We resume our game, the tension rising as we slowly lose articles of clothing. Kaia first removes her jacket, shivering slightly but giving me that confident grin of hers nonetheless. "Your move, Beck."

I follow suit during the next round, pulling off my own jacket and tossing it aside. Our breaths come out in small puffs of condensation in the chilly air, but we're too caught up in the game to care.

One by one, our clothes are slowly shed, the stakes of the game growing higher with each hand. The chill in the air is soon forgotten as the heat between us flares, our bodies growing closer and closer.

It's not long before Kaia's peeling off her shirt, revealing her shivering body underneath. "See? Not so bad."

I rake my gaze over her from head to toe, admiring her, the sight of her bare, glowy skin sending a flare of heat up my spine.

We continue playing the game, the sun fully set behind us now. The pile of discarded clothing grows, and the air between us is thick with anticipation and desire.

Finally, with just a few critical pieces of clothing left, we reach the final hand. Kaia studies her cards, biting her lip nervously. "Alright, Beck. This is it."

"May the best player win."

We reveal our cards, and for a moment, we're both stunned by the outcome. Kaia's hand beats mine by a single fucking point.

"I won!" she squeals with delight, throwing her arms around my neck, her thin, lace bra the only barrier between our chests. "I can't believe it!"

I laugh, the fact of my loss momentarily forgotten in the face of her joy. "Congratulations, Karras. You've earned it."

She grins, pressing a triumphant kiss to my lips. "I get to do the lectures."

"Absolutely," I agree, wrapping my arms around her, sharing our warmth as we huddle close. "I wouldn't have it any other way."

"What do you mean?"

"Well, I don't exactly have time for it with our practice

schedule, anyway. But I still wanted to see if you could beat me on your own merit. Fair is fair, after all."

"I should've realized you were playing games all along. But, you know," she says, giving me a mischievous smile. "You still need to uphold your end of the bargain regardless."

"Come again?"

She raises a brow, gesturing toward my boxers.

"Ah, come on," I say, reluctant to give in to her request.

She folds her arms across her chest and mocks, "Fair is fair, after all."

With a sigh, I loop my fingers through the elastic waistband and pull my boxers clean off. My cock, thick and heavy between my legs, springs free. She lets her eyes roam across my body, slowly, without shame, licking her lips as they land directly on my prized possession.

"You look hungry," I tease.

"I am," she says, her voice sultry and confident. With a daring glint in her eyes, she grips my growing erection, her fingers wrapping around me as she slowly strokes her way to the base.

The heat of her touch sends a wave of pleasure coursing through me, and I grow thicker, harder, in the palm of her hand. She's teasing me, her movements deliberate and slow, her gaze never leaving mine.

Without another word between us, she maneuvers herself onto her knees and sucks me between her lips, shocking the hell out of me. The sensation of her warm, wet mouth sets my senses on fire, and I let out a low groan.

Her tongue swirls around my shaft, teasing and tormenting, before her lips envelop me once more. She bobs her head, taking me deeper with each movement, and the tension builds and builds until it threatens to break.

"Kaia," I breathe, my hands tangling in her hair as I try to regain some semblance of control. "If you keep doing that, I'm not going to last long."

She releases me with a wet pop, a devilish grin playing across her lips. "That's the idea," she says before diving back down and taking me even deeper than before.

My body tenses as the pleasure mounts, my breaths coming in short, ragged gasps. Her skilled mouth works me relentlessly, driving me closer and closer to the edge.

"Kaia, I'm—" I manage to choke out, the warning clear in my voice. "*Fuck, yes.*"

She doesn't stop, only increasing her pace, her fingers gripping my thighs as she takes me further down her throat. I can't hold back any longer, and with a strangled groan, I reach my climax, my body shuddering with the force of it.

As I come down from my high, Kaia releases me and sits back on her heels, a satisfied smile on her face. "Well—" she says, wiping her mouth with the back of her hand. "—I think that was a fitting reward for my victory, don't you?"

I nod, still catching my breath, and pull her up for a heated kiss, tasting myself on her lips. "Fucking Christ, yes," I murmur against her mouth. "But don't think this means I'm going easy on you next time."

She laughs, her arms wrapping around my neck as we lie back on the blankets, our bodies flush. "I wouldn't expect anything less."

As the sky outside the lighthouse darkens, night falling over us, I think about how perfect this day has been. The competition, the shared laughter, and now the intimacy—everything just feels so fucking right.

Still, an insatiable desire courses through me even now, the need to have Kaia in every way imaginable.

I brush a strand of hair from her face, my fingers trailing down her neck and across her collarbone before gently cupping her breast through the lace of her bra.

"Kaia," I say, my voice low and full of need. "I want you."

Her eyes darken with lust, her lips parting slightly as she nods her agreement. "And I want you."

Wasting no time, I move over her, my fingers deftly unhooking her bra and tossing it aside. My mouth descends on her exposed nipple, sucking and nipping as she gasps in pleasure.

As I tease her with my mouth, my hand slips down between her legs, finding her already wet and ready for me. I rub her clit with a practiced touch, watching her face contort with pleasure, her hips bucking against my hand.

"Please, Beck," she begs, her voice breathy and desperate. "I need you inside me."

I smirk, positioning myself at her entrance, teasing her with the head of my cock. "You want this?"

She nods, her eyes wild with desire. "Yes, please."

With a firm thrust, I bury myself deep inside of her, her body yielding to mine as she moans in pleasure. I hold her down, my hands gripping her hips as I set a punishing pace, each thrust driving me further into her, our bodies slamming together with a primal urgency.

My free hand moves to her throat, fingers lightly circling it, feeling the rapid pulse beneath her skin. As her gaze locks onto mine, I slide my fingers into her mouth, and she sucks them off, her tongue swirling around them.

My arousal builds, climbing higher and higher, until I let out a string of nonsense swear words, my voice a low, rumbling groan.

Her nails dig into my shoulders, her body writhing beneath me, desperate to meet each of my thrusts. Our eyes lock once again, and the connection between us is undeniable, fucking magnetic.

As I continue to pound into her, her walls clench around me, her body tensing as she nears her climax. "I'm so fucking close," she whimpers, her eyes pleading with me now.

I lean in, capturing her lips in a fierce kiss as I increase the intensity of my thrusts, determined to bring her over the edge with me. "Let go, baby," I whisper against her mouth. "Come for me."

With a moan that echoes through the lighthouse, Kaia's body shudders and convulses, her orgasm washing over her like a tidal wave. The feeling of her clenching around me is too much, and with a final, powerful thrust, I join her in ecstasy, our bodies pulsing together.

As we catch our breath, I pull her closer, our sweat-slicked bodies entwined, the warmth of her skin against mine shielding us from the chilly air. Our breathing slows, our hearts gradually returning to a normal rhythm.

"God, that was so fucking good," I rasp, burrowing my face into the crook of her neck.

"So good."

"Hey, Kaia?" I murmur the question of her name against her soaked skin, pressing a kiss against the tiny beauty mark just there.

"Yeah, Beck?"

"I love you."

"I love you, too," she whispers back, her voice full of contentment, and it feels like I'm in fucking heaven.

In this moment, at the top of the lighthouse with the moonlight streaming in, I feel like we've truly found something special. That there's this unbreakable bond that's woven its way between us.

And as we lie here, entwined beneath the stars, slumber tugging at the edges of our consciousness, I know that there's nothing—in this entire goddamn world—that could feel any better than this.

# Chapter Thirty-Seven

KAIA

The cold air nips at my cheeks as I stand outside the rink, waiting for Holden to finish his final practice before their ten-day recess. I'm excited to spend the upcoming holiday season with him, even if it means breaking my usual traditions.

Lately, I've been getting back into my CBT workbooks, practicing some nightly journaling along with the exercises. With winter break starting and applications finally out of the way, I've had more time to dive in.

It feels good knowing that I'm actively working towards being happier and healthier, and with Holden's support, the journey seems a little more manageable.

As I wait, I spot a familiar face in the parking lot, but I can't seem to place him right away. It's a man, tall with dark hair, leaning against the bed of his truck. I stare at him for a moment too long, and he approaches me with a slightly guarded expression.

That's when it all clicks inside my brain. It's Elio's older brother, Luca, and he must be out here waiting for his wife to finish up. I haven't seen him in a long while, not since last Christmas, but I've known the guy since I was eight years old.

"Hey, Luca!" I call out, waving enthusiastically.

"Kaia." He nods in acknowledgment, his face serious but not unfriendly. "It's been a long time."

"It has. How have you been?"

"Just fine," he says. "Yourself?"

"Great, actually," I say with a grin. "Just waiting for my boyfriend to finish up in there."

As I move in for a hug, I remember too late that Luca isn't much for physical affection. He stands stiffly, clearly uncomfortable but not in a rude sort of way. I quickly brush it off, not wanting to make him feel any more awkward.

"Sorry," I mutter, my cheeks reddening.

He waves off my concern. "No worries."

"So, what brings you here?"

He scratches the back of his head, his gaze flicking away for a quick moment. "Harper had to run some errands, so I thought I'd pick her up after practice and tag along."

"Oh, that's nice of you," I say, sliding my hands into my front pockets. "How's she doing?"

"She's good." His expression softens as he thinks about her. "Busy, as always, but good."

"And Juney?" I ask, curious about their daughter.

"Good. She's with Ma today."

"It must be nice that she's around to watch her sometimes."

He grunts his agreement, and we stand there for a moment, an easy silence settling between us. I glance back toward the rink, wondering how much longer it'll be before Holden emerges.

"So," Luca starts, looking at me with a hint of curiosity. "Are you coming over for the holidays again this year? Elio mentioned you might be, but he wasn't sure."

I shake my head, feeling a slight pang of guilt for not spending Christmas with Elio and his family like I usually do. "Actually, I'm going to spend it with Holden this year," I say. "I figured it'd be nice for us to have our first Christmas together, you know?"

He nods in understanding. "Good for you two."

"Yeah, it will be. You know, I was gonna tell you that I'm glad that Elio could take in Bentley. I think it's been really good for him."

"Yeah, Taylor figured it might be," he says. "Should've just trusted her from the get-go."

"What do you mean?"

He shifts uncomfortably on the balls of his feet, avoiding my questioning gaze. "Er, nothing really."

"Spill," I playfully demand. "I can keep a secret."

He rubs at the back of his neck. "Just—Harps and I really wanted to take him on, thought it would be fun for Juney and all. We were gonna hire someone to walk him during the day, but in the end, Tay thought Elio should have him. That it might, I don't know, spark something good in his life."

"Ah, I agree with Taylor. He needed a little bit of sunshine."

"Well, good, then."

We chat a bit more, catching up and reminiscing about past holidays spent together. Despite Luca's initial stiffness, our conversation flows easily, and I'm reminded of the years I spent growing up around his family.

Before long, the rink doors open, and a group of players spills out, chatting and laughing as they make their way to the parking lot. I spot Holden among them, his face lighting up when he sees me.

"Hey, baby!" he calls, jogging over with a grin. "What are you doing out here in the cold?"

"Waiting for you, obviously," I say, wrapping my arms around his neck as he pulls me into a warm embrace.

As we walk away, I glance back at Luca, who waves and

offers a tight-lipped smile before heading into the rink to find his wife.

Once we're tucked inside the warmth of Holden's car, I let out a contented sigh, snuggling into the heated seat. "It was nice seeing Luca again," I say, glancing over as he starts the engine. "I didn't expect to run into him here."

"Yeah, I've heard he's a pretty decent guy. He and Elio seem nothing alike, though. I'm always shocked that they're related."

"Yeah, in some ways, they're very different," I say, tucking my nose into my scarf. "But in others, they're more alike than you might expect."

He makes a noncommittal sound as he pulls from the lot. "Well, I'm glad you two had the chance to catch up, especially since you'll be spending Christmas with me this year."

As we drive, I focus on the upcoming holidays and the changes they represent. Spending Christmas with Holden and his family will be a new experience, one that I'm anxiously anticipating.

I'm also acutely aware that, in the coming days, I'll be hearing back from the schools I applied to for early admission. The anticipation of those decisions is a constant hum in the back of my mind, and I can't shake the feeling that everything's about to change—for me, for us.

Holden squeezes my hand, sensing my growing anxiety. "Hey," he says softly, his voice full of reassurance. "No matter what happens in the next few months, we'll figure it out as a team, okay?"

I look over at him, my heart bursting with love and gratitude. "Okay," I agree, squeezing his hand back. "You're right. We're a team now."

. . .

THREE DAYS PASS, and Holden and I find ourselves seated in my bedroom, my laptop balanced on both thighs. I've received a notification from all three early decision schools, and it's officially time for me to sift through them.

My hands tremble with anticipation, and Holden's arms encircle me, providing both solace and reassurance.

"You've got this, Karras," he murmurs, pressing a gentle kiss to my temple.

I pause to center myself and click on the first portal, my heart pounding in my chest. The screen loads, and I can barely breathe as I read the words, "Congratulations! We are pleased to inform you that you have been accepted, early admittance, to Dayton University—Master's of Science in Biomedical Engineering."

A gasp escapes me, and I turn to Holden, my eyes brimming with tears of joy. "I got in!" I exclaim, practically shaking with excitement.

He grins, pulling me in for a tight hug. "I knew you would! Congratulations, baby!"

I can't contain the grin that spreads across my face, my heart swelling with joy as I open the next portal. This out-of-state school was more of a spontaneous application, but to my pleasant surprise, I'm greeted with yet another acceptance.

An accompanying scholarship catches my eye, offering me a generous grant to attend their program. While it wasn't a top contender before, this boosts its spot in the ranks for me.

Finally, I click on the last remaining portal. This one is for Coastal's program, where I've always envisioned myself attending. As the page loads, I know it in my heart even before I see it —it's another acceptance.

"Hell yeah." Holden hugs me again, his pride for me clear

on his face. "I knew you could do it. Smartest fucking woman I know."

Initially, I'm overjoyed by the news. But as the excitement fades away, a new wave of anxiety washes over me. Now that I've been accepted into all three schools, I have to make a decision—a decision that will impact not only my future in academia but also my future relationship with Holden.

The out-of-state school offers the most scholarship money, which would mean I wouldn't have to rely on my parents for financial support. But it's also the furthest away from him.

As I weigh my options, I think about making a compromise. It's never been my desire to put a man's needs before my own, to be someone's trophy wife. To sit on a shelf and make my decisions based around someone else's desires.

I suppose there's nothing wrong with that, per se, but it doesn't align with the plans I've always had for myself, for my future. I've been determined to put my own ambitions and dreams first. But now, faced with the reality of our relationship, I wonder if compromise isn't such a bad thing.

If choosing a school that's closer to Holden—and his future with the Tornadoes—might be the best option for both of us.

He must sense my inner turmoil because he gently takes my hand, eyes filling with concern. "What's wrong?"

I hesitate for a moment before I determine that it's best to be honest and up-front, laying all my concerns on the table from the beginning. "I know I still have a few weeks to decide, but I'm struggling with my options here. I don't want to base my decision wholly on our relationship, but I also don't want to be apart from you any more than I have to."

"I get that, Kaia." He squeezes my hand. "It's a tough decision to make. But whatever you choose, just know that I'll support you one hundred percent. Of course I want you to be closer to me. But mostly, I want you to be happy and to follow your dreams, just like I'm following mine. We'll make it work, no matter the distance."

His words curb my anxiety, and I lean into him, grateful for his unwavering support. "Thank you, Beck. It means a lot to hear you say that."

As I consider my options, I find myself gravitating toward Dayton. It wasn't my first choice all along, but I was impressed by what they had to offer at the symposium. And it's not only closer to the city—which means I'd be closer to Holden's home base—but it also offers everything I want in a school.

Based on the hours I spent combing through their website, they appear to have a strong academic program, diverse research specialties, and the opportunity to make valuable connections in my field. The only thing Dayton doesn't have is Dr. Khatri, but I'm almost certain I can find another professor to latch onto.

It feels like the perfect compromise, a way to prioritize my ambitions without sacrificing my relationship with the man I love.

"I'm gonna put a deposit down with Dayton," I finally tell him, my voice steady and full of conviction.

"Not Coastal?"

"Nah, it's about time for me to get some distance from Boyer, anyway," I tell him, feeling satisfied with my decision. "Besides, I'll still be close enough to home, to Elio, to Amber Isle."

With a warm smile gracing his lips, he pulls me in for another hug. "I'm so fucking proud of you, baby. I know you're going to do amazing things there, and I'll be cheering you on every step of the way."

As we sit there, wrapped up together, I feel a sense of utter peace. Contentment like I've never felt before. It's true that our lives are about to change drastically, with Holden's burgeoning athletic career and my own academic pursuits, but I have faith in our ability to make it work, no matter what.

"You want to know what else I've been thinking about lately?" I ask, snuggling in closer.

He chuckles, his chest vibrating against my cheek. "Probably a million things all at once."

"Well, yeah," I admit. "But I mean, in particular . . . I've been thinking about how I wanted to be the first one to say I love you, but then you beat me to it."

"Oh, of course you did," he teases, a playful glint in his eyes.

"Come on, Beck. I don't mean it in a competitive way."

"You sure about that?"

"Okay, well, maybe that played a tiny, minuscule part in it. But mostly, after everything, I just wanted to make sure you knew I wasn't simply parroting your feelings. That I really fucking mean it when I say the words. And even if you didn't love me back, or you weren't the one to tell me first, I'd still say them anyway." I smooth my hands across my thighs. "What I'm trying to say is that I really, really like you *and* I love you, so much more than I ever hated you."

His brows shoot up in mock surprise. "You hated me?"

"No, but I tried to tell myself I did," I say with a self-deprecating laugh. "I don't think you're supposed to think about someone you hate that often. And I especially don't think you're supposed to have dirty dreams about them."

A smirk forms on his lips. "You dreamed about me, Karras?"

I roll my eyes, the heat rising in my cheeks. "Only a couple of times. Completely against my will."

He leans back, grinning wide. "Knew you could never resist me."

"Beck . . ."

"Yes?" he prompts, his voice soft and tender.

"You have anything else you want to say to me?"

"I love you, too, baby," he says, pulling at a strand of my hair. "And I really fucking like you, just as much as I love you. Always have, and always will."

"That's good to know."

"Oh, and Karras?"

"Yeah?"

"You think you'd want to be my girlfriend now?"

As I pull away from him, shocked laughter spills free. After all this time together—all the hours we've spent confessing our feelings, our fears, and our hopes for the future—we're well past the stage of defining the relationship.

"You know what, Becker? Ask me again when it's not an afterthought."

# Epilogue

## HOLDEN

I'M BACK on campus today, walking through Navy Square, eager and ready to attend my girlfriend's guest lecture. I didn't imagine that I'd be back at Coastal so soon after graduation, but Kaia was invited here by her favorite professor, and she couldn't pass up the opportunity.

Thankfully, it aligned with a break in the hockey season because there's not a chance in hell that I'd miss this.

The campus is bustling with students, and it feels surreal to be walking amongst them as an alum. So much has changed, yet being here today feels a lot like coming home.

I stroll through the courtyard, lost in thought, reminiscing about the days when Kaia and I were just starting to navigate our relationship, wondering what the future held for us.

The past two years have been a whirlwind, filled with ups and downs, but through it all, our love has only grown stronger. We've both been pursuing our passions relentlessly, with me continuing my professional hockey career and Kaia excelling in her studies.

The distance between us has been challenging at times, especially when I'm on the road, but we've remained committed to making our relationship work, no matter what obstacles we face.

As I enter Weyerhaeuser and make my way into the lecture

hall, I take a seat near the front, wanting to have the best possible view of the podium.

The minutes tick by, and anticipation builds inside of me. It feels like the first day of freshman year all over again, and I'm about to lay eyes on the most stunning woman I've ever seen.

When Kaia finally walks to the front of the room, I'm brimming with pride. She appears poised and confident, her hazel eyes shining with excitement. I can tell she's eager to share her knowledge and insights with the class, and I know she'll captivate them all.

She begins her lecture, her voice clear and steady as she dives in. She's discussing her research on brain signals associated with OCD, a topic she's become increasingly passionate about over the years.

As I watch her speak, I'm reminded of the countless late-night conversations we've had—hours spent discussing her aspirations, her dreams, her unwavering determination to make a difference in the world. It's inspiring to see her standing up there now, bringing her vision to life, and I couldn't be happier for her.

Throughout her lecture, Kaia remains articulate and self-assured, her passion for the subject shining through in every word she speaks. The students seem interested, listening intently, and I'm in awe of her ability to command the room.

It's sexy, empowering, and it makes me even more excited about my plans for tonight.

As she reaches the conclusion of her talk, she receives a short and sweet round of applause. I'm so fucking proud of her that I give a standing ovation, clapping enthusiastically as she beams at the crowd.

After the lecture officially ends, Kaia cozies up with Dr. Khatri and a select group of students, eager to discuss her work further and ask questions. I watch from a distance, allowing her to bask in the well-deserved attention.

When the crowd finally disperses, I make my way over to her, wrapping her up in a warm embrace. "You were incredible, baby," I say. "I knew you'd be amazing, but you surpassed my expectations a hundredfold."

She smiles, her eyes shining with happiness. "Thanks for being here, Beck."

"Wouldn't miss it for the world." My voice drops, low and sweet as I add, "That was really fucking sexy, by the way."

"Oh, God." She swats at my arm, laughter bubbling out of her. "Please take your student/teacher fantasies elsewhere."

"Don't mind if I do."

Before we leave Coastal's campus, the two of us grab a quick meal with Dr. Khatri, and the day quickly fades into night.

Now, it's the perfect time to put my plans into action. I'm taking Kaia back to our lighthouse, back to Bluewater Cape, because I can't think of a better location to ask her to be my wife.

I've been planning this moment for months now, maybe even years, wanting to ensure that everything's perfect for the woman I love.

As evening falls, I take us on a walk down memory lane, driving through Amber Isle, through Boyer, and then taking the long route over to Bluewater. The sun is setting, dipping well into the blue hour, and the sight of the lighthouse standing tall against the sky fills me with nostalgia.

We climb the steps to the top, where the stars are freckling the sky, and Kaia's entranced, her eyes fixed outside. It's fucking beautiful out here tonight, serene, and I can tell that she's already lost in thought.

As she continues to gaze out the window, her attention fully captured by the night sky, I take a deep breath and prepare myself. This is it—the moment I've been waiting for for so long. I slowly, quietly get down on one knee behind her, the engagement ring I've chosen clenched in my hand.

"Hey, Karras," I say, my voice steady despite the pounding of my heart.

"Yeah?" she asks, not bothering to turn around, her eyes still glued to the stars.

"I know you've got a lot going on right now, but do you think you'd be at all interested in marrying me?"

At the sound of my words, she whips around so quickly that I'm afraid she'll lose her balance. Her eyes widen as she takes in the sight of me, down on one knee, the ring held in my outstretched palm.

For a moment, she's speechless, her eyes darting from my face to the ring and back again. Then, with a grin that lights up the entire room, she breathes out, "Um, yeah, you could say that I'm interested. Are you . . . ? Is this really happening?"

"Yeah, this is real," I say, my voice cracking with emotion. "Kaia, these past two and a half years have been the most incredible journey of my life. We've faced challenges and overcome them together, always emerging stronger and more united than before. I can't imagine my life without you, and I never fucking want to. You're my rock, my inspiration, my everything."

I pull out the small velvet box from my pocket and open it, revealing the engagement ring nestled inside. "Kaia, baby, will you marry me? Will you be my partner—my teammate—as we continue to chase our dreams together?"

Tears glisten in her eyes, and her lips curve into a wide, beaming smile. "Yes, Beck," she whispers, her voice filled with certainty. "Yes, I will marry you."

I wrap her up in my arms, and I can perfectly envision our future stretching out before us, laid out in plain sight. It's a fucking beautiful thing, unbreakable, and it reassures me that we're ready to face whatever life has in store for us—together, no longer as adversaries, but as partners.

In this life and the next.

# Acknowledgments

Thank you for reading Fault Line. I appreciate you all so much—from the readers who've been here from the beginning to those just now joining me. I'm so grateful that you took a chance on my stories!

I want to first thank my sweet little family—my husband and baby girl—for giving me endless inspiration, and for showing me perfect love.

My wonderful author friends (and yes, also very real friends)—Becka, Erin, and Hannah—for always being there when I need them.

My icepop princess, Ellie, for being the best cheerleader.

My alpha reader team—Megan, Nikki, Sierra, and Sinead—for being the first people to lay their eyes on this story. My ARC readers for their unending support. And all of the bloggers/reviewers for creating, reposting, and sharing my content. I owe a huge part of my success to you all!

My editor, Sandra, for lending her talent to my work.

And lastly, one final thank you to every person reading this. I'm so grateful that you've chosen to spend your time on my imperfect little words.

# About the Author

Ki Stephens is a romance enthusiast who finds comfort in the happily-ever-after . . . with just a little bit of angst along the way. She has a special interest in works that include neurodivergent characters like herself. When she's not daydreaming about books, Ki enjoys working with kids, creating art in her backyard studio, and spending loads of time with her baby girl, her husband, and their three pets.

She released her debut novel, Spring Tide—Book 1 in the Coastal University Series, in December of 2022.

**www.kistephens.com**

Made in the USA
Las Vegas, NV
23 May 2023